FOLLY

Also by Maureen Brady

FICTION

Give Me Your Good Ear
The Question She Put to Herself

NONFICTION

Beyond Survival: A Writing Journey for Healing
from Childhood Sexual Abuse
Daybreak: Meditations for Women Survivors
of Sexual Abuse

FOLLY

by **Maureen Brady**

Afterword by Bonnie Zimmerman

The Feminist Press
at The City University of New York
New York

Published 1994 by The Feminist Press at The City University of New
York, 311 East 94 Street, New York, New York 10128

97 96 95 94   1 2 3 4 5

Book design by Mary A. Scott
Typesetting of *Folly* by Martha Jean Waters

Library of Congress Cataloging-in-Publication Data

Brady, Maureen.
   Folly : a novel / by Maureen Brady ; afterword by Bonnie
Zimmerman.
      p. cm.
   ISBN 1-55861-078-2 (cloth) : $29.95. — ISBN 1-55861-079-0
(paper) : $12.95
   1. Strikes and lockouts—Textile industry—North Carolina—
Fiction. 2. Women textile workers—North Carolina—Fiction.
3. Mothers and daughters—North Carolina—Fiction.   I. Title.
PS3552.R2435F6   1994
813'.54—dc20
                                                        94–5905
                                                           CIP

Cover design: Paula Martinac
Cover art: *Self-Portrait with Anita* by Audrey Flack, 1955. Oil on
   canvas, 25 x 36". Collection Thalia Gouma-Peterson and Carl
   Peterson, Oberlin, Ohio.

Printed in the United States of America on acid-free paper by
McNaughton & Gunn, Inc.

This publication was made possible, in part, by public funds from the
New York State Council on the Arts and the National Endowment for
the Arts. The Feminist Press would also like to thank Ellen Bass,
Janet E. Brown, Joanne Markell, Nancy Porter, and Genevieve
Vaughan for their generosity.

To Judith McDaniel

Acknowledgments

I wish to extend deep gratitude to the women mill workers of North Carolina who granted me interviews about their lives. Thanks to Nancy Bereano for her enthusiastic ushering of the manuscript to print the first time around, and thanks to Susannah Driver, Florence Howe, Paula Martinac, and others of The Feminist Press for bringing it out again.

There are some women who like factory work. They like the feeling of running a sewing machine, seeing piece work eventually turn into finished products. It is hard, physical work, but under the right conditions many women enjoy it. Some of the women in the Blue Ridge strike felt that way. . . . Not long after the strike ended, a few women who had walked the picket line decided to start their own sewing factory. They wanted to own, manage, and operate a workplace where the women in Fannin County, Georgia, could work without unfair production rates, without the tension and tedium which are day-to-day factors in the lives of most garment workers. They wanted to make a new kind of factory—the kind that did not exist in this country. And they did it.

Kathy Kahn, Hillbilly Women (1972)

School wasn't even out yet and already it was so damn hot and muggy the new flypaper over the kitchen table had curled up. Folly sat in front of the fan in the old wicker rocker. She could feel the small, broken pieces of wood pushing into her legs below her bermuda shorts. She stared at a page of her new mystery story that Martha had just finished and loaned her, but she couldn't read. She thought maybe after the summer she'd start on a new budget and try again to get them out of the trailer and into a house. They were all tripping over each other, all the time tripping over each other. Mary Lou filling up with hotsy-totsy ways, bungling around in there. She'd leave her room a shambles. How could you read a mystery with such a fast growing-up, noisy kid in the next room and that wall between you so thin if you put a tack in the one side, it'd come out the other?

Skeeter was out mowing lawns. There was a good kid for you. He wanted some money of his own and he wasn't scared of working a little. Mary Lou would drop her allowance on the first thing that came along and then hitch from town when she didn't have change for the bus. Folly felt her worries about that girl as regular as clothes getting dirty. With Tiny, it was too early to tell. He still minded. He was only ten. She remembered nursing them all in the wicker rocker, Mary Lou nibbling at her nipple. Seemed like the other two had taken more easily to it.

Mary Lou came out in her cut-offs that she'd sat fringing for two hours the night before. She wore a skimpy T-shirt and a scarf tied around the crown of her head as if she were going out to sweat in the fields. "Did you sleep some today, Momma?"

"Not much. Too hot." Folly worked the night shift at the factory, putting zippers in polyester pants. She looked back down at her page.

"Yuck. Do we have to have that stupid flypaper right over the table?"

"Mind your own business, sister. I don't see y'all working out with the fly swatter, ever. That's the reason we need it."

Mary Lou stood sneering at the yellow strip and didn't answer. Folly had to admire the way her daughter's body had grown so nice and tall and lean. Graceful, too, as it perched on the uppermost portion of childhood. Her hair was brown—short and curly and soft around her face, and her eyes were green and full of clarity, seeing always the nakedness of things—the flypaper, the ratty condition of the sofa, worn so the stuffing showed through in the pattern of the backs of a pair of legs. Mary Lou saw these measures as their failures, and with some shame that they didn't have better, Folly sensed. Her face was so clear, so young and open and unmarked, except for the occasional pimple which she attended to and fussed over as if her pretty puss was the mainstay of the entire family. Folly remembered holding this baby, herself not much older than Mary Lou was now, landing kisses all up and down the child's face, tears in her eyes at the wonder of this soft baby skin having come from her, almost as if she were kissing herself.

Mary Lou did a sort of reverse curtsy, going up on her toes and putting her hands behind her back and said, "See ya later."

"Where you goin'?"

"Out."

"Out where?"

"To town."

"You stay away from the A & P, you hear, child?"

Mary Lou didn't answer.

"I don't want you hangin' around with that Lenore. She's too old for you."

"Mom, she's only nineteen," Mary Lou said, exasperation puckering the corners of her mouth.

"That's too old. You're sixteen."

"You don't have to tell me how old I am."

"Who told you she was nineteen, anyhow?" Folly asked. "She's been around that store for at least four years now."

"I know. That's cause she dropped out of school the end of tenth grade."

"That's what I mean. I don't want you runnin' with that sort. She'll be givin' you ideas about droppin' outa school."

2

"But Ma, she's smart. She's so smart she can study on her own. That's why she dropped out of school. She had to work anyway so she figured if she worked all day, she could get her some books and study what she wants to at night. She does, too. You should see all the books she's got."

"I don't care how many books she's got, she ain't smart," Folly said, her voice rising. "People don't drop outa school from being too smart . . . and I don't want you around her. I want you goin' to school and lookin' for a job for the summer." Folly turned her book face down to keep the place, heard the brittle spine crack, leaned forward so the chair was silent, and tried to penetrate Mary Lou with her eyes as if to stamp the statement into her. It was too hot to fight if you could help it.

Mary Lou held on to the back of the dinette chair and matched her stare. She was thinking of what to say. Finally, she said, "School's stupid. There's no way I can explain to you how stupid school is."

Folly rolled her eyes up in her head to dismiss the point. "You're goin' to school, that's all. You get you a job for summer and then you'll know how easy you got it. I oughta send you to the factory a couple nights. Let you sit in front of that damn sewing machine for eight hours." She wiped the sweat from her forehead. Jesus, she didn't want to fight. She was just scared for Mary Lou that she'd end up like her or worse. She tried to lower her voice and it came out scratchy. "Look, I'm working my ass off to try to get us out of this rotten trailer. I run off with Barney when I was sixteen cause I thought he was hot shit with his tight pants and his greased back hair and his always having change to buy me a coke at the drug store. They kicked me outa school cause I was pregnant, but I figured sweet shit on them, I already knew everything. Then I had to work cause Barney kept on goin' out with the boys and gettin' drunk and losin' his job, then I was pregnant again . . . . Then, you know the rest."

Folly looked at the flies stuck on the flypaper instead of at her daughter. She was sorry she had gone on so. That wasn't what she had meant to say.

"Ma. It ain't my fault you married a motherfucker," Mary Lou said.

"You watch your mouth. You watch how you talk about your father."

"Well, he was . . . ." Mary Lou kept her mouth in a straight line though both mother and daughter were aware that she was probably grinning underneath. She had always had a grin to go with her defiance. Folly had pretty much slapped it off her face by the time she was twelve, and now she was sorry. She'd rather Mary Lou would just grin and then she'd know for sure it was there. Instead she picked up her shoulder bag and made a sort of waving gesture out of the way she hiked it up on her shoulder.

"Anyway, Lenore's trying to get me on at the A & P for the summer," she said at the door. Then she was gone.

Mary Lou was gone and Folly was left with a picture of Lenore standing behind her meat counter, quartering the chickens, her strokes swift and clean. She had always kind of liked the girl. She got up from her rocker and moved the flypaper to an old nail stuck in the wall by the kitchen window. She looked out at the back yard, crabgrass trying to root and spread on the hard clay, some clumps making it and some scuffed away. A lot of folks wouldn't even call it a yard, but it was; it was the only one they had.

She registered how badly the windows needed washing. She should plant some flowers along the back border, she thought. It wasn't too late yet to get them started, but she had no fertilizer.

She took the wash off the line out back and called across to Martha to come on over. The two women sat at the table on the concrete slab of Folly's porch, and Folly folded the laundry into two piles. She folded neatly, trying to keep the ironing pile low. As it was, she never seemed to reach the bottom of it. On the other hand, she didn't want the kids going to school looking sloppy poor.

Folly's appearance reflected this balance in herself. She was not at all fancy or emphatic in the way she presented herself, but she was careful. There was little waste in her movements. She was a small woman. Mary Lou had surpassed her in height already, but she was strong, and her hands moved quickly and decisively. Martha noticed the firmness of the muscles in her arms without realizing what she was doing.

"How's your ma?" Folly asked her.

"Oh, she's getting back to her old crabby self. She woke me up at noon to make sure I wasn't hungry . . . you know, in my sleep I'm gonna be hungry and not feeding myself. Then all afternoon it's, 'Go lie down, you didn't get near enough sleep.' I couldn't go back, though, with her bumping up and down the sitting room with the cane. She's not near as steady on her feet as she was before she took the pneumonia. I can't help myself from peeping out at her, waiting for her to fall. Lotta good it's gonna be if she does, me lying there peeping."

Martha had come to live with her mother there in that trailer of Daisy's after Daisy's second stroke. Folly had a lot of respect for what she put up with, but whenever she said anything about it, Martha would say, "Look at your own load, Fol, and the way you take care of it." Once she'd even said, "I swear you were born a solid rock."

Folly thought about how Martha always seemed like the rock to her. She kept her awake at work making jokes about the boss. She'd touch her shoulder when Folly was nodding out and say, "I wish I could just give you a pillow but you know old Fartblossom'll be making his rounds soon." Coming home in the early mornings they always came back to life for the fifteen-minute drive and concocted tricks they would do on Fartblossom once they were ready to quit the factory. That was Folly's favorite time of day. Once you'd come out into the sun and sneezed the lint out of your nose, the air always seemed so sweet and fresh. She often wished they lived a little further from the factory so the drive wouldn't be over so fast.

"Did you finish that mystery yet?" Martha asked.

"Nope . . . hardly got started on it. I been tryin' to figure that Mary Lou again."

"Yeah. What's she been up to?" Martha turned to face Folly more directly.

"I don't know if it's anything or not. You know that girl behind the meat counter at the A & P? Short, dirty blond hair brushed back?"

"Lenore? I think she's the only woman."

"Yeah, you know her?"

"Not much. Only from going in the store."

"She's queer. Least that's what the guidance counselor down at the school says. She called me in to tell me that Mary Lou's been hanging out with her."

Martha pulled back to herself almost as if she'd been socked with Folly's bluntness. "I didn't think Lenore went to school."

"She don't. The guidance counselor says she comes by in her car when school lets out and picks my Mary Lou up every now and then. What do you think?"

"I don't know, Folly. Did you talk to Mary Lou?"

"I told her I didn't want her hangin' out with no one that much older. She's a smart-ass kid, got an answer for everything. She ended up callin' Barney a motherfucker."

"What's he got to do with it?" Martha asked.

"Good question." Folly shook out a pair of jeans, then placed one leg over the other and smoothed them with her hand. She could hardly remember how Barney got into it. "He sure was a motherfucking bastard. Serve him right if his daughter turned out queer. Him runnin' back, just stayin' long enough to knock me up with Tiny." Her face felt hot. The anger always rushed to her head when she thought of him.

"I sure have to agree with you," Martha said. "It never sounds like he done you any favors."

"I was pretty stupid," Folly said. She tried to get back to thinking about Mary Lou. She didn't want her mind wasting time on that bastard. The thought struck her that at least if Mary Lou was messin' around with that girl she wouldn't be gettin' herself knocked up. She didn't say that to Martha, though. It was a weird way for a mother to think.

Martha sat, quiet and patient, waiting for Folly to get back on the track. She ran her fingers through her hair. It was then that Folly realized Martha's hair was cut just about the same as Lenore's. It was the same color, too, except for the temple parts where she had most of her grey. Folly looked away and tried to pretend she was immersed in her laundry. Ever so strange, the feeling that had crept up on her. How could it be that you live next door to this woman, you know exactly how she looks, you know she came up to North Carolina from Florida seven years ago when her ma first took sick. She works all night in the same room with you, she sleeps mornings in the next trailer, she knows every bit of trouble you ever had with the kids. They mind her like they never minded you. She loves them. She's like family. Folly was realizing that Martha never had talked about sex. Never. She'd never talked about any man. She'd never talked about not having children. She'd talked about her girlfriend in Florida when she'd first come up, about working citrus groves with her; then Folly had become her best friend.

This all slipped furtively through her mind in a few seconds and she could only glance sideways at Martha. She was husky. She flicked her cigarette ashes with a manly gesture. "For Christ's sake," Folly said to herself, "so do I." Then it hit her that she never talked about sex to Martha either. Except to bitch about Barney. But that was because she didn't have any. She didn't want no man within a clothesline length of her. No thanks. She did just fine living without.

Folly stooped forward and fished around in the laundry basket for more clothes, but she was down to the sheets. She sat back again and scrutinized the ironing pile just to make sure she hadn't put anything in it that could go right on over to the other pile and be done with, but she didn't find any mistakes. Then she searched out two corners of a sheet, and Martha came around and took the other corners just as she would always do if she were around when the wash was taken in. They stretched it between them.

"Listen here. I just don't want no trouble for Mary Lou," Folly said. "You know, she seems cut out for gettin' herself into things."

"Yes, but she's pretty smart about getting herself out of trouble too. Least she don't come crying to you most times. I bet she didn't go to that guidance counselor on account of wanting guidance."

"Uhn't uh. Matter of fact if you ask me I think that counselor is a snoopy bitch. She'd probably like to have somethin' on Mary Lou. Said Mary Lou is a rebellious girl, that's what she told me."

"What of it?" Martha said. "Ain't nothing wrong with that. I bet that counselor don't like any kid that don't run around with a runny nose and a whiny voice asking for guidance." Martha shook her end of the sheet vigorously as she spoke. "That's a fine girl you got there. Reminds me of someone I know real well."

"What do you mean?"

"You know what I mean. I mean you. Remember when you ran around getting us all ready for presenting that petition to big Sam when they wanted to raise production to ninety? They tried to give you some guidance. Remember that? You saying, 'Piss on them, they'll never get me outa here till I'm ready to go.'"

Folly tried to keep her mouth down to a flat line but the grin was there anyway. You could see it if you knew her as well as Martha did.

2.

Driving to work later, Folly said to Martha, "That sounds like a damn fool thing to say."

"What?"

"That they wouldn't be gettin' me out until I was ready to go. You know as well as me, Martha, they could've scooped me up and dished me right out the door any time they damn well pleased."

"Yes and no," Martha said slowly.

"How you figure that?"

"Sure, they could, but . . . you had them scared. They don't expect anyone standing up to them. They bank on keeping us so damn busy and tired we won't even have the idea. And they figure they got us all scared to death we'll lose our jobs or get shuffled to a different machine if we don't keep up the production. Course, by and large we are . . . after all, how many places are there to work in Victory? Besides, they don't credit us with enough smarts to see that every time they pull off some trick to up production, they're making more money and we're still in the hole."

"You can say that again."

"Least we got them to hold production to eighty-five. That ain't much but it's better than ninety. We wouldn't have gotten that if you hadn't stood up to them and took them off guard. They don't expect any of us to have a backbone."

They rode in silence for a while, Folly remembering her anger the day that Fartblossom had announced the plan to up production. They had taken the top workers, usually women who had been on the same machines the longest and had built the most efficiency into their movements; then they had calculated that everyone else would get paid on the basis of ninety percent of their production. Women who didn't come near it would be working under the constant threat that they could be shifted somewhere else or down the road. No one would make more than minimum wage unless they beat the ninety. Folly's backbone had bristled rigid. In the lunch room she had found the women huddled in small groups, talking with panic about how they couldn't possibly make it. She had stood up and told them it was ridiculous, of course they couldn't make it, and the only thing to do was to tell Fartblossom that they knew it was ridiculous, and that they wouldn't even try. She had asked for help to say this. Emily, a tall, Black woman, a whiz at her sewing machine, quiet in her manner, had come over and sat down next to her and right then and there they had written up a petition and gotten all the signatures and had taken it to Fartblossom, and the factory had agreed to hold production to eighty-five.

"Any day now they're going to try to pull that again," Folly said.

"You bet your sweet ass," Martha agreed.

They drove into the parking lot. "I hope it ain't tonight," Folly said.

"I reckon next time they'll try out some other shift first. Graveyard brings out the witch in us."

"And then some."

They stood in line waiting to punch the clock. There was a din of voices of people making greetings, razzing each other, joking and teasing. The folks headed out were waking up to vigor from the stupor of the last two hours of their shift. It often struck Folly this way at shift change—that those who were arriving had a certain amount of energy and enthusiasm about them. They had been away from the factory for the most possible hours. They had tried to sleep, to eat, to feed their children, to get some things done at home, and now, somewhat restored, they waited to punch in. The others moving toward their homes were beginning to hear distinct voices again instead of the hum. While their eyelids had wanted to droop and fall a few minutes before, their eyes now popped open and seemed to acquire a gleam in the place of vacancy. It was almost as if the departing shift stole the energy of the arriving shift as they passed each other at the clock. Most of the time people didn't look at each other one to one during this passing. They concentrated on moving up as smoothly as possible, preparing to aim their arms at the right slots for their cards. They weren't exactly in a line. More in clumps. Black and white clumps. About fifty-fifty now in this mill. Folly was concentrating on the simple act of moving forward in coordination with the crowd.

9

Effie's voice threw her off for a second. "My boy home?" she asked.

"His motorcycle's there." Effie was Folly's other next door neighbor in the trailer park. Her son had been chasing after trouble for the past couple of years.

"Good. See ya later," Effie said, flashing a smile at the fact that she was on her way out.

"Right," Folly said, her arm poised, almost there.

Inside, Folly and Martha's machines were located next to each other. There were two rows of zipper machines, then the inseam line. Although they were close enough to reach across and touch, it was almost impossible to talk because of the concentration required in the sewing, and because of the constant level of the noise, which seemed to have made them all slightly hard of hearing. Often they dropped a conversation in the middle of a sentence when they reached their machines, then picked it up at the same place as they went out for first break. Folly had told Martha as they went in that she had gotten to read some more of *Agatha Webb,* which was the mystery Martha had loaned her. As they started out for the break Martha said, "What do you think of it?"

"Well, it's something else the way that girl, Amabel, is made out to be such a bitch. I hope she gets smart and just takes the money and runs . . . forget about that boy and marrying him and blackmailing him. I don't see why she's a bitch at all. She says straight out what she wants is to go forward . . . that how else can a poor girl like her get out of her position than to hook on to someone like him . . . and her a lot smarter too."

"I hadn't thought about it that way," Martha said. "She did seem kind of spooky standing out in the yard and knowing right where the blood was. You didn't finish yet, huh?"

"No."

"Well, I don't want to spoil the end for you."

"I'll try to finish tomorrow. You got more by this same author?"

"I got a couple more same time I got that one down at the rummage sale."

"The one I really feel sorry for is Batsy," Folly said. "Look at her. She gets it for nothing. She just happens to be cook for the lady that gets murdered, so she dies too."

"You think we're supposed to think she's *bats* because her name is Batsy?"

"I don't know. Don't care either. She ain't bats in my book."

10

Martha nodded agreement. "She's so shocked she has a heart attack."

"I don't understand why her body was hanging halfway out the window. I'd think she'd have doubled up on the floor."

"The idea was that she went to call for help."

"Oh, yeah," Folly said. "That's right."

The rest of the night Folly kept thinking about poor Batsy. She could almost see her hanging from that window. It was a more likely fate of the poor than for that Amabel to pull off marrying into the fancy house she'd started off taking care of. In the end, Folly thought, that girl's going to get it good, no matter what else. Poor Amabel. You got it coming, honey. You ain't got much to lose, but you're going to lose it all. Then she'd have a second thought which was more like hope. There's got to be a way out and maybe this Amabel will find it. Maybe Mary Lou would find it. She hoped Mary Lou wouldn't start thinking about dropping out of school. Not that she'd gotten a whole lot out of her own experience in school. When she tried to think back and remember something she had learned, she couldn't come up with much. She could remember her English teacher standing up at the board and pointing with her pointer to various parts of a sentence that she had put slash marks through to show the clauses. The tap of the pointer on the board —the same idea over and over. Mrs. Penny would put up a sentence and chalk a big X over one word. For instance, if the sentence was— "When are you going to get yourself up and out of bed?"—she would X out the 'get.' Only use 'to get' if you could use 'to obtain.' Folly could still hear the even admonition in her voice. She had learned it (some of the kids never had gotten it) even if she hadn't adopted it. But what good had it done her? I've got to be able to think, she thought, without all this obtaining. If Mary Lou could go to college, she'd keep her from starting at the mill. She had to get her to finish high school and keep her from messing around and getting pregnant.

The stitch of the zipperfoot was a straight line, but her mind zigzagged as she started on a new piece of work. If she could sew up the holes in their lives . . . . If she got Mary Lou to go to college, what about Skeeter? How could she afford it? There were community colleges now where the kids could work their own way. Skeeter was a good worker, but slower in school than his sister. She thought of him as having more chances for other ways out, right down to the most basic level. Such as, he could hitchhike out of town if he wanted to go somewhere else to look for work. Mary Lou thought she could too, but Folly didn't want her doing that. She worried about her. Mary Lou was her own life over again.

She remembered herself, at sixteen, walking home from school—tired, bored, slow. The sun hot, sweat smelling strong in her arm pits, her books heavy, her feet scuffing the dirt at the side of the road. She didn't want to go home. Her Ma worked the 3 to 11. She was the oldest, had to cook dinner. It wasn't a fair deal. Barney came along on his motor scooter and offered her a ride. He attached her books on the rack over the rear wheel. She had to sit right up close to his back and hold around his stomach with her arms. It was awkward with a skirt, but she managed. The wind blew on her sweaty arm pits. Barney's stomach was hard and tensed as he leaned forward to get up more speed. She felt excited. She felt she was being loved because he had encouraged her to hold her arms around him. He rode her to the drugstore and bought her a coke, and they hung out with the others there, which she had never done before. They all sat and talked of how boring it was in Victory. One of the kids would come in: "Hi, y'all. What's new?"

"Nothing." NOTHING NOTHING NOTHING. The word echoed in the high ceilinged space. Barney said Victory reminded him of a turtle who got tired crossing the road and just stayed there, right where he'd get run over. "Dead," he said. "This is Deadsville. I don't know why anybody would live his whole life here."

"You going somewhere?" Folly had asked.

"You better believe it, baby," Barney had answered, smiling with one side of his face and strutting his weight from one leg to the other. "Come on, let's ride."

She had been glad to ride but sorry to leave the drugstore so soon. She had liked the idea of sitting slouched lazy in a booth, complaining of the nothingness in the atmosphere while surrounded by rows and rows of objects on the shelves. She wished she had nothing to do. No cooking. No babysitting.

Every day for a week Barney took her by the drugstore for a coke after school. They never talked about if that meant they were going steady or what. He rode her home and played with her sisters and brothers, acting the big dude, holding out promises for rides on his scooter someday. One afternoon he followed her into her room when she went to get something, and he closed the door and took her by the shoulders and planted his lips smack on hers and kissed her for a long time, working his tongue into her mouth. She had kissed other boys before but not like that. She had felt the excitement like riding up close to him on the motorcycle. Then he had wrapped one leg around behind her knee and pressed the back of it to make her collapse down on her sis-

12

ter's bed, and she had pushed away from him, saying, "No, stop, Barney. We're messing up Junie's bed."

The next afternoon he rode her out the dirt road across from the Victory Mill, and down in there a couple of miles, he parked the scooter and walked her in through the woods to the stream. He led her to a place where they were under some big pines and the ground was a spongy cover of pine needles. They stood there kissing the way they had in the bedroom only he had his arms around her and squeezed her intermittently, as if he were making orange juice. She felt hot, and she understood finally the jokes and stories she had heard about people getting hot. She had been pretty dumb about the whole thing. That was that. Barney had put down his windbreaker on the pine needles for her to lay on. He had felt her up under her blouse and under her bra. She had said no a couple of times, but he had said, "But I want you *so* much. I need you," as if his whole life depended on what happened next. "Say yes, please, say yes," he had said. She had never said yes but had felt her face flush. Felt red, hot, scared. He had lain on top of her and squeezed her some more, awkwardly, which had made her feel loved. Then he had unzipped his pants and taken out his swollen big thing, and holding her pinned with his legs, he had pulled her skirt up and her underpants down just far enough to get his penis stuck between her pants and her body, and then he had slid it back and forth while she had stayed still, trying to get used to the shock of all this and to fit his penis to all the words she'd heard like hot dog, wienie . . . and she was the bun.

Folly was suddenly aware of a presence, a pants leg in her peripheral vision. It was Fartblossom standing between her machine and Martha's, supervising. She did not look up. She made it appear that she was moving the material through her machine at a steady rate while she actually accelerated her activity in a gradual, calculated way so that he wouldn't know he had caught her at a drifting moment. Each time her eyes darted laterally, they landed on the light green of his polyester pants, a hole worn from carrying keys in his right front pocket. His wienie was on her eye level. She wished he'd move on so she could see Martha, and finally, he took one long stride, stopped between the next two machines. She and Martha caught each other's eyes—checked in.

Barney had pulled her pants the rest of the way down, pushed inside her. She had lost the hots at that, had gone cold, pale, still, while he pushed through—no longer kissing, no longer squeezing, just pushing, piercing, breaking. When he stopped she felt the pine needles poking at her rear. Who could have told her that this was going to change her life, that she was giving up chances to be another Folly? She had not even thought of pregnancy. She would rather have been in the drugstore saying there was nothing to do in Victory.

She wished still for that time in her life with nothing to do. She heard the expression come out of Mary Lou, regularly. She had tried to tell her, don't go so quickly, wanting to fill that nothing. Live with it a little. Let it fill with yourself, with your joyful, baby self from when you didn't know there was anybody else in the world but you. Let that come back in you. Let yourself know you're something.

Fartblossom strode back by her machine, caught her off guard again and reminded her of the guidance counselor. She had felt guilty because she didn't know where Mary Lou went most afternoons after school. There was only so much she could keep track of. Her zipperfoot hammered away. For sure she was not going to make eighty-five unless she concentrated on getting more speed.

3

Mary Lou had been by the store asking about her job for summer. Lenore wished she could have said, "You're on. It's all arranged," but Peters had said he had to wait until he had all the vacation schedules worked out. Peters might have been the fastest bagboy in the South but, in Lenore's estimation, he wasn't worth shit as day manager.

"He's the molasses type," Lenore had said to Mary Lou. "I reckon he's gonna take you on my recommendation but he's got papers piled up in there on his desk, he ain't got the first glimmer 'bout what to do with them." Lenore packaged stew beef as she talked. She distributed a mound in each cardboard container, rounded it with cupped hands, then ripped off cellophane and wrapped. Mary Lou watched her hands.

"I'll try to pin him down," Lenore said, "but I 'spect I won't get his attention 'til the first day he comes up short when someone goes on vacation. Then you'll be on."

"Yeah," Mary Lou said, "long as I get the job." She frowned and that was when Lenore had wished she could've said it was all arranged.

"If you hang out 'til I get off we can go get a coke down at the diner."

"I better go on. Ma's bitchin' at me. Maybe tomorrow." Lenore nodded and Mary Lou turned and headed down the aisle. Lenore was sorry to see her looking so troubled. She wiped her fingers across her stomach on the big, white apron and watched her walk until she was out of sight. Then she went back to packing.

Lenore was the best butcher they'd ever had in that A & P. She was fast, neat, efficient, clean, reliable and courteous to customers. Besides the fact that she had it in her to be these ways, she made sure she worked her job fast, neat, efficient, clean, reliable and courteous because she couldn't stand people being shit on, and this way nobody had anything on her. Produce was a mess and Peters knew he could go on over there whenever he wanted to be a bastard. Still, they had never gotten around to getting her a butcher's apron the right size. This one fit around her waist twice and ended up being tied in the front. Furthermore, she had to tie a knot in the loop that went around her neck; otherwise the bib would've started at her waist. The apron reminded her of home, of wearing Angie's hand-me-downs. They'd both always been skinny but Angie had been extra long-waisted, and Lenore had spent her whole life with a belt marking her middle. Way back in the first grade she could remember the waists of the dresses falling on her hips, her pulling them back up under the belt until they were in the right place. That left her with goddamn tucks around her ribs where it should have been flat. Jesus, how she had hated those tucks, how she would have liked to rip those dresses to ribbons. It had been even worse when her breasts had started to grow. Even though they never grew very big, they were there, but you couldn't tell with those tucks just below them. Made it look like they were in the wrong place.

When Lenore had complained to Peters about the apron, he'd said, "Ain't many lady butchers, you're probably 'bout the only one. They don't make 'em for no one small as you."

"Yeah," Lenore had said. "Well, if they'd make 'em, there'd probably be more lady butchers."

Roland was her relief, and he was late again. It didn't much matter since Mary Lou hadn't waited, and that left Lenore thinking about her choices of what to do when she got off, and thinking about the choices was a whole lot easier than deciding, which is what she'd have to do when Roland got there. She could go to her room and fix herself some supper and finish her book, she could go over to the diner and hope that Sabrina would be waiting the counter and maybe it wouldn't be too crowded and they could talk, or she could take a package of hamburg and stop over at the house and make sure Perry got fed.

It had only been two days since she'd had the last fight with her ma and she'd said, "Get out. You don't belong here no more. You split, now you stay outa my way." Swinging the bottle around in the air—"You leave me and Perry alone. We get along okay." And Perry holding her hand and squeezing it tight but sounding real cool in her voice, saying, "You better go on, Lenore." And knowing that meant—if you make her any madder she'll beat up on me—and turning away, dropping Perry's hand, dropping down the steps, knowing not to step on the places where you'd go through. Then driving out Route 15, the tears burning in her eyes. She knew the road. She had walked it before she had been old enough to drive. She went a long way out from town trying to clear her head of the mixed up fury about her mother. She caught herself thinking . . . if mother would die, if something would happen to her, then Perry could come to live in my room, and I'd take good care of her. Then she'd felt almost sick, goose bumps had run down her back as she'd pictured Perry standing beside the grave site, her eyes staring into the earth and her lips held in a tough pout. That took her back to when she was Perry's age and Angie was eleven, and it was one of those days her mother declared they were going to have fun. "A hot time in the old town," she would say, and if they were downtown she'd take them in the thrift shop and tell them to pick out her "dancing duds" for her, and they'd find some frilly, shiny dress off the super, super bargain rack and all trot home. Then she'd try it on and prance around and say all the lines she could remember from the movies she'd seen, with her thrift shop cigarette holder clamped between her teeth and Lenore and Angie would roll around on the floor laughing, laughing till they were so sore they had to say, "Wait, stop, wait, my stomach."

That was back when she still worked at the diner and she'd put on an extra thick Southern drawl and imitate herself telling off the customers. "So you think you like the looks of this here package, honeychile. You got your eyes wide open and your tongue's hangin' out and it ain't but breakfast time . . . . Oh my goodness, I'm sooo sorry I dropped them grits on your pooo little lap."

After a while she'd point at Lenore or Angie and say, "Okay, your turn," and whoever it was would get-up in the clothes, their ma's high-heeled shoes and all. Lenore and Angie took to imitating whichever of their teachers they didn't like, and their ma would sit at the dinette table and roar. When they were each done with their shows, they'd put on music and all dance together, and Lenore and Angie thought they had the best, funniest mother there ever was to have in this world.

That was when she only drank beer.

When Lenore had quit school her mother had said she was a wise ass, and she was sorry she'd ever laughed at all those teacher jokes, that was what had made her a wise ass. Lenore had tried to tell her that wasn't the reason.

"They put me on full time at the store," she had said, "and I can bring home the money. You and Perry and me, we can have more things."

"Big deal," her mother had said.

"Angie quit school," Lenore said.

"Angie didn't know no better. Angie was a dumb fool gettin' herself pregnant. Besides, Angie didn't take to school."

Somehow that made Lenore mad, the idea that just because you were good at something you had to keep doing it. "No reason to go," she said.

"Who do you think you are, girl?"

"Nobody special."

"That's for sure."

They had stood then with their eyes locked in a stare down until Lenore had dropped hers. Her mother could have left it alone at that but didn't. She had picked up the bottle on the table and turned it upside down to demonstrate how empty it was. "Okay hot shit with all the money and the steady job, go on out and buy me a bottle of whiskey."

Lenore noticed her mother hadn't combed her hair yet that day. Nor had she gotten out of the old terrycloth robe and the slippers that flapped on the linoleum when she walked. "No," she said.

"You ain't too old to be beat," her mother said.

"I am too," she said. "But not old enough to buy at the liquor store."

"Shut that smart trap."

Then they had both gotten louder and nastier, and Lenore had ended up telling her ma all the real reasons why she had to quit school, including that she was part of this family in which the mother was a mess of a drunk, Perry wasn't getting taken care of, and them being on welfare made her stomach knot up. Then she had run out the door before her mother could see she was crying and walked and walked down Route 15 and hated her in a way that stung.

Three months later she had walked out and gone to Mrs. Henry's and rented a room with a kitchenette. At least Perry had been there and seen her ma go to get the strap, and Perry knew that the reason she had to leave was because she couldn't let anyone ever beat up on her again, least of all her ma.

Roland came in whistling and caught her with her mind way off loitering in her troubles. He was tying his apron, and she noticed out of the corner of her eye how it was the right size for him. He didn't mention his lateness, but they both knew the clock had noted it.

"See ya tomorrow," she said and went in the back to drop her apron in the laundry bin. As her card clicked in the time clock, she made her decision. She went home to read the book that Betsy had sent her from Alaska.

4.

Lenore picked up the mail and went inside. She tucked the fat letter from Betsy under her arm to open the door and left it there while she went to the refrigerator, took a beer, then settled into the deep old chair with the stuffing hanging out the bottom that Mrs. Henry had proudly furnished with her room. It was one thing to anticipate a letter that hadn't yet arrived. Lenore knew the disappointment that could lead to so she had set herself a policy of not expecting Betsy's letters, not allowing herself to stand around at work thinking maybe one would come that day, but it was another thing once the letter was there—in the box, in the quiet of her room, in her armchair. She made herself open it slowly, read it slowly. She held her gratitude, her eagerness, under a type of control that would lengthen the pleasure of the experience.

Dear Lenore,

I got your letter and just when I needed it. It came on a day when I was feeling pretty discouraged about being here. I was out on the job and this guy, Buster, was up on the truck lifting and throwing down these big iron mothers. He's part of my crew so I figured I should help him out. They were too heavy for any one person to lift alone so I called up to him—Buster, you sure got a high estimation of your own strength. How'd you like a hand for lifting those damn two-tons. He mumbled back about how it would take four girls to lift one of them. I said I doubted it. So he said he'd do half and leave the other half for me to do by myself. Big shit. No deal, I said.

So he thought he'd proved that women shouldn't be up here on these jobs. I said I wasn't crazy or dumb. I said—a brain 'll take up a lot of slack in your muscles, Buster.

Willy, the one I share my lodging with, she and I had just been talking the night before about how these guys get to you. There are a whole bunch of them I'd like to beat the shit out of. Willy and I decided the best thing was to just ignore them, not let them know if you were getting razzed. Anyway there I was the next day telling this jerk off. Then I got your letter and I said to myself—you wouldn't catch Lenore taking any shit off these guys. I didn't know how Willy would be because she's kind of different from anyone I ever knew, like she makes up rules for herself, things like getting up earlier than we have to for making it to work in the morning. To me it's glory not to have my pa making up the rules. She comes from a real classy family. Her father's a doctor. I don't understand what she's doing here. Anyway we'd sort of made the rule together that we wouldn't let these guys razz us, but when I told her about Buster, she laughed and said she'd wished she'd been there to see me tell him off.

I'm learning so much being away from home. I guess you did too when you moved out from your ma's but for me it's really something to be so far away. No family to fight with. You wouldn't believe how strong I've gotten. My muscles feel like steel, and I really like this feeling in my body like there are no soft spots. Willy says by the time this pipeline is finished, we'll be in shape to start the women's army. She says she thinks I have a soft spot here and there. She means for you.

How are you? I miss you very much. I lie in bed at night and I try real hard to imagine you with me and there are times when I think I can feel you in my arms. There's nothing else that was ever as good in my life as finding you to love. Willy and I talk about you and Robin, that's her lover in Oregon, all the time, sometimes late into the night when we should be sleeping. I can't imagine if Willy wasn't a lesbian. Then I wouldn't be able to talk about you. I feel pretty lucky. Lots of the other women up here are probably lesbians too, I think, but I don't know for sure. Willy just came right out and said it, so maybe the rest of them will too when they get to know me better. What I haven't figured out is whether they seem like lesbians because of the jobs they do, or whether they know jobs like welding and stuff because they're lesbians. Get it?

I was thinking maybe it sounds weird to you since I never said the word or anything back home to hear me calling myself a lesbian. I just know I could never go the other way so why not. The other reason was because of reading that book I sent, <u>Sappho Was A Right-On Woman.</u> Did you read it yet? You probably did, you're such a good reader. Can you imagine me reading a whole book in a week? You must've been a *good influence on me. Anyway it sure wasn't like any book I ever had to read in school. When you finish tell me what you think. I'll send you more if you want them. The woman who gave it to me, she's the only other one I know for sure is a lesbian, she comes from San Francisco where there are gay people all over the streets, and she has friends who send her lots of odd books and things, and she says when we're finished with them, we should pass them on to someone else, and then that person should pass them on, too, sort of like a chain letter. What I want to know is who in the world are you going to find in Victory that you can pass that Sappho book to? (Ha, ha.) Got any ideas?*

How's Perry? I hope things have been going okay. I know how that tears you up. How are things at the store? Write to me soon. It makes me real happy to get your letters. Be taking good care of yourself.

Love,
Betsy

P.S.   What do you think of me changing this way? I suppose Victory is getting along just fine without me but I don't know if it'll be ready for having me back.

P.S.S.   Willy says hello. She feels like she's getting to know you.

Lenore put out her cigarette and closed her eyes. She left the letter lying in her lap and tried to picture Betsy. Having never been out of North Carolina it was impossible for her to imagine Alaska other than as a cluster of igloos and penguins and Eskimos eating hunks of fat as they'd been shown in the school books. She could see Betsy lying in bed, one arm up with her hand propping her head and her dark underarm showing. That was a soft spot. Betsy lying there in her bed on a Sunday morning while she was at the counter pouring the coffee. Betsy looking at her that morning after the first night they'd spent together when every time Betsy had looked up and caught her eye, Lenore's heart had tripped, the feeling of missing a stair in the dark. It had been her first night ever sleeping with a woman and she had wanted to think out what was happening to her, but she couldn't because each time she would look in Betsy's eyes, she would get this warm feeling as if it were the perfect day with a clear sky and just the right amount of breeze, and she was all shook up with excitement but calm at the same time, and this smile would break away on her face that she couldn't have stopped if she'd tried.

"It seemed pretty natural, didn't it?" Betsy had said, speaking of their love making.

"Yes, oh yes," she'd replied in a soft voice which she hardly recognized as her own.

"Have you ever slept with a man?" Betsy asked.

"Once. It wasn't like this at all. He was big and heavy, and I didn't tell him, but it hurt. It sure wasn't what it's chalked up to be . . . . Have you?"

"Yeah. I'll tell you some other time. Let's just be alone now."

Lenore remembered nights when they lay side by side on their backs with all the lights out and talked until real late with maybe just their feet and their arms touching. She wondered about how the lodging up in Alaska was arranged. Did Willy and Betsy sleep in the same room? When they talked into the night were they already in bed or sitting up at a table somewhere? She imagined them in narrow beds arranged on opposite sides of the room. Somehow that seemed most likely. She tried to fix that picture in her mind so as to avoid having to think about them being any closer. True, it was good that Betsy had someone to talk to and could talk about them, but that didn't make anyone for Lenore to talk to, much less give the book to.

Lenore's room was actually a sun porch with the addition of a small kitchenette at one end. A counter marked the boundary between the kitchenette and the remainder of the room which contained the chair with the stuffing hanging out, a bookcase, a step table, and the bed. Two walls of the room were made up of jalousie windows. Everything in the room belonged to Mrs. Henry right down to the sheets and the glass dancing figurine that had been set out on the corner shelf in the kitchenette for decoration.

Lenore got up and pulled the blinds down to block herself from being on view to the outside. Doing so relieved one tension at the same time it brought on another—she would be making herself suspicious by being invisible. At the store Lenore was hardly ever conscious of herself the way she was in her own room. Alone, blinds down, it was as if she developed a shadow, a double. The doer did. The watcher watched. Her eyes lit on Mrs. Henry's dancing ballerina. She didn't want it on her shelf. The doer got up and walked to the shelf, took it in her hand and fingered it while holding it behind her back. Thin legs. Easily breakable. The watcher watched Mrs. Henry coming up to the jalousies during the day, shading her eyes from the sun, squinting, straining, searching for the ballerina. Lenore put the ballerina in an empty drawer in the kitchenette, one she had not yet found anything else for. The ballerina rolled over as she slid the drawer closed. She went back to her chair and looked at the shelf. A simple shelf; it was more like her.

Lenore had run to this room in a rage from her mother's house. She had gloried in the aloneness at first even though the raw, hollow pit in her stomach had burned and burned and called for someone, when there was no one, to soothe it. She had toughened herself against all the feelings that came with her being there, except for when Betsy had come along and touched off this other Lenore that she hadn't even known was inside her.

She didn't like the idea of Betsy calling herself names, but in spite of not liking the idea, she was drawn to the word: *lesbian.* She was not sure why, but it seemed as though the word had strength to it. Betsy sounded proud of using it. She read the letter over again. Her mind kept going to the part about Betsy and Willy talking into the night. She wished Betsy would've said something about what Willy looked like. Stephanie Pritchett was about the only one she had ever known who had a doctor for a father and she was sure Willy didn't look like Stephanie Pritchett, just as she was sure that Stephanie Pritchett would never have gone to work on the Alaskan pipeline.

Willy says hello. Lenore didn't like that. It made her feel like someone peeping in between the blinds. She got up to make her supper. She figured she would answer the letter after she ate, but she wasn't about to say hello to some complete stranger.

5.

Folly knew something was wrong as soon as she sat down at her machine. She looked across at Martha and saw a wary look about her. There was something more in the air than lint dust.

The story came around in whispers. "Did you hear about Cora? Cora's baby? A horrible thing . . . Cora's baby dead . . . during Cora's shift . . . with her daughter, Bonnie . . . tried to call Cora at the factory . . . Fartblossom, the fuck, he called the police . . . sent them to Cora's house . . . never let her know . . . told her to go home . . . told her her kid was sick (as if she didn't know) . . . last night this happened." Folly felt sick. She stared at her zipperfoot which was stuck and hammering out a wad of thread at the same space. She knew she was behind already, but she couldn't think how to fix it. All she could think was were her own three children home safe, asleep and okay. Even though they were getting old enough to take care of themselves, she pictured them younger like they had been when she'd first had to work nights and leave them alone.

The next round of whispers set Folly back in motion. "Cora fired . . . first arrested, then fired . . . keep your work up . . . Fartblossom's nervous . . . comin' round . . . what's to be done . . . wait for coffee break."

Reasons. Folly wanted to know what were the reasons. Why did Cora's baby die? Why did they arrest her? Why did they fire her? Why was her machine getting stuck every time she looked up? She wanted to scream her questions. She wanted to bang her fists on her machine. She glanced over at Martha and saw that Martha was trying to give her the signal—patience, have momentary patience, hold on and wait and we'll think this thing out and do something. We won't just let them take Cora away. This statement was made by the serious look of justice in her eyes and by the way she sat, her weight looking stubborn in the chair. Martha, the rock. Folly swallowed her screams. She tried to set her mind to catching up production before the break.

It was not the first time that Fartblossom had ever stood his large, obnoxious self up there at the front of the room and swayed stupidly between line two and line three and announced that the first break would be skipped because they'd been working slow so far that shift. It was not the first time but still, the announcement had a grating effect, and in the light of Folly's need to have the break, it seemed momentarily impossible that he had dispensed with it. She thought about being a school child, about Mr. Hickey, the science teacher who went right on talking after the bell rang and no one dared move as long as he had stared out at their desks. She understood why Mary Lou might be tempted to drop out of school. At that age she had thought the faster you grew up, the sooner you wouldn't have to pay any attention to something like Mr. Hickey's eyes telling you what to do. But there was Fartblossom dispensing with their first break that they'd all been waiting for, and already crawling back into his plastic office before anyone had even gotten a mouth open to say, "No, you shit, you're stealing from us."

He sat behind his wall of plastic which was designed to keep the lint out of his nose and glared out at the women who cursed him, called him thief under their breath.

As soon as Folly caught Martha's eye, she rolled her own back toward the bathroom. Martha stood and inclined her head toward the restroom door so Fartblossom would know where she was going. Folly waited till Martha had been gone a few minutes, hoped he'd have forgotten she was in there, then stood and putting a pained expression on her face to indicate she was sick, headed for the back, practically running down the aisle. It was not that one was actually required to get permission to go to the bathroom. Rather the management *highly recommended* one care for these needs on break time. But then, Fartblossom had made short of that.

As soon as Folly came in, Martha took two cigarettes out of her pack, put them both between her lips and lit them with the same match. She held one out to Folly and took a long drag on her own. Then she stooped down on her haunches and leaned her back and head against the wall. "Fartblossom see you?"

"Yeah. He's all eyes. I played sick."

"Shit."

"Damn right."

"That poor Cora," Martha said.

"This goddamned place," Folly said.

After that they smoked in silence, sadness and silence. Their thoughts were on Cora, who was a perfectly good one of them. Good worker, didn't bitch a lot, didn't cheat, didn't steal, didn't talk behind your back, didn't play up to the boss, didn't ask for anything special.

"What can we do?" Folly asked Martha.

"I don't know. Maybe find out more what happened later."

"I'm about ready to walk out," Folly said. "I'm about ready to not put up with this Fartblossom ratfink. I'm about ready to stomp in there and I don't know what, Martha."

"Wait," Martha said. She closed her eyes so that Folly's being so excited wouldn't affect her so much. The house. Folly was forgetting about the house. In her anger Martha knew she was forgetting about all the time, the work, the saving, that she had done for the house. Martha got an empty feeling similar to hunger whenever she tried to imagine living without Folly and the kids in the trailer next door, but that didn't keep her from wanting them to have the house. She knew so well how happy Folly was going to be when finally she had it.

"Let's just think this out," Martha said. "You know we can't afford to be outa work much."

"Negligence, my ass. You know how many times I had to leave a sick kid at home? You tell me what right Fartblossom had callin' the cops on Cora?" Folly's voice was husky and cracked and demanding.

"None," Martha said. "None of his business. It's all wrong . . . ."

"I'm going to ask him," Folly said. "I'm going to ask that bastard what right he had. You comin'?"

Of course, Martha was coming. She followed with proud, sure strides. It was too late for the house. Folly was fired up and Martha might as well let herself get fired up too. This was one time they weren't marching back to their machines to sit and stew.

Martha marched behind Folly feeling in awe of her bravery. By the time they reached Fartblossom's door they were side by side.

He stood up, opened the door. He puffed his breath at them. No one spoke. It seemed a long time. The women stopped sewing one by one and the drone of the machines faded to silence. Martha put her hands on her hips in such a way as to make her body say *showdown* because facing down Fartblossom that way, being so close to his clammy skin and all, had taken her words away from her.

He exercised his jaw up and down a couple of times before he spoke. His double chin wobbled with the motion. "What's your problem, girls?"

26

"We want to know what happened to Cora," Folly said.

"You're holding up the work," he said. "If you'd like to speak with me when the shift is up, I'll see to it you have an appointment."

"What right you got stealing our break?" Folly asked. "What right you got callin' the cops on Cora? What right you got makin' her come to work when her kid was sick? Answer me that?" As soon as the words were out, Folly held her breath.

They hadn't even realized that Emily had come right up behind them until her voice came from there. "Yeah. Answer us that," she said with gravity. She stood straight and still in the silence, her body emphasizing her statement. Martha felt more strength to her balance from the presence of Emily behind her, enough to look around and discover that several other women, Black and white, had stood up at their machines.

"No one made Cora come to work," Fartblossom said. That was all he had to say for himself. His breath puffed away at them. His face was pink. Martha had a childish feeling of wanting to smear it with a mud pie.

"Every one of us has to come to work every single night whether our children are sick or not, or you wouldn't keep us on," Martha said, "and you know it." Because she was one without children she felt strange as soon as she had made this statement, but no one acted as if she shouldn't have said it. In fact, Emily said, "That's right," and Folly nodded.

"We ought to have time off even if there's no pay for it so nobody's got to run off and leave a real sick baby just so's they don't lose their job. I know'd Cora since the first grade 'til now. Went all the way through school with her, sitting next to her most of the time because of our last names falling together. She didn't do nothin' none of the rest of us wouldn't have done. Ain't no fairness in your callin' the law out on her. Law ought to be called out on you." It was Shirley White who made this speech and made it clear from the back of the room where her machine was located right next to Cora's empty one. Her voice echoed all across the room, the sound strong and strange in this place which usually had a hum to keep the whispers from being heard. Shirley might have been a preacher for the feeling of reverence that flowed behind her words. The concentration which centered on her, fluttering in the breast of each woman there, pulsed almost audibly while her statement hung in the air. This attitude of concentration completely transformed the sewing room. A factory was a place in which each woman's mind wandered off to its own escapes, meandered on voyages that were designed for passing time. Here, time was stopped. Every eye was on Fartblossom. Every woman could feel the others' feelings and Shirley had spoken their mind.

27

Fartblossom worked his jaw for a second and Martha thought maybe he was going to say he was sorry about Cora's baby, but he said, "You girls can't afford to hang around chomping like this on work time. You've already shot your production to hell. You better get on back to your machines if you're fixin' to hold down these here jobs of yours."

Folly knew he was trying to scare them. She knew because the fright came on her immediately. Admit it? Never. She couldn't help the images that came right before her—her charge list down at the store growing quickly to several pages, Skeeter never really full, eating endless pancakes if you let him. She did as she had been taught as a child to do with a snarling dog—got a steady hold on her fear and hid it. Then she realized the other fear which was even worse—would the other women retreat, slide back into their seats, man the machines? Would the first foot press the pedal, start the whir of the zipperfoot, leave her standing face to face with Fartblossom, forget the sound of silence in the factory? She reached for her own control again as if another snarling dog had to be met on the other side of the street.

Shirley's voice came clear from the back again. "You ain't answered our questions, Mr. Blossom." She made the Mr. Blossom sound real polite.

"I've no intention to," he said.

"I've no intention to go back to my machine then," Folly said. She looked over at Martha. So many times they had talked this out on the way home and said all the things they would say just before walking out on Fartblossom. Now Folly didn't feel she had anything more to say and Martha didn't look like she did either. Martha just nodded and made the first step toward the door. Folly followed. Emily had been standing behind them all along. She followed Folly, but Folly still wasn't sure Emily wasn't going back to her machine until she went right past it. A couple more women stepped out from the first row and made a single file line behind Emily. Folly couldn't believe it. She thought maybe she hadn't heard Fartblossom declare second break or something. The way people exit from a church they were getting up, one right after the other and falling into line. She didn't dare turn around to see what she knew was happening. There was silence except for the sounds of feet walking until they got past the door, and then there was everyone talking at once.

6.

There was an extra catch to Martha's feelings. It had been moving along
just underneath the surface in her ever since the day when Folly had
talked to her about Lenore and Mary Lou, about the counselor saying
Lenore was queer. The feeling was both a worry and an excitement. It
had certainly not been consciously on Martha's mind when she and Folly
had been standing up there staring Fartblossom down, or when the
whole string of them had filed out past the machines, or when they had
reached the outside and turned around to see the beautiful sight of every last woman coming out too, but that is when, joyous and without
intention, she and Folly had opened their arms and fallen into a whoop-
ing hug together, and Martha's heart had felt the extra catch, a snag, an
odd step.

All day long they had worked side by side on the picket line explaining to the women on the other shifts why nothing was going to work
right unless everyone joined in. Over and over they told the story of
how they had walked out in the middle of the night, how they had left
Fartblossom standing all alone to fart his heart out. They didn't talk
money. They talked about Cora and principles and being treated like
shit. To themselves they wondered about their pay which was due the
end of the week. By the time Folly and Martha got in the car to go
home, their voices were hoarse and their bodies were heavy with fatigue.
Still, Martha glanced over at Folly and remembered the hug, and the
shock which had come inside her body came again just with the remembering. She was surprised at the strength of her reaction and at her body
for acting almost as if it were on its own, without her permission. A
warm glow came into her face. She felt shy and stopped looking at Folly and hoped she hadn't noticed anything different. She held her secret
thoughts close and drove in silence.

"I reckon we'll sleep fine tonight," Folly said. "Regular hours and all."

"Better watch we don't get spoiled." Martha tried for an even voice.

"I ain't willin' to worry none about going back, least not before morning."

"Damn straight," Martha agreed.

The kids were home from school and knew all about the walk-out by the time Folly walked in. It was the most exciting thing to hit Victory in a decade, since the time the escapees had gotten out of the state hospital up on Black Mountain, and everyone had stood around wondering and speculating on whose house they were likely to show up at when they got hungry and would you recognize them when they did if it was yours. Cora's daughter, Bonnie, was in Skeeter's grade and hadn't been in school. Mary Lou was wide-eyed, full of questions and torn between hiding her pride or showing it.

"Is it true you was leadin' the line, Mama?"

"No, that was Martha who went first."

"Is it true you told Fartblossom to go piss in his pants?"

"No, where'd you get that?"

"Is it true Cora's gone to jail?"

"Yes, that's true enough. That's why we went out."

"Is it true . . . ."

"Ma, Mary Lou's been tryin' to boss me around all day," Tiny broke in.

"So," Folly said, directing her eyes at Tiny. "I called her up this morning and told her to be the boss." Her fatigue hanging on her like a weight, she went for the rocker.

"I can take care of myself," Tiny said.

"So can't we all, but we still got bosses and most of us don't like who they are."

"Well, they ain't as bad as havin' Mary Lou." He turned his lip out in the direction of Mary Lou who, as utterly as possible, ignored him except for the brief correction, "*aren't,* stupid."

Skeeter sat at the dinette table and drummed his fingers nervously. "Do you still have a job, Ma?" he asked. Concern sounded in the quiet of his voice.

"I vowed not to think about that today," Folly said. "We're gonna have a party before we start figuring anything out. Mary Lou, you ride your bike down and get me some extra hamburger at the A & P, and Skeeter, you go on over to Martha's and tell her plan on bringing Daisy over for supper tonight. Tell her I'll help walk Daisy over in about an hour. I'm going for a quick nap first.

Folly couldn't sleep. As soon as she closed her eyes she saw Fartblossom standing up there in his doorway, red-faced and puffy, and she saw her and Martha planted solid, facing him down and talking back. The memory felt like a big smile inside of her. Then he grew bigger, and they grew smaller, and she was shocked at her own audacity, shocked and frightened and awaiting his wrath. She fantasized the possibility of Fartblossom or even the mill owner, Big Sam, coming to see her, coming into her front yard and up to the front door, rapping on it, of course not realizing that they had furniture across it, that everyone had to come around back. Everyone. No matter who they were. That brought the smile back. But Fartblossom coming around back, finding her door, seeing her back porch, seeing her children . . . . The blue lights of a police car out front . . . Cora going home to that . . . to the dude with his holster slung in line with his balls . . . her baby gone blue without breath. What right would they have, bringing a police car to her house? None. She wished she had a shotgun. Fartblossom stumbling around looking for the back door. She'd hide around the corner. Wait. Face him down the sight. "You mister misery ain't got no right on my property. You best get on. You make me nervous." She imagined Fartblossom trying to run from a shotgun on his birdlike legs.

Often when she couldn't sleep Folly would conjure up pictures of the house she was planning on getting them eventually. It didn't make sense to do that now, since if they stayed out at all, her savings would be gone right away, and she'd be back to starting over, but she did it, anyway. She pictured a large yard like some of the ones that Skeeter mowed. She had all her heaviest furniture across the front door, and he wouldn't dare just walk around back of that house.

She was tempted to get up and go sneak a look at her savings account balance as she couldn't remember exactly what it was. She didn't, only because she was the one who had declared the pact with Martha that they wouldn't start worrying until the next day. She did decide there was no sense lying there, though, with her mind flying off all over the place, in spite of the fact that she hadn't slept in what seemed like a week.

"Hey, who wants to have a party?" Folly said in the kitchen.

"Me," Tiny said, his hands clenched, backing away from the T.V. Then, as if his sixth pace released him from a circumscribed cage, "Me, me, me, me."

He wrapped his arms around Folly and she enclosed him and swayed with him gently back and forth. The purpose of the embrace she knew was to comfort him, and yet, it comforted her. The others had already gone from her in this way. "All right," she said. "Let's get this barbecue going, then."

Mary Lou was taking longer than her errand demanded. Folly had tried to avoid asking her to pick up things at the A & P ever since the counselor had called her in about Lenore, but she couldn't do right all the time. She lit the charcoal, yelled in to Skeeter to bring out one of the hardback chairs for Daisy and went over to Martha's.

"Ready, Ma?" Martha asked Daisy.

"Ready as ever," Daisy said. She walked to the back steps herself but had to be helped from there. Daisy gave her cane to Folly and put her arm around Folly's shoulder. Martha, on the other side, took Daisy's paralyzed arm. They waited for her to take the first step. "Just go slow," Daisy warned. "My eyes ain't used to outdoors."

She was a shrunken old woman and Martha and Folly could easily have carried her down the steps and across the yard, but Daisy wouldn't have allowed them to. They all three bobbed down the first step, then the second, moving in unison. Then they set out across the grass, Daisy establishing the pace.

"You want the shade or the sun?" Martha asked.

"Lord, give me shade," Daisy said. "Might as well be able to see somethin' while I'm out here."

Martha detached herself from their unit and moved the chair. Daisy and Folly followed, still attached. The older woman's grip on Folly was a fearful one. It reminded her of the way babies had sometimes grasped onto her and not been able to let go. She was about to drop Daisy onto a chair when Daisy stood up even more rigid. "One of you better go after a chair pillow for me. My bones'll go straight through this here seat." Folly called Skeeter to bring one out, and they all three sighed when Daisy was finally situated.

"I'll be right back. I'm goin' to get the beer," Martha said.

"How ya feelin'?" Folly asked of Daisy.

"None too bad," Daisy answered. "Little fresh air feels good."

Folly studied Daisy's hands. One was fisted up tight from the stroke and never opened at all any more. The other rested gently on top of the fist and Folly stared at the ends of the fingers which were bent at almost ninety degree angles. This was the arthritis that everyone got at the factory eventually from pushing the material through the sewing

32

machine. She realized that her own fingers were stiff sometimes when she woke up and wondered how soon they would start to angle off like Daisy's. Folly's eyes moved to Daisy's face and studied the wrinkles, the droop of her mouth on the one side, the set of her neck which gave her the same look of determination that Martha had. It was one of those features that told Folly they came from each other, even though the ways they were different were more noticeable. Daisy was wispy. She looked like a strong wind could blow her away, whereas Martha was heavy but firm, both taller and broader than any woman in her family had ever been. Daisy had been the wind itself when she was younger— strong and sharp and ready with a sassing for whoever needed it.

Daisy's eyelids were drooped part way down and she appeared to be thinking far away, so Folly didn't talk but continued to watch her. She realized that she and Martha were more than half way to Daisy's age. Daisy seemed old for her age but then so did they. Daisy was sixty-six.

Martha returned with the beer and held out a can to break Daisy's spell. "What about you, Ma?"

"Y'all go on," Daisy said. She waved the can away from her. "Them water pills for my pressure, you know. They keep you exercised . . . all day, back and forth to the pot."

Martha sat back and let herself take up the whole lawn chair. "A night off," she said, raising her beer can to Folly.

"Damn right," Folly said. "Cause for celebration."

"I say you girls done all right," Daisy said. "I ain't seen Martha coming home from work with such a look of glory since she won the jackpot down at the bingo game way back when she was no more than a girl."

Folly looked at Martha who had moved forward in her chair and was looking down at her shoes the way Mary Lou did sometimes when Folly talked about her to someone else in her presence.

Her bicycle basket jumped and bangled with the bumps in the road, putting Mary Lou in mind to everyone sitting there listening awhile before she actually appeared in the back yard. When she did appear she dismounted her bicycle with flair, flipped the package of hamburger through the air in the direction of Skeeter, who was standing in the doorway, with the last second instruction of "catch," pitched the bike against a tree, and shaded her eyes with her hand to better see Martha and her mother. And Daisy, whom she had forgotten would be there. She went over and stood beside the straight-backed chair and said, "Hi, Gramma Daisy."

Daisy patted Mary Lou's arm repeatedly, a brisk pat just less than a slap. "My girl," she said. "How's my girl?"

Mary Lou felt Daisy's frailty in spite of the vigor of her pats. She felt the freshness of her own movements in comparison and the oddness of her seeming older than Daisy, regardless of Daisy's age. She stepped back from the chair. "Guess what, Ma. You won't believe it. Guess. Come on . . . please."

"What? Give me a clue."

"Guess what just happened to me, just now since I saw you last."

"Something new about the walk-out."

"No."

"You stopped to rest and sat in chiggers."

"No, Ma. Come on. Be serious. Your jokes aren't funny anyway.

"I give up. Give me more clues."

"Vegetable or mineral?" Martha asked.

"Could be either." Mary Lou shifted her weight from one leg to the other to show how her patience was running out. "It has something to do with money."

"You found a golden egg down to the Hardy's where they let them hens run loose," Folly said.

"You hid it," Tiny added. "Where, where, where?" He ran in circles around the yard.

"Stop it," Mary Lou shouted. "Just listen here. I got a job. I go to work starting Tuesday and Thursday evenings and Saturdays down at the A & P, and soon as school's out, I work everyday when someone's taking vacation."

"Well, I'll be," Folly said. "Guess I wouldn't never have guessed." She gave Mary Lou a long, appraising look as she absorbed the news. She remembered the day she had told Mary Lou she didn't want her hanging out there. Getting work was not the same. She didn't know quite what to say without having time to think to herself. Finally she said, "You got another beer, Martha, for this here daughter of mine who's gone out and got her a job."

Martha pulled one from the six-pack, popped the top for Mary Lou and held it out to her. "Sure do," she said.

"You sure you're growed up enough?" Daisy asked.

"I reckon," Mary Lou answered, not sure if Daisy meant old enough for the job or for drinking the beer. She sat down on a cinder block next to Martha. It wasn't the first time she'd ever had beer, but it was the first time she had been given a whole can by her mother.

"What all you think you'll be doin' down at the store?" Folly asked.

"Depends. I guess a little of everything."

"I hope you won't be cuttin' off no fingers," Folly said.

The comment stung. Mary Lou chugged at her beer. "Ain't you glad, Ma? Especially now with the walk-out? Ain't it good I'll be able to bring something home?"

"Yeah, candy bars. Can you bring home candy bars, Mary Lou?" Tiny asked.

"Not without paying, same as you. Tell him, Ma."

"I just meant I reckon I'll worry a little," Folly said.

Martha slapped the hamburger into patties and Folly placed them on the grill. "You'd best move a little farther out for playing ball under the influence of beer," Martha said to Mary Lou, who had started a game of catch with Skeeter. Daisy's neck got exercised as she followed the ball back and forth from one to the other. The ease of them all there together the way that they often were, playing, talking, just sitting, was the mainstay of Martha's life. They had built up to this over the years. Daisy had already become a part of the family, spending more time caring for her children than Folly did, and after Martha had moved up, she and Folly had taken each other for neighbors with equal interest in good neighboring, women who had to work to pay their bills, leasers of two little plots of clay earth that shared a boundary, clots of crabgrass on either side, simple strugglers after a life that they took for granted was worth struggling after. Martha had never had to think in advance about what she might say to Folly. Just simply she had said anything that had come to mind to say over all these years, until then, when suddenly, she couldn't get herself to ask the question that was on her mind—was Folly still worried about Lenore, and especially now, if Mary Lou had a job at the A & P? Folly hadn't brought it up. Could she have forgotten? Martha was just about to say something when Folly flipped one of the hamburgers too high, then moved, fast, intercepted it on its way to the dirt. The current ran through Martha again, just as it had in the car. She had to force herself to let her breath out quietly.

"How long do you think we can stay out?" Folly asked.

"I don't know."

"Come on. FOOD," Folly announced as she gave the beans a turn in the bowl and began dishing them out.

"We'll have to think on it," Martha said.

The kids had cleaned up after the picnic and then been sent inside to do their homework. Folly could hear the T.V. going. She wished some-

one would rush in on Tiny or Skeeter or Mary Lou, whoever wasn't doing their homework, and punch the "off" button and stand right there
in the spot in front of the tube and light into them about how television
would turn them into jelly people, how idiotic it was most of the time.
All those shows to show them what they didn't have, she didn't understand why they didn't get fed up with it themselves. She didn't have
the energy to do it, having done it so many times before. And she had
nothing new to say, and what the children needed was to be taken by
surprise. Martha would do it if she asked, had done it before, but Martha seemed too remote to ask at that moment, so Folly tried to tune
the sound out and concentrate on the feel of the cooler air which had
come with darkness. She could count on the picture tube to go in the
near future.

Folly could only make out the outline of Martha's face in the dusk,
the strong jaw with its forward set, its severity broken by the roundness
of Martha's cheeks. She could feel that Martha wasn't with her on
thinking about the walk-out. She thought about turning the porch light
on but didn't. They needed the quiet of the evening.

She didn't want to force Martha into focusing on her but she wanted
her to be thinking on the same track. She didn't want to be out there
alone, Fartblossom pissing in his pants over their defiance, and them
not ready for the next step. She needed the strong look in Martha's
brown eyes to put her at ease. Martha had actually been first to turn
and show Fartblossom her back. Folly wondered about all the other
women that had followed. What were they thinking now? Were they
wishing they hadn't? There was no plan. Didn't anybody but her realize that there was no plan? There was no one but her to go tell her kids
to turn off the damn T.V. Martha would do it if she asked. Who was
going to make things work? She started to feel downright nervous, almost afraid. Cora's baby dead . . . blue in the face . . . the blue lights
of the police in the front of the house . . . no rights . . . lint in your
nose and you hardly got the right to sneeze.

"It ain't right the way age works," Daisy said.

"What?" Folly asked, as if she had just been roused from sleep.

"It don't seem fair," Daisy said. "You get old, and then you don't
have to care much. You got a stake in each day and that's about all.
So you could really run off your mouth but by then you've lost your
teeth or your speaking ability or you can't walk, like me, so who's
gonna listen to you. Or you're just plain weak. See, if I was a little bit
stronger I'd plant myself right up at that mill on a picket line, and I'd

stick my tongue out at them and tell them they couldn't budge me with a bulldozer. When I was younger I would've been scared. Now I'm old enough to be past all my fears but I can't hardly stand up. Can't stick my tongue out either. I've tried it in the mirror. That's one of the things this here stroke will do to you." Daisy's voice was feeble in timbre but strong in pitch.

Martha had leaned forward in her chair and was listening fully to Daisy. "That's all right, Ma. We'll be takin' your spirit."

"What's gonna happen tomorrow?" Folly asked.

"What do you mean?"

"What are we gonna do? What are we gonna say? They're all gonna ask us questions?"

"Who all?"

"Fartblossom . . . the women on the line."

"One at a time. Okay?"

Martha was right there with Folly, and Folly breathed relief. They fired questions, fired answers back. Daisy followed their voices as she had followed the ball landing first in Skeeter's glove, then in Mary Lou's. They worked together this way—clear, direct, smooth but excited. They edged toward the front of their seats as they went along. "What about the union?" Folly asked.

"I don't know," Martha said. "We've got the guy's number. They'd help us, but then they might scare some of the girls off too."

"Would they give us money?"

"Maybe." Martha went to silence trying to picture the union. She'd met a guy hanging around the gate one night, an organizer, and that's whose phone she had. She'd known a few people who had belonged to unions, but she wasn't sure what they had done for them.

"Ma, what do you think about us bringin' in the union?"

"They'll all be men, you can count on that. They might do something for you, but they won't care much about Cora's baby. That's all I'd know for sure."

"The way I see it, we gotta put it to a vote before we call in anyone. See what the other women want," Folly said.

"Right. Tomorrow we take a vote on how many want the union man to come talk. That's all—not do anything but just let us ask him questions."

"Good. And we set up who's to come when to be on the line, and who's to look after the children of the picketers and who all's gonna be on the walk-out committee to decide when we'll go back . . . ."

"Yes, what we'll be satisfied with, and who's finding out about Cora and collecting the money for bail." Martha was orchestrating with her hands when Folly grabbed them both for a brief second.

"We did it," she said. "We goddamn walked out on the old fart." She laughed out loud, a laugh that came from deep inside her and rolled out across the back yard.

Martha had her hands back to herself, but she could still feel Folly's touch as if a memory imprint had been planted on them. She felt childish, as if she were playing a mystery game with a shadow, holding herself enraptured with the various possibilities. She wanted another beer but was reluctant to touch the cold can with that same hand that Folly had squeezed in the middle of a gesture.

As if she were a mind reader, Folly got up and brought out the last two beers. She handed one firmly to Martha so that there was no choice but to open the palm and take it. Martha took too large a gulp which made tears come to her eyes.

7.

Martha pushed her cart to the back of the store, wandered up and down the meat counter, and saw that no one was tending it. She saw the sign: RING BELL FOR SERVICE, but she wasn't the type to ring. She went on around the store, picking up the rest of her groceries, then returned to the meat counter. Still, no one there. She seriously considered the buzzer. Daisy needed her liver. As if she had heard Martha's thoughts, Lenore's head appeared in the oval window of the door to the back room, and her eyes caught Martha's. She pushed through the door with a tray of packaged chicken and set it down.

"Hi. What can I do for you?" she asked.

"I need a piece of liver."

"About a pound?"

"Fine." Martha didn't bother trying to calculate how big a piece it would be. She knew that Lenore was assuming it would be for her and her mother and would make it come out right.

Lenore went back through the swinging door. She had the walk of an athlete—a friendliness with her body, a slight bounce in her stride. Martha thought of Cookie, of how she had liked watching her move as she packed a crate of oranges. She brought the liver and displayed it to Martha before she wrapped it. "Looks fine," Martha said.

"I've been hearing about y'all down at the mill," Lenore said. "How's it going?"

"Not easy but we're holding out."

"I saw Cora's out of jail."

"Yeah. That much we got done. When it came right down to it, they didn't really have nothin' to keep her on. But it took bringing in a lawyer to tell them that."

"Well, that's something," Lenore said. She wanted to say more, to express her admiration for what they were doing, but she couldn't think of how to say it. And she didn't know if Martha'd believe she was really on their side. She didn't know if Martha knew about her mother going in as a scab.

"We're staying out 'til we get some kind of policy on taking time off for sickness at home."

"I imagine it ain't going to be easy to get anything out of that old Fartblossom, but I sure hope you do," Lenore said.

"What he's up to now is trying to hire a whole new crew, as if our jobs didn't take any skill or practice or anything. He's going out trying to find every woman in this town who doesn't have a job and stick her behind our machines."

"That's lousy," Lenore said. "That's plain lousy." Martha must not know about her mother or she wouldn't be talking to her like this. Either that or she was one of those people who realize that you don't have to be forever after associated with your mother—you can be someone different on your own. Martha had come to her mind when she had been trying to think of someone to pass that Sappho book Betsy had sent on to. She had her suspicions about Martha based on nothing but an inkling, that and the fact Martha had never been married. This was the longest conversation she had ever had with her.

Martha put the liver in her basket and scanned it for other needs. Lenore had to say something fast, or she was going to leave. "Do you like to read?" she asked.

"I do," Martha answered. "I read a lot."

"What kind of books?" Lenore asked.

"Mostly mysteries."

"Oh."

"I'd best be gettin' on," Martha said.

"If I can do anything for the strike," Lenore said, "I'd like to do something, but I don't know what I could do."

"I'll think about it," Martha said. "I'll let you know if I can think of something."

Victory was a straight and narrow town, Betsy always said. It felt to Lenore as if the town were wearing a belt, tight in the middle, to hold itself from bursting. Or was that just the feeling inside her as she offered to help, while her mother was offering to scab? She drove from the A & P on down Main Street to the diner, only three blocks. She might have walked, but it was in the direction of her room on Back

Street. A stretched out straight and narrow town—Main Street, Front Street, Back Street. Front Street was where the classy buildings were, Main Street was business, Back Street was where the less than high class whites lived, cracked sidewalks along one side of the street. The Blacks lived up past the A & P on a couple of streets running the other way from Main, dirt roads really, no sidewalks on either side. Victory was supposed to be peacefully integrated, but integration was a word that didn't mean much anymore—politicians spoke it with quiet drawls, trying to make it sound something like nutrition, and it certainly had little to do with neighborhoods. Beyond Colored Town was a long, flat swamp extending far back on either side of the road, then a couple of hills and beyond them, the trailer parks that had come in when they had opened up Victory Mills.

You could sit out there by the marsh at night and turn your engine off and listen to the swamp noise. Lenore and Betsy had done it together sometimes. The noise would start out quiet, almost distinct. Crickets rubbing their legs, a hoot owl far off, the glog of a bullfrog. Then everything would start mixing together and the noise would grow and grow in your ears. Screeches, saws, haunting calls. They would hold hands, sharing their fascination. Lenore had tried once after Betsy left to do it alone, but she had not been able to enjoy it. She had been nervous and felt too much like a spectator.

Lenore bounced up the entrance steps to the diner. It had once been painted bright yellow but now was back to an almost pure silver look since most of the paint had worn off. Sabrina looked up and nodded a greeting as Lenore rounded the corner at the end of the counter and sat on the last stool. This stool was more home than Mrs. Henry's room to her. The slits in the vinyl of the seat were covered with strips of black tape, as they had been for all the years since Lenore had gotten her first pocket knife. Her mother had been waiting the counter then, and absentmindedly, without even knowing who she was mad at, Lenore had cut two slits along where her thighs had straddled the stool, her dime coke sitting idle in front of her.

"What'll you have?" Sabrina asked.

"Apple pie and a small coke."

The next day Evelyn had come home from work and told Lenore and Angie about discovering the slits in the stool. "Some folks ain't got no respect for other people's property," she'd said, elevating herself into the category of those who did. Lenore had reddened with shame, looked out the window, smiled behind her mother's back at the sense of possession she had of that stool, and for once, kept her mouth shut.

41

She had a regular habit now of checking in, reaching down without looking and feeling the edges of the tape. She watched Sabrina set out the pie and cut her piece. Many a day she had sat here with her papers spread out in front of her, pencil clenched by her teeth, supposed to be doing her homework, but watching her mother work instead. Watching her estimate an eighth of the pie, the knife drawing tentative lines so she could still redo it if her first guess was off, then the cut, the pie spatula sailing to the plate, Evelyn's index finger swiping the lip of the pie pan, into her mouth with the crumbs the same sec her eye checked the customer to make sure he or she wasn't watching. Lenore had seen her divert her finger, almost miraculously, to the apron, when she had found the wrong eyes upon her.

If Sabrina had snuck the crumbs, she had been too fast for Lenore's eye, and Lenore had been vaguely watching her even as her mind wandered to her memories of her mother. Now she realized Sabrina had been waiting for her eyes to say yes to the scoop of vanilla ice cream she held poised over Lenore's slice of pie. Sabrina came toward her. "Trying to give you a bonus," she said.

"Thanks, looks good."

Sabrina's eyes danced, and Lenore smiled at her as she walked away. They were both the same age. Sabrina looked solid, stern about the mouth. She had dark brown skin, an Afro short enough to make her skull look close to a perfect shape. Lenore found herself constantly drawn to staring at it. It was in Sabrina's deep brown, playful eyes that she had seen and begun to recognize the friendliness that had grown up between them, almost too slowly to be noticeable, not too sure yet.

She had come to the diner, always, regularly, because it was a home to her. When her mother had been fired and Sabrina had replaced her, the first Black waitress they had ever hired at that counter, Lenore had continued to go daily to sit on her stool and have her coke, sometimes her pie and sometimes not. She'd been disappointed that the waitress was Black because she needed her to be someone she could talk to, and she knew she wasn't supposed to talk to Black people, really, other than to ask for what she wanted. But she'd continued to go in the mornings, too, for her coffee and donut. She thought of the counter as belonging to herself as one of the regulars, although she remembered her mother raging at that attitude. "Where the fuck do these folks get off thinkin' they own the place?" First she tried to absorb Sabrina as if she were just a piece of the familiar environment, only this had required constant blotting out of Sabrina's Blackness, both the fact of it and the implications which flew around, colliding in her mind's eye. Lenore wore down rapidly. For one thing, Sabrina's Blackness was striking; for another, Lenore found her own eyes over and over seeking to explore just who this woman was. She had no knowledge in herself of any Black person, one to one, but she knew there was a spark to Sabrina that she liked.

A few times Lenore had come in when there were no other customers and Sabrina had been standing by her stool, the same place her mother used to stand around waiting for business. They'd talked more then, still casual, joked about the weather and how slow things were in Victory. Once Sabrina asked her about her job. "Seems like a right good job," she'd said. "It is," Lenore had agreed. "I'm not complaining. I could be a whole lot worse off." She didn't say anything about how bored she got with it sometimes, so that she felt like she could fall asleep on her feet. "Do your feet hurt after a day here?" she'd asked instead.

"They sure do."

"My ma used to complain about that. I get it sometimes at the store, too."

"I don't know how these older womens takes it," Sabrina said. She took one foot out of her loafer style nurse's shoe, placed it on the floor and exercised the toes. Both of them watched her toes stretching and curling. Lenore noticed that Sabrina's toenails were nearly the same color as her own.

Peters, Lenore's boss at the A & P, had come in then and sat midway down the counter. Lenore had felt momentarily conspicuous about him catching her talking to Sabrina when she prided herself on her reputation of unfriendliness to him. She nodded a greeting, then looked down. "Too bad, other foot," Sabrina muttered and went off to wait on him.

Peters was slow on decisions, and Lenore noticed that while he pondered what to have, he stared at Sabrina as if he were looking right through her. There were times when a person needed something to fix the eyes on to think clearly. Lord knew how many hours of Lenore's life had been spent staring at the stainless steel plungers for the fountain flavors. But for Peters to stare at Sabrina that way, as if she were a fixture . . . . She hoped she'd never done that, but she had an uneasy feeling which probably meant she had.

She couldn't stop watching Peters. She kept herself on Sabrina's side of the counter though she knew she was breaking some unspoken requirement that she be looking from Peters' side, the white side. She noticed Sabrina's foot tapping quietly to no music, calling up a reserve of patience, Sabrina's mouth opening and closing as she gathered in long, deep breaths. Finally Peters ordered a hot fudge sundae and Sabrina, released, went about making it. Loudly, vigorously, she flipped the steel refrigerator covers over the ice creams open and closed. She distributed a handful of chopped nuts on the sundae as if she were shooting craps. The instant whipped cream farted out. Then she pinched the cherry with her agile fingers, poked it onto the white mound, and glided to Peters, napkin and spoon in one hand, sundae in the other. She glided back to Lenore's end, put her elbows on the counter, her back to Peters. She rolled her eyes up in a gesture of frustration. Lenore felt as if her own eyes were furtive, almost hidden by comparison to Sabrina's, whose eyes seemed to talk more than any she had ever known. Sabrina took Lenore's empty coke glass and refilled it from the fountain. They both watched while the foam ran down the sides of the glass before she brought it back. Lenore leaned over and whispered, "Hey, is there still mold in that hot fudge?"

"Yeah, all around the edges," Sabrina laughed. "How'd *you* know that?"

"My ma used to tell me. You never saw me order hot fudge in here, did you?"

Sabrina inclined her eyes, this time to signal who was eating the hot fudge mold. She bent over, laughing. Lenore snuck a glance at Peters who was licking his lips, oblivious. She restrained herself, thinking it was just as well that Peters remain oblivious, otherwise he'd take it out on her. But this had been a point in opening up the two of them together, which had led to Lenore coming more and more to find the times when the counter would be empty and she and Sabrina could talk.

The counter was empty now and Sabrina had one shoe off and was massaging the bottom of her foot on the corner of the ice cream cooler.

"Easy day?" Lenore asked.

"Easy to starve with business like this. Slow . . . real slow. Must be connected to them being out at the factory."

"Yeah. It's slow at the store, too."

Lenore had finished her pie. She squashed the few small crumbs on her plate with the fork.

"What's eatin' you?" Sabrina asked.

"My ma." Lenore looked down, weighed her need to tell against her shame.

"So what else is new?"

"You know what she's done?"

"What's she done?"

"She's gone down and took a job at the factory. She hasn't worked since she left here three years ago. Now those guys want anybody they can find with two legs and two arms . . . . They'll take her and that's all she cares. She thinks she's going to get herself all straightened out this way."

"Maybe she will."

"Maybe," Lenore said, without conviction. She had a momentary flash of her mother getting ready for work in the mornings back when she was younger. She could see the crisp, white uniform suspended in that short period of staying-clean-time before the ketchup and mustard stains of midday. "It's not that I don't want to see her work. It's just that she doesn't understand how people like her willing to do it ruins the whole thing for those women on strike. And she'll be dumped right out when they do go back. I told her that. She says, 'Oh, no, they won't dump me. They don't want them women back. That Mr. Blossom told me, once the women went out on them that way, no way they'd *ever* take 'em back.' "

"Reckon she'll find out," Sabrina said. "One thing for sure, you can't tell her nothing. My ma says when it comes to work, you gotta take everybody on her own terms, because how hungry you are makes a lot of difference."

"Your ma sounds nice," Lenore said.

"She's okay."

Lenore tried to picture Sabrina's mother but couldn't. Her imagination was blank and she didn't understand the vacancy there. She felt uneasy, as she had when she'd watched Peters staring at Sabrina, so she went back to thinking about her own mother.

8.

Folly walked the picket line beside Effie, wearing a placard across her front that said: WOMEN OF VICTORY MILLS UNITE. A young woman across from her going the opposite way wore one saying: WE DEMAND HUMAN WORKING CONDITIONS. It was the middle of May and hot, and Folly passed the word back to slow the pace. "I hope we don't have to be here all summer," Effie said.

"Damn tooting," Folly said.

"I don't see how we could."

"What?"

"Stay out that long."

"Depends on what we get," Folly said.

"You think we'll get something?" Effie's tone was wistful.

"We better."

"Why should they give us anything? I mean here we are messing up their schedule, aggravating them and all. I bet they're damn mad."

Folly looked slowly around at Effie, stared as if she were in a trance. For a moment Effie's words sat on her brain, and she held the idea that they were crazy to be doing this—just plain stupid, foolish, dumb, crazy. Then she broke the spell and spoke sharply to Effie. "Hey, look at what we do in there. You know how many garments we turn out every shift? They need us. *Us.* You and me. They got to give us something to get us back."

"Looks like they practically got the whole place filled up with them scabs so it ain't no skin off their backs," Effie said.

"How many of them you think is meeting production at eighty-five?" Folly had found her anger again and stayed with it. "I bet they got half them machines all balled up with threads. They probably got

46

a triple crew working on repairs. They're gonna have more seconds than firsts coming out of that place. Not everyone you pick up off the street can sew, you know."

"I reckon," Effie said.

They walked for a while in silence, pacing in a long oval so that there was no beginning or end to the line. Folly liked watching how the line grew in front of her just after she had rounded the turn, then feeling the sense of the line extending longer and longer behind her, while woman after woman passed through her frame going the other way. As a child, she had taken a train trip with her mother once and watched the backs of the houses passing her by. She had felt privileged then for this glimpse of life away from home. Now she felt privileged to be part of this march of proud women. She looked at each face for the brief second it passed her and each seemed so definite, strong and clear. She knew that others were afraid, as she was, as Effie was, but their fury had triumphed and was shining on their faces. The mill stood in the background with its closed front, windows from the original construction bricked over. They were in the foreground, where they should be, the basis of operation of the mill, walking in the sunshine, beaming to each other, experiencing the power of their unity.

Folly glanced up to the manager's office windows, but with the glare of the sun, she couldn't tell if anyone was watching them from there. She could feel the eyes of Fartblossom and Big Sam, though, from wherever they were perched, glaring, and she imagined them puffing and fuming, if they had gotten over their disbelief. She couldn't see anyone at the other set of windows which were in the lunch room, either. From the perspective of walking the picket line, the building looked more like a prison than she had ever realized before. She tried to picture it inside, what was going on, which scab was at her machine. She wondered would she get it back when the strike was over? Although they all looked alike, everyone knew that her own machine was slightly different from every other one, and once a woman was used to hers, she could work better on it than if she had to keep switching around. Folly felt very protective of her machine, that and the fact that her place was right across the aisle from Martha's, which made her job a whole lot more enjoyable than it would be otherwise. She passed Martha going by in the picket line. Martha smiled with her eyes, and Folly nodded in return. She could tell Martha shared her excitement, and even though they were still riding high, she knew the next layer down was worry and was glad they were meeting with the guy from the union that afternoon.

Folly made the turn again and saw Fartblossom standing in the road, a few feet back from the line, watching her and waiting. She straightened up taller and looked directly ahead at Emily's back. When her part of the line approached where he was standing, he stepped forward. "Can I talk with you a minute?"

"I'm walking," Folly said. "You'll have to walk too." She never missed a step. Neither did the women right behind her who were next beside him. He stepped back again. He had papers in his hand. It seemed like it took hours for Folly to get all the way around again, but it must have only been a couple of minutes. He was still there. This time he stepped up, saying, "I've got an injunction for you here," and when Folly kept walking, he fell into step beside her. Effie looked as if she were about to swallow her tongue.

"What's that?" Folly asked.

"It's a court injunction that says you can't picket here. So you better call in these here women if you don't want them getting hauled off to jail." Women passing them were hiding their snickers at the way Folly had Fartblossom walking the picket line.

"It ain't no private road," she said.

"You're not just out for a walk."

"I am if I say I am." It sounded to her like one of Mary Lou's smart ass comments, but it stopped Fartblossom for a minute.

"I'd advise you to read them papers." He indicated the envelope he had handed her. He was finished, but they were on the wrong side of the road, so he stayed in formation and walked beside her until she came back around to the mill side, the pride of the women surrounding him so strong it didn't require any concrete form to be felt. Then he veered off and went up the hill.

Fartblossom didn't realize how good his timing was. He couldn't have known that they all had to break for the meeting with the union man in a half hour anyway. Folly passed the word: "Fifteen minutes 'til we break," and stuck the envelope in her pants pocket without opening it. She knew she was taking a chance on him sending in the cops before the fifteen minutes was up, but she wasn't about to walk off right behind the man.

She read the injunction out loud to Martha as they drove to the firehouse. It prohibited them from picketing *en masse* and allowed for only two pickets at a time.

"You know what they'll try to do to two women alone on that road, don't you?" Martha asked.

"What?"

"Run 'em over." Martha was spitting fury. "What a bunch of chick-enshits we're dealing with."

"You got it." Folly said, but her attention had left Martha and the injunction. They had driven up to the block the firehouse was on and parked across the street, catty-corner from the building. Her eyes followed the gaze of the other women arriving before them, who couldn't avoid the figure of the lone man, standing on the hot asphalt, passing leaflets to anyone who ventured within arm's reach.

"Must be him," Martha said.

"Yeah." Neither of them made a move to get out of the car.

The first thing Folly noticed was that he was short and soft, easy to beat up if Fartblossom wanted to put someone onto him. The next thing she noticed was that he was wearing the kind of pants they made in the factory—dark green poly. He wore a light green, short-sleeved shirt, no tie, and most of his head was bald. The fringe that was left was grey. She figured him for early fifties. He looked downright relaxed passing out those leaflets while all she could feel was nervous—no telling who might drive by and put him out of commission before he ever got to tell them what the union had to offer.

"What do you think?" she asked Martha.

"He looks okay."

"A little spongy," Folly said.

"Come on, now, let's not pick him apart before we meet him." Martha slammed her shoulder hard into the stubborn car door and sprung it open. She got out, hoping this would go well, that this man wouldn't be a jerk. She liked the way he looked.

When he handed her a leaflet, she introduced herself and he turned to face her broadly, shook her hand and spoke warmly. He had started without a welcome, but was glad of one now. He asked her questions about the women: what experiences they had with unions, and how the picketing was going. She told him that the women, herself included, didn't know beans about the union, beyond that it might mean trouble, which was what they were in pretty deep already. She told him about the injunction and introduced him to Folly, who let him read the papers, which he did very intently while Folly got the meeting started.

Someone had rolled out a cart of fold-up chairs and Folly stood on the riser they used for a stage at the firehouse and looked out at a lot of familiar women opening the chairs and seating themselves. The building had a high roof and concrete walls which made the metal of the chairs chatter against the echoing of conversation and greetings. This noise which normally would be driving her crazy, seemed almost joyous, though Folly's spirits had been somewhat checked by the injunction.

When the first lull came, she started. She thanked everybody for coming and told them how good it had felt, being out there that morning on the picket line with all of them. They let out a long, vigorous cheer for their picket line. Then she explained what Fartblossom had handed her.

"Why?" Shirley called out.

"Don't ask me," Folly said. "It's the best thing for them. Keeps us separated."

"But I mean why does a court give it to them?" Shirley moaned.

"Now there's a good question. How many people you suppose there are in this town can afford to buy theirselves a judge?" Folly saw several nods of understanding.

Mabel, a large, Black woman, who was standing in the back, asked with a level voice, "Can we do anything about it?" Folly didn't know her. Nor did she know how to answer her. She realized how little any of them knew about legal matters, and while she wanted this union man's place in the meeting to be limited to what he was supposed to be there for, she ended up suggesting that perhaps they could ask that question of Mr. Jarvis after he talked. Then she introduced him and went down and took the seat he'd been sitting in next to Martha, while he went up and announced he liked to be informal, call him Jesse, please.

Soft, spongy and informal, Folly thought, then decided to give him a chance. He was either nervous or hot, she could tell by the way the sweat circles around his armpits were growing. He started out telling the history of the union, but he didn't stay with that long. He seemed to sense the girls getting antsy. "You can read more about the union in that leaflet," he said, "but let's get right down to business." Folly looked around toward the back, saw the Black woman who had asked the question nod. She pointed her out to Martha. "Mabel," Martha whispered. "In some ways you've already done the hardest thing," Jesse said. "You've all gone out over something you agree on. You've all acted as one unit, and you are, right this very minute, showing the management down there at the mill, how valuable you are to them, by your absence." He spoke slowly, pausing to let his words settle before he added on. Folly liked hearing the deep, calm tones of his voice. It was good to have someone who wasn't all stirred up inside the way the rest of them were. "It isn't going to be easy from here on out." She saw the faces of the women giving recognition to their worry. "They're not going to want to negotiate with you, whether you're in a union or whe-

50

ther you try to simply negotiate with them as individuals. In the best of worlds for them, they'd like to control you completely. They'd like to say jump and see you jump. But you've already showed them you won't do that. The best chance you have to make yourselves heard is if you can stick together. And that's what the union is about."

Getting preachy, Folly thought, but just then he threw it open to questions. A bunch of hands went up at once, and he called on Gilda. "Say we voted the union, then what would happen?"

"Then we represent you as a collective bargaining unit. You decide what you're willing to settle for and you elect a couple of representatives from amongst yourselves, and they go in along with me and sit down and negotiate a contract with the management." He made it all sound very simple, almost dreamy, though he certainly did not seem to intend to delude them, and he was not at all heavy duty. Folly realized she had half expected someone who would run all over them, talking like a Fuller Brush Man.

Mabel spoke. "Sir, I beg your pardon, but what if the management ain't willin' to give nothin'? Which if you knew them, you'd understand why I ask the question."

"It's an important question," Jesse said. "There are ways in which they maintain the upper hand, the position of power, such as, they own the mill, they opened it, and they could close it. But you've begun to force them to recognize your power, too. They're counting their losses right now. How many dollars for every day they don't have you working? And that's usually the motivation for negotiating. Sometimes it means staying out on strike long enough to get them to see the light."

The top of Jesse's head was shiny and there were beads of sweat on his upper lip. Folly thought about if they didn't have someone like him to help them out, what would they do, where would they start to try to negotiate? At the same time as she could look around and see the energy in their faces and feel pride in what they had done so far, she came up against a blank trying to go the next step.

"There are other possibilities," Jesse was explaining. "If an impasse is reached, and the two sides seem to have no chance of coming to agreement, the contract can be given over to binding arbitration, in which case an outside agent makes the final decisions which both parties, yourselves and the management, are then bound to accept." One question followed another and Jesse went on in the same quiet, factual manner until he had explained the whole process that would go on if they chose to join the union—them signing up until there were enough committed to petition the National Labor Relations Board with a request to hold

51

an election, then the election: what would be on the ballot, the rules by which it would be held.

Finally there was a lull, no new questions, and then a buzz started up—the women talking to each other. Jesse let it rise for a minute, then held up one hand to call for their attention again. "This is a lot to take in. I know you need to talk it over amongst yourselves and come to your own decisions. I'll be available the next couple of weeks whenever you want to ask anything of me. No matter what your decision, I know you're not looking at a picnic, you're looking at a struggle, and I want you to know I have great respect for the courage you displayed in your walk-out." He nodded and moved off the stage. The applause echoed and Folly found herself blinking to clear her eyes of tears. He was right to respect that courage.

The hum filled the space rapidly again. Effie was arguing across the room with two other women about whether you'd have to belong to the union even if you didn't vote for it. "Of course you wouldn't," she said loudly. "Can't make anybody join unless it's of her own mind." Someone posed the question to Jesse and he explained the right to work law, which they had in North Carolina, and which made it illegal for anyone to be forced to join a union in order to secure or retain their job.

"Told you," Effie said, elbowing the woman next to her.

Jesse declared that these laws were anti-union, that the states which had them had kept labor organizing to a minimum in the South. "If we didn't have a right to work law in this state," he said, "and enough of you signed union cards to warrant an election, you could vote on whether or not you wanted a union shop, which would mean everybody had to belong and pay dues."

"But ain't it better anyway to have everybody join of her own choosing and not to *make* anybody join?" Shirley asked.

"It might *seem* better, but realistically, it's almost impossible. Besides, when you have an open shop, which is what you'd have, you have to spend a lot of energy watching over the management so whenever they hire new folks, they don't get away with checking out how they feel about the union and only putting them on if they're against it. Otherwise, you start out in a majority and next thing you know you're in a minority and they're calling for another election." Jesse gestured with a shrug and empty hands, the powerlessness of the minority.

"You sayin' that if we do go union, we gonna have to worry about this?" Mabel asked.

Jesse nodded. "Nothing in this state is designed to make it easy for you. The best thing you got going is yourselves and the way you've already started out by acting together. If you can speak to them with one voice, all of these voices," he spread his arms out to encompass the women on both sides of him, "then they have to listen to you."

"What about that injunction?" Emily asked.

"For the time being I think you have to obey it. If you decide to start signing up cards for the union, then we'll go after trying to get it overturned. Otherwise, you'll have to get some legal help of your own to fight it."

Then he left, and the fear that had not been voiced, came out rushing to fill the space he had vacated. Birdlike, Patsy Pinder fluttered her hands in the air, her fingernails dark red talons that might land anywhere. "We're in trouble." She spoke with a tremor in her voice. "What're we gonna do? That Fartblossom and that Sam, they must be burning up so furious with us. I wouldn't be surprised if they wouldn't even *let* us come back."

Most of the women stepped away from her, moving back to take their seats again. "We got Cora out," Effie said. "That was the main thing. Maybe we ought to just go back now and say we'll work. We've showed 'em we wouldn't let them lock Cora up."

Mabel was standing in the back again. "What about Cora's baby?" she asked them. "What about next time your kid is sick and you have to go off to work?"

Folly looked around to make sure that Mabel was finished. She took Mabel into her view, fully, realizing this was the first time she had ever done so, though surely they had passed at the clock millions of times when the shift changed. Her chest full of emotion, Folly broke the silence. "We've already gone past behaving ourselves the way they want. I say we might as well go all the way. Union or no union, I think we have to make up a list of what we're willing to settle for, print it on our placards and march it up and down out in front of that mill from now 'til the day they invite us to sit down and talk."

"And what if that day never comes?" Emily asked slowly.

"I don't know. I'm for being too damn stubborn to think about that."

"What about the injunction?" Gilda asked.

"We'll have to picket in two's until we can find out more."

"With a car full of us sitting by the side of the road to keep an eye on the two," Martha added, "just in case anyone tries to get smart." She scanned the faces, asking for others to say how they felt.

"I'm with Folly," Gilda said. "I don't see the generosity likely to come just pouring out of Big Sam. I don't expect we'll ever get anything we don't put up a damn hard fight for."

"I felt good marching on the picket line," Sandy said. "I felt strong, and oh . . . another thing. I sure did like the way you had Fartblossom walking the line with us, Folly."

They laughed, remembering. Someone clapped, someone hooted. Then they all started standing up, clapping and hooting and smiling at each other. For that moment they stomped out fear. They signed up their hours on the picket line and their times for sitting guard. They formed a committee for drawing up the demands. Folly and Mabel were on it, as well as others. Folly felt lightened by their readiness, their solidarity, their pride.

9.

Mary Lou and Lenore had gone to supper together at the diner, then back to work until nine. When they met at the time clock on the way out, Lenore invited Mary Lou to stop by her place for a beer or a cup of coffee, and Mary Lou said yes right away. Since she'd started working, she had been searching for ways to assert the feelings of being grown up that came with laboring for someone other than her mother, and Lenore was the best example she had of what a woman of independence could be. She remembered her mother's set conviction that Lenore was too old for her and felt the energy of rebellion as she slid in the passenger side of the car. A 1968 Oldsmobile, it was ten years old but looked new. Lenore had waxed the two tone exterior shiny, and the interior was spotless. The few times Lenore had picked Mary Lou up at school, Mary Lou had felt convinced that anyone watching couldn't help but notice she was getting into one of the best cared for cars in town. She couldn't wait to get her license. Not that it would take her far. She couldn't imagine when she'd ever be able to get a car unless she went to work full time. Even if she did, and her mother would never permit it before she finished high school, the family would need her earnings, especially as long as the strike was on. She could dream. That was about all.

"What'll you have?" Lenore asked.

"What are you having?"

"I think I'll make a pot of coffee."

"I'm not too big on coffee."

"How 'bout a beer? Or grape soda?"

Mary Lou took a long time deciding because she really wanted to have the same thing as Lenore, but she couldn't stand coffee. Learning

to drink it was one of the measures of adulthood that she didn't savor
any more than having a splinter removed. She thought she'd like to
have a beer, but she'd have to try to get some chewing gum before she
went home so her ma wouldn't smell it on her. Also, she didn't like
the idea of drinking beer alone. As if she were a mind reader, Lenore
said, "Maybe I'll have a beer, too, if that's what you'd like."

"Split one with you," Mary Lou volunteered.

"Make yourself comfortable while I get it."

Mary Lou, hands in her jeans pockets, wandered automatically over
to the bookcase. The thing that had stuck most in her mind since her
first visit to Lenore's was the fact of that bookcase with its three long
rows of books. Everyone knew Lenore as the butcher at the A & P,
and Mary Lou was sure most of them figured her for anything but a
brain. She was a good butcher. That was as far as Victory could think.
But Lenore had read as many books as anybody Mary Lou had known
in her life, and Mary Lou found herself amazed by that.

Mary Lou's hand went to the last book on the shelf, pulled it out,
and looked at the cover. *Sappho Was A Right-On Woman: A Liberated View of Lesbianism:* two authors—Sidney Abbot and Barbara
Love, one male and one female, Mary Lou thought. She stuck it back
on the shelf as fast as she could without being conspicuous. Her hand
felt as if she had just touched something red hot. She put it back in
her pocket. Wow, she thought, be cool. Her eyes went to the framed
photograph of Betsy that sat on top of the bookcase—Betsy in her work
shirt and overalls ready to go to work welding. She had known about
Lenore before, hadn't she? She just hadn't thought about it directly.
Wow. Wow . . . kept popping into her head. So what else is new, she
said to herself. Act normal.

She slumped down into the big arm chair with her beer while Lenore
sat on the floor facing her, her back up against the bookcase. Mary Lou
couldn't get herself to be as cool as she wanted to be, but tested her
voice. "It must be neat to have a place of your own."

"Yeah, I like it. You can keep things the way you like them."

"No little brothers bugging you to death."

"I wish I could have my little sister here," Lenore said.

"Where is she?"

"Out at the house with my mother."

Mary Lou had never really known why Lenore had left home but
assumed she'd done it out of sheer desire for her independence as that
was the reason Mary Lou was thinking along these lines for herself.
Lenore told her about her fights with her mother. She searched the

backs of her own hands as she talked, keeping her eyes away from Mary Lou. Then she told her about her mother scabbing. "It's weird telling you this," she said, "your ma being one of the main organizers for the strike and all. I tried to talk her out of it, but getting her to listen to me, that's just about hopeless. I feel bad about her doing it."

Mary Lou's first reaction was to be shocked. She didn't expect to know any of the scabs. She had pictured them much like the word—crusty, degenerate, not quite human people. True, she didn't *know* Lenore's mother, but she knew *her.* She avoided thinking further about who Lenore's mother might be, and gathered herself by remembering her mother talking about the scabs. "Ma says the scabs make things harder for them, but it's really the owner their fight is against. So I don't think you should feel so bad. Besides, you got me a job, and that's a help to my ma."

Lenore looked straight at Mary Lou then. "I suppose." Her eyes were a deep green but full of light. She had a gold cap on one of her front teeth, otherwise her face was soft and even. "Anyway, I'd like you to meet Perry some day. She's a neat kid."

"I did," Mary Lou said. "That one Saturday I was here."

"Oh, yeah. I forgot."

Lenore went back to the refrigerator for another beer, leaving Mary Lou with her feelings about Perry. She remembered her round, sweet face, her eyes eager for Lenore's attention, her dimples which deepened with her smile. Mary Lou yearned to be cared for the way she could see Lenore cared for Perry. And Betsy. Though with Betsy maybe Lenore's caring was something different. This was confusing and distressing because she wanted to be able to talk easy with Lenore, and if she were a lesbian, how could she then sit in that chair and talk casually away to her? She wouldn't let her know she had seen the book. If Lenore didn't know that she knew, if she could keep cool, then nothing would be different.

Lenore refilled both of their glasses, and Mary Lou took a long swig. She realized she was beginning to feel giddy. Lenore got back down on the floor, only this time she stretched out flat on her back and closed her eyes, let her arms fall to her sides, took a deep breath, then let the air out in a sigh. Mary Lou watched her make this effort at relaxation, while trying to picture her elsewhere—inside a secret life—a dark bar. She imagined Lenore standing up against a wall, dragging hard on a cigarette, her eyes darting about, trying to make out the contours of others in this wicked, beer-smelling place, her body defined and tensed against the probable intrusion of strange touch. Her mother was a scab.

Only trouble was none of this fit with the Lenore who got her the job at the A & P. She felt as if she were doing a puzzle and was down to the last space with only one piece left, and she had to turn it around and around and upside down, and still it wouldn't seem to fall into place.

Lenore sat back up and found Mary Lou's eyes on her. "Pardon the desertion," she said. "Just tryin' to get that store out of my bones."

Mary Lou felt caught. Lenore always seemed to know what she was doing. She was orderly, and straightforward in her thinking. Perhaps Betsy would go to a dark bar but not Lenore. "What do you hear from Betsy?" she asked.

"She's fine. Working hard and stashing away her wad, and I reckon she'll be up there another year or so."

Mary Lou hadn't really known Betsy other than to recognize her. In fact, she hadn't known Lenore either until after Betsy had left for Alaska. There wasn't anybody in Victory that didn't at least know *of* Betsy since she'd gone off, displaying such rare courage as to wake up the memory of the gold rush.

"Must be cold up there," Mary Lou said.

"That is for sure."

Maybe they were just good friends, she thought. Maybe that was one way of being lesbian—having no use for men and pairing up with your best friend and helping each other out. "You must miss her," she said.

"Sure do. We been like this," Lenore closed two fingers tight together, "ever since we were little girls."

Maybe Lenore wasn't a lesbian with Betsy, maybe it was with someone else. They couldn't have been lesbians when they were little girls. Mary Lou finished off her beer and went home.

The following Saturday night found Mary Lou at the drive-in movies with Roland, fighting him off the whole time. When he had asked her that morning, she realized she had given him extra attention all week, putting on a smile whenever he passed her in the store. Whatever was known as flirting, a phenomenon she had never associated with herself, was probably what she was guilty of. It had felt awkward and uncomfortable—the sensation of underpants on backwards. In fact, Mary Lou had rarely had a date and didn't know why. Boys most often didn't ask her out. The ones she liked she felt shy with, and her shyness seemed to erase her from their vision. The only ones who ever asked her out were the ones classified by the other girls as leftovers. Usually she said no, but thinking so much about Lenore being a lesbian, she had decided she ought to try to date more.

The movies hadn't been going ten minutes when Roland started with his wet kisses. Mary Lou had expected they might talk and get to know each other a little, but she hadn't been able to think of what to say before he had moved in. She had struggled with him, feeling as if they were engaged in a territorial battle, the territory under siege—her body. His hands had fought for possession everywhere she didn't want them; she had arrested them here, there, moved them away, only to find him coming on again, stronger, more insistent, almost hostile. She realized she didn't know him at all. She was sexually excited, but she didn't want to be. She felt pinned. She remembered her daddy when she was small, flexing the muscles of his arm until they bulged and holding it out to her, saying, "Hit me . . . hit me harder . . . I can't even feel it . . . you sure you're hitting me?" She remembered the feeling of futility as she hurt her own small, tough fists, packing them into him with her full power.

They ended with Roland giving up on everything else and locking her hand up against his penis and riding it. She figured what the hell. She figured if he didn't mind getting off to an instrument, her hand could afford to be the instrument. For now. She could feel his zipper, and she thought about her mother at her machine, sewing zipper after zipper, handling the empty crotches of zillions of pairs of pants. She thought of Skeeter and Tiny running around after a bath with their noodles and balls dangling, extra parts, vulnerable with their lack of muscle. She worried about how easily they could be pinched. About Roland's, she didn't worry. She waited and wished he would hurry up. She felt humiliated by her own participation, and she wanted to be home, safe and free and able to think.

When he left her off in front of her trailer, he cooed, "Sweet girl, I want to go out with you again real soon," holding her chin firmly in his hand so she couldn't look away.

"Yeah, Roland. I'll see you at work. I gotta go in now." He gave her one last, sloppy kiss before releasing her.

All the next week, Mary Lou built up her nerve to ask Lenore if she could come over after work Saturday night. She had hoped Lenore would suggest it herself, but she hadn't. Roland hadn't asked her out either, but she worried that he would. The nights she'd worked, he'd come up behind her and bumped her with his skinny rear end, as if accidentally. She had been cool in her responses, but that seemed to be the way he preferred it. Friday afternoon he stood at the meat counter where he could see down the soup aisle while she stacked the new shipment of Campbell's, and she saw him staring at her and licking his lips. She couldn't wait until he got off and Lenore came on, and as soon as she saw Lenore, she asked her, "You doing anything after work tomorrow?"

When Lenore said no, she asked if she could come over and talk, and it was settled that she would. And Roland came, sure enough, walking jaunty down the aisle, asking her to the movies again.

"Sorry, I've got other plans," she said.

"What you doing?"

"Visiting Lenore."

"Oh, oh, oh," he said. "You watch out, baby." He made his voice extra deep. "Roland knows. You ain't her type."

"You're obnoxious," Mary Lou said. She could feel blood flushing in her face. She wanted to know what he meant, but she knew better than to ask him.

"I try," he said. He ran his hand across the back of her jeans, possessively, as he walked away.

Lenore bought a six-pack as they were leaving the store. Mary Lou offered to split the cost with her when her paycheck came, but Lenore said it was on her. "I hope I'm not contributing to the delinquency of a minor," she said.

"I guess not. My ma lets me drink beer at home with her sometimes."

Lenore's apartment was exactly the way Mary Lou had remembered it—contained and clean, nothing out of place, nothing strewn around. The books were in their same places, including the one she had taken out to look at. She pictured her own apartment being just like this—a home for every object, every piece of furniture. In the trailer they were forever moving things around, chairs from the dining room over to the front of the T.V., dishes from the table in to the sink so homework could be done on the table, dishes back to the table or the counter or the drainer because they didn't all fit in the cupboards or the sink. Something was always lost. Someone was always on a search. Mary Lou imagined herself living in a place like this, and once a week she would have her mother and Skeeter and Tiny over for dinner. When they were gone, she would put away the dishes and not take out more than one of anything again for the next week.

60

"Want a glass or a can?" Lenore asked.

"Can's fine."

They both sat on the floor. "What's on your mind?" Lenore asked her.

"Nothing much." Mary Lou looked away and neither of them spoke for a moment. Finally she asked, "What do you think of Roland?"

"Roland Tucker?"

Mary Lou nodded.

"I think he's a turkey."

Mary Lou laughed. "That's pretty good." She thought of Roland's penis and a turkey neck and laughed some more.

"I get along okay with him as long as I just have to pass him at the time clock. We hardly ever work at the same time."

"I went to the movies with him last weekend," Mary Lou admitted.

"Oh." Lenore became guarded. "How was it?"

"Well, I wouldn't of minded seeing the movie, if he'd let me."

"He was on the make?"

"You might say."

"From what I hear, he always is."

Mary Lou could feel the intensity of Lenore's dislike for him filling up the room. "He *is* a turkey," she said. "I didn't give him a thing." She knew it wasn't true as soon as she said it and suspected that Lenore did, too.

They were sitting in silence, contemplating this, when the phone rang. Lenore picked it up, and surprised, turned to Mary Lou. "For you." Mary Lou's heart shot adrenalin out to the ends of her limbs. No one knew where she was except Roland.

It was Folly saying Daisy was having another stroke. The ambulance was coming and they were taking her in to the hospital. "I want you to see her," she said, "in case she dies. I know how she loves you."

"Oh, Ma." Tears formed in her eyes and Mary Lou's throat closed up so she couldn't speak more.

"I know it's hard," Folly said. "Can you get someone to bring you down to the hospital?"

"Yes, Ma. Okay. I'll be there. I'll get Lenore to take me right over."

Lenore stood, restless and helpless, as Mary Lou told her what had happened. "My gramma . . . she's having another stroke. She's not really my gramma. She's Martha's mother. She lives next door."

"Come on. I'll run you over to the hospital." Lenore was already collecting her keys and her handbag.

"I think I have to use your bathroom," Mary Lou said.

"Go ahead."

While Mary Lou splashed cold water on her face to try to calm herself, Lenore paced the room, looking for a place to put the energy that was in her arms. She saw Roland, an octypus with his arms crawling all over Mary Lou trying to make her, and she couldn't even open her arms to soothe her without worrying that someone might think she was weird.

She opened the door on the passenger side first, and when Mary Lou was seated, she pressed the door closed securely with both arms, as if the car door might be capable of communicating her embrace. Then she went around and got in herself and drove them to the hospital.

10.

Mary Lou put her books in the chair in the corner of the room and went to Daisy's bedside. Daisy was asleep as she had been every day since they'd brought her to the hospital—semi-comatosed—the doctor said. When he jabbed her feet with pins, Daisy groaned. Sometimes she seemed to come partly awake and would utter a long wailing series of "oh, oh, oh, oh's." Mary Lou had spent hours of the past few days watching and wondering what Daisy could feel in her coma.

Right then she was very still. Her body looked as if it were turning into a skeleton. Her arms were on top of the sheet, and Mary Lou noticed that her left hand wasn't fisted up anymore the way it had been for years from earlier strokes. Mary Lou froze for a second, thinking that maybe Daisy was dead. She had had this moment every day for the past week at the beginning of her visit. She stared at Daisy's chest, trying to detect movement. She thought she could see movement. Then she thought she had made it up. She hadn't ever seen a dead person. Would she be able to tell? Would Daisy's hand go back up into a fist? *Please, Daisy, don't die,* she prayed, but she prayed less fervently than she had earlier in the week. The only one she had ever known to die was her real grandmother on her mother's side and that had been when she was only five, and she hardly had a clear memory of her. And her real grandmother had never lived next door. She felt like an adult when she thought of the idea of having to go on without Daisy. She put her hand on Daisy's arm and felt reassured by the warmth of Daisy's skin. There were red splotches under her nearly transparent skin on her forearm. Mary Lou covered the ones on her right arm with her own hand and watched Daisy's left arm. When did these splotches come?

They seemed to appear between one visit and the next. She thought maybe if she watched long enough she would see one come.

What would become of Daisy if she died? Mary Lou's mind brought that question to her over and over, then seemed to brake at thinking further. She didn't believe in Heaven or Hell because her mother had never followed any religion. Her ma said people soaked up religion to try to feel full when they were hungry. "I try to keep us in enough food," she said. That was fine for eating, but what about death, Mary Lou wondered. She tried for a minute to believe in Heaven and think of Daisy dead, Daisy's body floating in some heavenly sky. That picture did not seem at all right to her. She thought of Daisy in a grave. She felt a hollow feeling inside herself. She understood then, in the passage of that moment, that this was what her feelings were about—the lonely hollow of Daisy's absence in her own life.

Daisy stirred and let out a long sigh which brought Mary Lou up to full attention. She opened her eyes and stared at Mary Lou with a stern look. Mary Lou was astounded that Daisy looked so wide awake and stared back. Daisy formed her lips as if she were going to say something. When she opened and closed her mouth, nothing came out but, "ef . . . ef . . . ef . . . ef . . . ."

"What?"

"ef . . . ef . . . frumbled," she said. Then she closed her eyes and smiled. Spit bubbles formed on her lips behind the word.

"I know," Mary Lou said. "I remember. That was my word."

She tried to get her back. "Gramma . . . gramma?" Mary Lou repeated louder and louder, but Daisy seemed to have gone back into the coma.

Mary Lou remembered their game. She must have been about seven or eight because Daisy hadn't had her first stroke yet. Her mother was working second shift. The bus would bring her and Skeeter home from school and drop them off a few minutes before Folly had to leave for the factory, unless something happened to make them late. A substitute driver, a fight on the bus, a kid forgetting his books—what it was didn't matter—just the knowing that they were going to be late and probably miss their mother was upsetting to Mary Lou. She understood that her ma would be in trouble if she waited for them and was late for work. Still, when they got to the door and Folly wasn't there, she felt small and insignificant. She knew they were more important than her job, but the proof was lacking. She would take Skeeter by the hand then, and they'd walk over; Daisy would be watching out the back door for them, Tiny already with her. Mary Lou would sulk those days and Daisy had to prod her into playing with anything. "What's the matter?" she would ask.

"Nothin'."

"You look pretty mucky."

"I do not."

"You do so."

"Do not."

"How do you feel?"

"Not mucky."

"Yucky?"

"Leave me alone." Mary Lou would say this with great scorn as if to declare it the final word.

Daisy would change to an appeasing voice. "Come on, sugar. Give me a word. Try me out with a new one. Make one up."

"Frumbled," Mary Lou had said.

"I know exactly how you feel," Daisy had said as soon as Mary Lou came up with the word. "I've felt that way sometimes myself."

Mary Lou didn't believe her at first, but then Daisy went around the trailer saying, "This whole day has been right frumbled from start to finish. First the pilot light went out. Then I had to wait two hours for Shelby Johnson to get off the party line so I could call about it. While I wasn't watching, my coffee boiled. I tell you, girl, I know what you mean. Frumbled is a pretty good word for it."

Mary Lou had ended up laughing at Daisy. She tried to think of the other words. Grotchetty, barrowed, urchy, meech. Meech was a scream with me in it. There were more she couldn't remember. She searched Daisy's face, but it didn't look frumbled. Maybe because she had said it. One always felt better afterwards—at least Mary Lou had. She went to the chair and started on her homework, glancing from time to time at Daisy. She couldn't see her face but she could see her chest through the bars of the bedrail, and she imagined she saw it rise and fall each time she looked.

Folly and Martha came straight to the hospital room from their stint on the picket line, greeted Mary Lou, and went one to each side of Daisy. They were sweaty and grimy, Folly with a dirty smudge on her face which Mary Lou was sure she didn't realize was there. When she thought of them marching back and forth with their signs, Mary Lou was fiercely proud to know them and wished she were a few years older and a worker at the factory so she could be out there picketing, too.

"Daisy the same?" her mother asked.

"She is now . . . but she opened her eyes and spoke to me before."

Surprised, they both turned to her. "What'd she say?" Martha asked.

"Frumbled."

"What?" Folly asked.

"Frumbled. It's a word we used to say in a game when I was little." Mary Lou got up and looked down on Daisy. "She opened her eyes up and stared straight at me and she stuttered a little and then she said 'frumbled,' clear as day."

"What's it mean?" Martha asked.

"It's hard to explain," Mary Lou said. "It means *frumbled.*" She caught Folly's look which was one of no messing around, kid. "Sort of like frustrated and mixed-up feeling. Like nothing's going right today."

Martha was listening carefully. "Do you think she was trying to say something else?"

"Nope. She even smiled, like she was playing with me."

"Then what happened?" Folly asked.

"Nothing. She closed her eyes again and went back out. I tried to call her, but I don't think she heard me." Mary Lou tried to remember if the smile had stayed for a while or what. Why hadn't she kept track? Daisy's lips looked dry and lifeless now, and Mary Lou couldn't really picture the smile.

Martha leaned over Daisy, jostled her arm gently and called her, "Ma . . . Ma . . . ." Her voice was husky. "Can you hear me, Ma?" Nothing from Daisy. Martha tried a few more times, then moved away from the bed over to the window. She looked weary and depressed.

"How about a cup of coffee?" Folly asked.

"Y'all go on and have one," Martha said. "I'll stay with her a bit."

Mary Lou was reluctant to leave, but her mother signaled her, and together they went down to the cafeteria. There was nothing to watching Daisy when she was like this, yet they had all hung close to her for a week now, with growing anticipation. Mary Lou was glad she had been alone with her when Daisy had spoken, although she felt badly that she wouldn't wake up for Martha.

She sipped at her coke and kept to herself. The cafeteria was empty except for them and the maintenance man who was mopping the floor. He had indicated the dryest corner to them and they had taken two chairs and turned them over on their legs and sat down. Now they looked out on a sea of chair legs poking up from the tables around them, and Mary Lou was casting through visions of living in an upside down world.

"So fumbled is when nothing goes right," Folly said.

"Frumbled."

"That's what I meant. It sounds like this day."

"What happened?" Mary Lou looked at her mother and noticed the smudge again.

"Couple of Fartblossom's boys tried to run us over."

"*Really?*"

"Yeah, really. That's what *I* said. I couldn't believe it. They came aiming right for us. I jumped one way and Martha the other or they'd have smeared us both. The other girls saw, too, from where they were sitting in the car. We all chased after them into the parking lot like a flock of banshees, hollering at their backs. You shoulda heard the language. We told them what we thought of them."

" 'You shouldn't be walking in the road,' one of them said out the window." Folly's voice was shaky. "Goddamned bastards. They had to get men to do it, too. I bet they tried to get those women who are scabbing to run us down, but you can't get women to do stuff like that. It ain't in 'em. It's in men."

Mary Lou felt panic at the idea that her mother was in danger. Her strong, loud, outrageous, speak-out mother. She had always imagined her protected by making enough of a fuss to scare others around her. Now, suddenly, she realized that was what made her a target. "You must've been scared," she said.

"You better believe it. I very nearly flew away. You never knew your ma to have wings, did you? Neither did she, before."

"You think they'll try it again?"

"I wouldn't put it past 'em, but probably not. They figure they got us scared now . . . and that fear'll wear on us. Some of the girls already started talking this afternoon about shouldn't we go back."

"You think they'll do it?"

"Over my dead body," Folly said, fuming. She was quiet for a minute. Then she softened. "I don't know. Maybe we should. I sure wish Daisy hadn't gotten sick now. I was counting on her for good sense."

"How come you think she talked to me, Ma?"

"I don't know. Maybe cause you're someone special to her. Then again, maybe just because you happened to be there when she woke up."

When they got back to Daisy's room, Folly asked Martha if she saw any difference. "She seems more peaceful," Martha said. "Still asleep."

The three of them stood looking down on Daisy in silence, each taking in her meaning to them. Folly finally interrupted this meditation. "I guess we ought to go fix supper. You ready, Martha?"

"I think I'll stay, if you wouldn't mind coming back for me later."

"Sure . . . or if you want to come home for supper with us, I'll come back down with you for the evening."

"Thanks," Martha said. "I think I'll stay now. I'll get something to eat later."

Mary Lou reached over and caressed Daisy's delicate, wrinkled cheek with the back of her hand. "I'll see you Wednesday, Daisy. I gotta work tomorrow. You sleep well." Then she got her books and went out to wait in the hall for her mother. She felt foolish talking to Daisy in front of Folly and Martha, but she was glad she had done it anyway because she had a feeling that Daisy could hear in her sleep. A superstition. Her ma didn't believe in superstition anymore than she believed in religion.

As they went out the Emergency Room entrance to the parking lot, Mary Lou remembered standing in that doorway the Saturday night before, waiting for Daisy's ambulance. A hot night but she had been practically shivering. She had wanted Lenore to drop her off and leave, had not wanted her mother to see Lenore, but Lenore had come in with her, gone to the desk and found out Daisy wasn't there yet, moved Mary Lou back out the doorway, saying, "Let's wait right out here." Mary Lou had never told her she wasn't supposed to be making friends with her. It would be embarrassing to say that her mother thought she was too old. That would make her ma sound like a stooge, which she wasn't. Anyway, she was glad she didn't have to wait alone. They had heard the siren coming closer and closer, Mary Lou's heart following the urgency of its pressing sound. Daisy had looked pale, pale white on the stretcher. Suddenly Mary Lou had realized that the siren had stopped, leaving a large, blank emptiness in her ears, almost like deafness, and that Lenore was gone. Daisy's eyes had fluttered as they had carried her past Mary Lou. They had been cloudy was the impression she had, but it had all happened so fast, and she wasn't sure Daisy had even seen her.

As they got in Martha's car, Mary Lou realized how far off she was from getting her own. Folly didn't even have one. They shared this one with Martha, chipping in for gas and some of the repair bills. She didn't even know if her mother would let her learn to drive on Martha's car. She stored this subject away in a place in her brain which she reserved for things to talk about the next time she caught her ma in a real good mood.

She remembered Daisy saying frumbled and the soft feel of her cheek. "What's for supper?" she asked her ma.

"I don't know. We'll have to think of something."

"Y'all probably think I'm an idiot, talking to Daisy when she's asleep."

"Maybe . . ." Folly said.

"I just got a feeling . . . ."

"You can go ahead and talk to her all day far as I'm concerned."

"Making a fool of myself," Mary Lou added.

"What's it matter," Folly said. "Look girl, don't let no worry about being a fool get in your way. You feel you should talk, talk. No sense holding your tongue when it's got an urge to move."

"I got a feeling Daisy hears us talking, sometimes."

"I think she's pretty far gone, but I sure hope she'll give Martha a word."

"Martha's pretty upset, isn't she?"

"I reckon she is," Folly said. "It's been hard on her, being out on the strike and then having Daisy in the hospital the way she is. Not that one thing has anything to do with the other. But it does tend to work on you that way. Here we are speaking out against the bosses and the way they run the show down there, and the same time, here's Daisy, laid low and silenced. It works on you to feel like she's taking our punishment. Martha ain't a fearful woman, but I reckon she's scared that Daisy's going to die; like as not she's scared, too, we're not getting anywhere with this strike and it's all gonna come to naught."

"You scared, Ma?"

"Here and there, I am, but I ain't gonna let fear rule me. When you do that is when you gotta wonder if your life's worth living. You ought to see some of them girls over to the mill . . . show them a union card and their teeth start to chatter . . . it's a wonder they don't fall out." Folly wiped sweat from her forehead with the back of her hand. "They don't speak their fears, they chatter them. All that does is spread 'em around, far as I can see. They're the ones who'll be first in line behind someone who's going to stick out her neck to get them something, but if the one with her neck stuck out moves aside, you watch out. They won't step forward unless it's time to cash in.

"You go right on talking to Daisy. You speak up whenever you think it's right to. There's plenty out there waiting for someone else to speak up for them . . . you don't need to be one of 'em."

Mary Lou took in her mother's words while inside her head she talked to Daisy. *Daisy don't die. Daisy, can't you hear. I know you can hear. They need you for the strike. You're a strong woman, Daisy. You always come back. We'll have a picnic out in the yard. I'll stop by your trailer every afternoon, except the days I work. I have to go straight from school to work some days. We love you, Daisy.*

Mary Lou, tears in her eyes, kept her head turned as if she were looking out the window as they drove the rest of the way home.

11

Mabel stirred the beans with a wooden spoon, lifted a spoonful up to taste. Her boy came over and stared into the pot, his ears sprouting plugs that led to the portable radio on his belt, his head dipping with the music. With a thoughtful look on her face, she tasted, then offered the spoon to Dean, who tasted, too, then pantomimed: so, so. She held the chili powder over the pot, pantomimed: more of this? He frowned, noncommittal. They were six weeks into the strike and Mabel was hot and tired and losing patience. She went through the salt, the pepper, the cayenne, Dean no help at all. With her thumb she ordered out, out of my kitchen, leave me alone. He went, stooping his head at the doorway. The week before he had informed her that not only had he surpassed her in height, but also his feet had grown to such a size that she would no longer be able to borrow his sneakers. She stirred the beans again, tasted, then covered them.

She still had to go to meet with the other organizers, though she had knocked off early from the rounds of people she was supposed to visit to get more union cards signed up. The thought had jumped into her in the middle of the day while she was visiting Miz Lucille Bailey that it wouldn't do for the Black women joining the union to get too far ahead of the white women, and she hadn't been able to put it down since. Now she realized it wasn't her idea at all, it was Miz Lucille Bailey's. An old woman, wise and worn, she walked with two wooden canes, swaying side to side. She looked weak to Mabel when she lurched out over, strong when she came back to her center. She'd said, "I be there when you ready, but I ain't too crazy about signin' up them cards. We gotta look out that the Black women don't get stuck out there riskin' our jobs, the white women deciding to pull out. You know what I mean? I got me only a few good working years left, but you watch out for your own self, Mabel, you hear?"

Yeah, Mabel thought, washing up the last of the dishes in the sink, always got to be watching out. Sometimes this seemed an enormous drain, sometimes just the way life was cut out for her—though not by her choice. She realized she'd been carrying this idea that Miz Lucille Bailey'd raised in her all along, but hadn't turned it over. It was like moss on the back side of a stone. Once you'd disturbed it, you couldn't put it back to rest in the same place. Neither did she feel firm about where to go with her feelings. She wanted the Black women to be able to be out in front, and to be proud of it, to fight with their own best strength and to feel the power of that, as she had these last few weeks, but they had to know their vulnerability, too. And they had to know that their fight wasn't just simply with the man. She felt her own mind sway the way Miz Lucille Bailey walked.

Before she left the house, she went in and pushed the OFF button on Dean's radio. He gasped as if she'd cut his lifeline, put a finger over a tracheostomy tube or pulled the plug on a respirator. Deliberately, while she had his full attention, she instructed him to mind Liza, Scott—the younger kids—because she had to go down to the meeting.

For a union headquarters Jesse had rented Bea Jones' beauty parlor over on Back Street, which Bea couldn't keep up working in because she had a slow growing brain tumor that made her hands shake. It still had mirrors the length of one whole wall and pink sinks every six feet and smelled faintly of permanent lotion. Tuesdays and Fridays those women who had been on the line that day and those who were going house to house, talking to the women who had not yet signed cards, checked in here at 4:30.

They sat in a circle, Emily and Mabel and Freena in a cluster opposite the mirror, which was partially covered with taped up flyers and announcements, but not so much that Mabel couldn't see herself and the other two Black women reflected in it.

"Where's Jesse?" Emily asked.

"I don't know but I think we ought to get started," Folly said, her voice weary.

"What's got you?" Gilda asked, chewing her gum vigorously.

"Ain't my day," Folly answered. "I struck out."

"How so?" Mabel asked.

"Got nothing but a headache going around today. No signers."

"I only got one," Gilda said.

72

"What's the story they're giving you?" Martha asked them.

Gilda put on an extra sweet voice: "I don't want to get involved. I'm just not the type to think about politics or anything like that . . . union. I never have understood them kind of things. I just try to go along and live my life without hurtin' no one else. I figure as long as my way don't hurt no one, I can follow it along."

Sure, Mabel thought, feeling closed in and hot in this place—don't notice who you hurtin' as you lay back.

"I've heard that one," Folly said, "but the one that really gets me is: 'I believe that the owners *do* have the right to decide how we should work—how much they want to pay us, when they give us time off.' I got that today, more than once." She perched her hands on her hips, imitating a woman she had visited. " 'This here house you're sitting in. It's mine. It ain't no big deal, but I own it, and that gives me the rights to decide what all I want to do with it, if I want to plant flowers out front, if I want to tear the back shed down, just what. So if I got that right, then those guys who owns the mill, they got their rights, too. I can't have mine if I won't give them theirs.' "

"What'd you say?" Martha asked.

"I told her we weren't talking about planting no flowers down at the mill, we're talking about sick time and how production goals get set and stuff like that. She said, 'All the same we're living in a free country, and I'm glad of it.' " Folly turned up her hands, helpless against this logic, and leaned back in her chair.

Free country, huh? That was something Mabel could hook onto from a whole other point of view.

"I hate that," Shirley said, "when they try to make you out to be against your whole country just because you're speaking up for your own rights."

"You shoulda asked her does she think we deserve less just because we own less?" Martha suggested.

"She woulda said yes," Gilda speculated.

They sat chewing on this a minute until Martha broke the silence. "Okay, if this is what we know we gotta fight, then how're we gonna change their minds?"

Mabel looked up and saw herself in the mirror. This helped to confirm her presence. She had round cheeks, which gave her face the appearance of softness, but she could see as well as feel how beneath the surface the muscles of her cheeks were drawn up tight, firm against her teeth. She wished this meeting was a resting place for her, as it seemed to be for the white women, but she could see in her face that it was not.

Black folks were still getting shot at for being Black. The KKK was riding around day and night. Maybe she was crazy to take up with these women here, but she felt she had to. Her fight was here as well as out there at the mill.

She cleared her throat and spoke, the strength building quickly in her voice. "You ain't heard from one Black woman yet. Now I know you ain't asked to, but you about to hear from this one anyway. You sittin' here talkin' like what those womens says in them houses you visitin' is the final word on why anyone and everyone don't want to join up . . . and that just ain't so. I been goin' round, too, and so has Emily and Freena and some other Black women, and we ain't about to set here and pretend we not here, even though that's what you seem to be doing." Mabel saw them flinch at her anger and added, "Whether you mean to or not. And this ain't the first time you've done it, either, but I wouldn't mind if it could be the last."

Mabel felt agreement coming from Freena and Emily beside her even though she didn't take her eyes from the white women to look at them. She didn't plan to go on until someone took up with her. She had plenty of time. In the silence, the smell of the permanent lotion seemed to grow stronger and stronger, a white woman's smell. She remembered the first day they'd set up in here, some of them talking about how that smell reminded them of home, of their mothers doing up each other's hair in their kitchens, making curls. Not her. It most certainly had not reminded her of home, of Black women doing their hair, which had a whole other smell, not to be confused with this one, and a whole other way as well.

Folly's take on what Mabel said was instant guilt and regret. She knew it was true—no argument. Not that the white women, at least herself, she should only say this for herself, had meant to do it, but the fact was, they *had*. She felt as if she'd fallen into a trap, too busy, too single-minded, had stepped right in. Now she was embarrassed to be found there, at the same time she was glad to know, she was relieved by Mabel's putting it in words. She felt as if this at least gave them the chance of springing the trap. She looked at Mabel, at the face that could break out into such lively laughter, now still and hard as a mountain. It was hard to imagine how her presence could ever have been ignored, and not just hers—Mabel and Emily and Freena made up nearly half the circle. How deep the blur this meant in her seeing, how deep the wound it must leave. She felt urgent in her need to be part of a repair, yet it was hard to step forward. She felt unsteady, weak in the legs, but she knew she could not have the familiarity of her old ground if that meant recognizing only half the circle, over half the women at the mill, nearly half the people who lived in Victory. She had a passing wish for Jesse's presence, for someone outside this circle to open up the contact. She didn't know where Martha and Gilda and Shirley were at all. In her mind they were flying all over the room, their mutual gripe session scattered.

Gilda spoke first, winding a strand of her blond hair behind her ear, "I don't see why y'all didn't just speak up when we was griping about those women who don't want to sign."

"I do," Folly said. "We got carried away thinking that the excuses we were getting were the same ones everyone was getting."

"Yeah," Gilda said, "because they didn't say nothin'."

"We didn't ask. We were goin' on our own ideas . . . . White ideas," Folly added.

The tension in the room was alive and nearly palpable. That's right, Mabel thought. Tell each other. Do. She wasn't sorry she'd exploded this, though she wasn't yet sure where it would go. She tried to rest her mind on Miz Lucille Bailey saying so simply, "Watch out for your own self, Mabel." Nodded at herself doing just that.

Martha broke in with the impulse to move on, asking Mabel, "What kind of reasons are you getting?"

Mabel turned first to Freena, then to Emily as if to offer them the floor, but they gestured silently for her to continue. "I haven't had no chance to talk about this with my sisters, so I don't know if they're gettin' the same thing. What I'm gettin' is a lot of caution about how we could be used." She saw the eyes of the white women widen. "Now don't y'all look at me like you never heard the first thing about the white person exploiting the Negro before, and us living in this here same town."

"How could you be used?" Gilda asked slowly, as if she were unable to understand Mabel's point.

Mabel wasn't surprised. She had encountered this attitude before— whites, who were perfectly smart, sharp even, suddenly seeming to be dumb when asked to comprehend the point of view of Black people. "It ain't too difficult to figure out," she answered. "If the Black women turn out to be the majority supporting the union, putting their names down on them cards, you watch how fast them white boys pull something to put us out on our asses. Set us all up against each other . . . ." Mabel hesitated but kept her will trained on Gilda, whose eyes were silent, not going to give away a thing. But Mabel could bet they were hiding her illusion of superiority. "And if you think this is my problem, honey, then you ain't gettin' it."

"Amen," Freena said quietly.

"I get it," Gilda said, not without an edge of insolence.

"What you think?" Mabel asked Emily.

"I'm glad you brought it up. I think it's real important we understand each other on this, and I've heard this same concern expressed by some of the women I've visited. Another thing I was thinking when Folly was talking about these women who don't want to sign . . . I don't think most of us in the Black community has many whatever you want to call them—illusions or delusions—about this being a free country."

"What about you, Freena?"

"I been mostly out on the picket line, not visiting with folks the way y'all been, but I see it, I don't have no illusions, or no trouble picturing the scenario. For every Black girl we get behind this, we gotta know you've got a white girl willing to stand behind her name on one of them cards, otherwise something bad gonna come down, that something bad bein' to hand over to Big Sam a way to get hisself back a lily-white mill and standing on a bunch of Black girls' bodies to make his ownself look tall."

Freena, so young, maybe twenty—Mabel was heartened by her quickness to comprehend the depth of the problem. She was not surprised that Gilda, the same age as Freena, had visibly pulled in her limbs, pursed her lips, and was translating the Black women's concerns into a discounting of her own hard work. "You can see we're behind you," she said, the chewing gum tucked behind her teeth now. "We're out there every day."

Folly put her hand on Gilda's arm, spoke directly to her: "They're not saying we—you and me—are gonna turn tail and run out on them, but we gotta know how easy it would be for the mill to set us up, white against Black, if we don't look out." Then she looked up at the Black women. "I'm sorry," she said. "I'm sorry we've been so dense on this. I guess this is a time when we can start changing that." As she spoke these words to the Black women, she realized she'd spoken first to Gilda, who meant little to her compared to Mabel, the way the fullness of Mabel's strength had served the strike, had served against Folly's own fears when they rose. So why had she spoken first to Gilda? Because of their common whiteness. Because the pain of Gilda's defensiveness, her need to stay blameless, was familiar, recognizable to Folly, and she wanted to touch it, to tamp it down with her whenever it rose in either of them. She knew that there were white women at the mill who'd be all for having a lily-white mill again, as Freena said, probably even some of those who were fighting with them for the union. They'd best get on with looking at this, both inside and outside themselves. She needed to know a lot more about what it meant to be Mabel and Emily, Freena and the others, to be Black women. She needed to know herself as a white woman who didn't just take it for granted that since she was white, she needn't bother with anyone who wasn't.

Mabel had noticed how Folly spoke first to the white woman, recorded it, but with Folly's apologies, she let go from sitting so tight to another level of concentration in which she could feel her body. She wiped sweat from her forehead. She'd seen Folly pull in tight in response to her, and hoped that didn't mean a wall. She thought her to be a person who saw things the way they were and didn't try to pretend they were different, but she had also learned not to trust that about whites without repeated evidence.

Martha suggested they count the cards and divide them up according to which were Black women and which were white women and see how they stood so far. Long before they got through, they could see that the white women had some hard work to do.

"I guess y'all can't give us lessons on what to say when we go rapping on these doors," Shirley said.

Mabel wasn't sure how to take Shirley. Was she saying, "Poor us, poor little white girls . . . got no advantage when it comes to being mill workers out on strike." She would have sprung back into her anger if she had answered the comment, but she heard Emily's cool voice reach out to Shirley. "I guess not. I guess you knows your own people better than anyone else. Only wait. I just got an idea out of what Mabel's been talkin' about." Emily smoothed her skirt over her crossed knee as she talked. "How 'bout . . . have you thought about maybe some of those white girls don't want to join up because we *are* workin' alongside of each other on this strike, trying to guarantee jobs for all of us, Black and white?"

Mabel looked in the mirror again, caught the smooth darkness of Freena's face, the leveling of Emily's eyes on Shirley. She let out a deep sigh.

12.

Folly woke with a start as if she had been interrupted in the middle of
a dream, turned over, and let herself lay in bed for a few minutes, her
body stretched out its full length. Voting day. She felt the knot in her
stomach. She remembered from her childhood the long days of anticipation waiting for the opening of the county fair, then the morning of
waking, the day having finally arrived, the flutter of the butterflies tick-
ling in her gut. This was the day. She had wanted to be well rested for
it, and here she was instead—tired, achy tired. She and Martha had
stayed up arguing late into the night, and then she hadn't slept well
when she'd finally gone to bed.

If having the election over with meant going back to the routine of
doing her shift, she wouldn't mind that. And she could surely use the
paycheck. In fact, Mary Lou's job had been feeding them the past few
weeks and she didn't know what they would have done without it. She
felt both let down and relieved by the idea that time was up, she was
done with spending her days talking herself and everyone who would
listen into supporting the union, talking down fears that she wasn't even
sure she shouldn't be holding onto, such as the fear that the union
would be one more arm of authority to come in and pinch off another
piece of their individual freedom.

The longer she let herself lay there feeling the weight of her bones,
the more she understood that Martha had been right about how they
were running out of energy reserves. She didn't know how she could
have argued against her, but she had. Since the day Mabel had brought
up the fact that the white women were lagging behind, it had come

clearer and clearer to her how vulnerable they all were, especially the Black women. She could talk big, they all could, but every single one of them needed her job. No one there worked in the mill for the pleasure of being out of the house. Folly and the other white women had gone after cards from more of their own and gotten commitments from some of them, but Folly felt often as if the white women were still in shallow water. She felt an urgency that the women who were coming over to their side understand what they were doing, the risks they were taking, rather than just allowing themselves to be talked into it.

She had argued with Martha that it was too early still for the election, that they should have held out longer to be sure of having a full majority, which would give them a stronger bargaining unit. That would make them all less vulnerable, less likely to get slapped around by the management.

Truth was, something in her wanted a hundred percent, always had. She knew that was a dream considerably off the road to reality, but she'd been like that about her work since way back. She held a pure crystal somewhere inside herself, turned it, looking at one surface after another, always wanted to come around full circle. She wanted to see Fartblossom hanging from the rafters, upside down, and them one hundred percent enjoying it, no one stepping forward to cut him down. She could hear him already conniving if the union won, how he'd play favorites with the girls who'd voted against it, trying to wedge them further apart.

She wished she hadn't fought with Martha. She didn't know why she had, really, except as Martha had said in the end, "If this ain't a good example of our exhaustion, I don't know what is." She recognized that wasn't all, but it was a good part of it. Since the walk-out, she hadn't felt that she and Martha had the same quiet sureness of the presence of the other as they'd always had before. Of course, they didn't have their routine, either. They didn't sit sewing for eight hours every night. They hadn't read a mystery the whole time. They'd hardly spent any time with the children. She remembered how they used to flop down on the chairs on the back porch and talk, slow and easy in the sun, while the children came and went.

All through the strike they'd been running around—picketing or standing guard, or going to meetings, talking their heads off to women who were hedging or had come down on the other side. Folly felt as if they'd been fire fighters assigned to a brush fire. Just as everything seemed under control, a spark would ignite here or there, and they'd go, spreading confidence like a blanket to put it out. Seemed like the elec-

tion could go the same, a fast sweep flaring up over all Folly's argu-
ments, all she had learned. Next to fear, the greatest problem they had
encountered was ignorance about unions. She and Martha, Mabel, Emily, Shirley and a few others had spent time with Jesse, learning about
the history of unions: how the labor movement had grown, what the
Taft-Hartley Act was for, and how restrictive labor laws had been en-
acted in states such as North Carolina after that. Folly felt as if she
could recite the rules of the National Labor Relations Board backward
about the rights of a worker to organize. Her mind contained a black-
board list of "unfair labor practices." Much of her talking had been to
impart this information to other women, but often they refused it.
Alice Crowley saying: "You don't have to go into all that with me, Folly. You say so, I believe you. I can go on your word just as well." But
Folly didn't feel right with this response. It was meant to compliment
her, but it didn't leave the other woman coming in with the same spirit.

Others used their ignorance as an impenetrable screen for their fears.
"Don't tell me nothing," they said, "I know. Where a union comes in,
there's trouble. You're bringin' in outside agitation, what can you expect?" "I been there sewing as many years as you," Folly was tired of
saying. "What's outside about that?" She was tired of trying to pierce
heavy armor with words. She knew that they were afraid of taking
what power they had and facing down Fartblossom with it. They had
all been so well trained in how to negotiate with helplessness, they
couldn't imagine actually sitting down with the management as equals.
And no wonder. Folly couldn't rightly say she could see it actually
happening herself.

She wouldn't want to put money on calling this election. It was
enough that all the past weeks were on the line. She thought of her
mother and father going out to vote for president, her pa changing out
of his farm clothes to do it. She remembered asking them over dinner:
"Who'd you vote for?"

Her pa: "Who you askin'?"

"You."

"Ask your ma."

She'd turned to her ma, who'd said, "Secret ballot. You're not supposed to tell."

"Just us. We won't tell. You can tell us."

"No," her ma had declared with finality. "Nobody knows. That's
what a secret ballot's for."

It was strange how this came back to her now, so vividly that she
could see the pearly gray surface of the table that everyone stared into

when they wanted to look away, and the tight line of their two pairs of lips, firmly closed. She had never been satisfied with their insistence on this silence.

She got out of bed and started dressing. Martha would be ready to go down and vote. She sifted through her drawers looking for something special to wear for this day but ended up settling for comfort—her old, blue, washed-out-a-million-times soft shirt and a pair of jeans. She caught a memory of Martha's face going near despair as she had paced the short space of Folly's living room the night before; Martha looking lonely as she explained how she thought if they tried to drag the strike out any longer, they'd start to lose women who were with them. Folly had felt this loneliness in Martha, almost as if it were her own. She had felt it sometimes when they were visiting Daisy. As everyone else had become more edgy over the strike, Daisy had become more calm. Even her paralyzed limbs that had been so strongly spastic seemed to have released most of their tension. She was awake more but unwilling to fight the weight of gravity that kept her still in the bed. She had talked to Mary Lou a few times, and twice she had talked to Martha, once about the strike.

"Cora. How's Cora?" Daisy had asked, voice scratchy.

"Quiet, pulled into herself," Martha answered. "She doesn't come down to the line or to the meetings or anything."

"Don't forget her," Daisy said. Then she had sighed deeply and her mind had moved away from Martha. Martha had leaned over and tried to get her to say more, and Folly had felt the loneliness of her not being able to get Daisy back.

When the women who had taken the place of the day shift went on mid-morning break, Evelyn rushed to be at the head of the line to the coffee machine. She kept her hands in the pockets of her housedress until it was her turn, then struggled to control them from shaking while she pushed the buttons: coffee with cream and sugar, extra cream, extra sugar. She'd take anything the machine would give. She could use something a little stronger, she thought, but at least the coffee did work to satisfy her craving somewhat. As she went to take the cup out of the small space it had dropped into, she spilled nearly half the coffee. Cursing under her breath, she went to the window, sipped it, and felt for its momentary calming effect. Two weeks since she had last had a drink and still she had the shakes. How long could this go on?

Her nerves were extra taut because the voting was going on. She could see the women pulling into the parking lot in filled cars, piling out and moving toward the door in groups. Fartblossom strode up and down the loading dock nearest the door, making his existence felt. Evelyn imagined that those women must feel his presence as they entered, much the same as she felt it when he strode up and down the aisles between the machines. Nothing caused her to make a mistake more, even now, when she was getting used to the machine. She knew she wasn't great, but she had improved on her sewing, and if she could keep this job, she thought she could get the skill down to a point where she'd be proud of her work. Behind that was the idea of showing Lenore a reason for respecting her.

Evelyn and the others inside hadn't been told what the vote would mean to them. First, Fartblossom had announced that they would be voting along with the striking women. "You are employed by Victory Mills," he'd said. "Therefore, when this here union election takes place, *if* it ever does, you'll vote right along with the rest of the employees of Victory Mills and you will vote for NO UNION. You have no need for a union. If you have any problems with the way you are treated here, please speak up to me about them right now." No one had spoken. They had felt reassured that they were to stay, no matter what. Evelyn had thought she would throw that up to Lenore next time she came by, but Lenore had not been by. Next thing she knew, Fartblossom had announced they wouldn't be voting after all; something about a ruling from the National Labor Relations Board. Only the women who had been employees before the walk-out were eligible to vote, and that was none of them.

Evelyn had finished her coffee and was about to walk away from the window when she thought she saw Lenore's car drive up. Now what on earth would she be doing here, she wondered. The car was shined up so there was no mistaking it. Two women got out of the front seat and two more got out of the back. Lenore stayed in the driver's seat. Evelyn was sure it was her though all she could see was her arm resting out the window, her shoulder sitting just so. Her eyes stayed beamed on that arm, that fraction of her daughter; the rest of her ran confused with why Lenore was there. Then she realized Lenore was serving as a driver, and that this was part of their fight. She gritted her teeth and walked over to the trash can to dump her coffee cup. Someone offered her a downer, and she dug up fifty cents for it out of the bottom of her purse and swallowed it dry on the way to the water fountain.

Martha felt as frustrated as Folly about them not agreeing on the timing for the election, and the two hardly spoke as they drove out to the factory. She ached to be in tune. At least she and Mabel were synchronized about the election; they saw things moving in steps. Folly wanted everybody ready to jump off the edge of a cliff if need be. What Martha kept coming back to was Daisy, the other time she had talked to her, her eyes coming suddenly from vacancy to full knowledge.

"You two."

"What do you mean, Ma?"

"Folly. You . . . two . . . ." Daisy had scanned the ceiling, searching for words. "Need . . . watch out for her . . . you . . . stick."

She'd meant stick together, Martha was sure of that. She hadn't told Folly. She felt almost always now her heightened attraction to Folly and how these sensations suspended her from feeling at ease. She'd never know how much Daisy understood, but she liked to think Daisy had a way of knowing right down to the heart how Martha felt. Certainly she hadn't been dumb to Martha's relationship with Cookie. She had visited them in Florida and Martha remembered her saying, "How nice it is you have someone the likes of Cookie caring for you." When Daisy had taken sick and Martha had come to stay temporarily, then gone to Florida for her things and come back for good, Daisy had asked if she would bring Cookie. "No," Martha had said, "her people are all there." She hadn't told Daisy that it was time for them to be finished anyway, that Cookie had taken to spending much of her time in the bars, her mouth getting louder with the juice, and leaving Martha wondering if she were the same Cookie she had loved.

She did not want distance from Folly, but she recognized that already the feeling of attraction stood as an opposition between them. There were times when Martha thought that surely Folly must feel it too, and not mind what she was feeling. Those times when they moved close in the small space of Folly's kitchen and Martha suddenly felt the current run through her, she had looked for a sign from Folly that she had felt it, too. It was hard to imagine that it could flow from one to the other and not be felt by both of them. She could never fully search Folly's face at these times as Folly would usually look away, busy with cooking, and Martha feared the embarrassment of being caught looking for something that wasn't there.

"Stick with her," Daisy had said, and Martha would. As she pencilled her X strongly in the union box, she willed for many other women to do so also. She was scared for them both that going back to the mill with an open shop was going to be bad news, but whatever it was, they'd go it together. She was willing to pool anything she had. She ached with the hurt Folly would feel if the union didn't have the strength they needed it to have, soothed that ache with knowing she could count on Folly's strength as well as her own.

Mabel and Folly, selected to be the watchdogs, sat directly across from each other at the table where the votes were being counted. The official from the Labor Relations Board sat at the head of the table, Fartblossom on one side of him, Big Sam on the other. Jesse took the seat at the other end. No one had spoken to them except Mr. Halibut, the official, who had explained that their presence was a mere formality to assure that someone from the workers' side could attest to the fact that the ballots had been counted fairly. He had a mustache which he shaped with his fingers as he talked. He took the ballot box, turned it over and opened the bottom with a key. One by one he opened the folded pieces of paper, smoothed them out slowly, marked the vote in column one or column two on the sheet he had before him. Folly kept straining to remember which was one and which was two. More votes under one, then almost even, then more under one again. That was the union. She and Mabel looked at each other and restrained themselves from expression or wild behavior. Fartblossom grunted and shifted his weight in the chair. Some of the ballots were folded over and over again, and as the man straightened them out, Folly and Mabel felt the nerves of the voting women in the folds. When Folly accidentally kicked Mabel's leg under the table and found her rigid, she knew Mabel wasn't breathing anymore than she was. They both avoided looking at Jesse as if the conspiracy among the three of them was unknown.

When the last ballot was on the stack, Mabel and Folly could see quite easily that they had won. Still they strained forward as the man from the Board counted. Fartblossom shoved back from the table. Mr. Halibut twirled his mustache. "One hundred and twenty-three for the union, eighty-nine against." Folly heard Fartblossom wheeze. His face was red. "Union wins," the man said. Big Sam got up and walked out as if he had more important things to do, which they all knew was bullshit; there was nothing more important to him than the fact he had just lost the election.

"When y'all expect to bring your troops back in here?" Fartblossom asked without looking up at them.

"We'll throw that out to them this afternoon," Folly said. "Probably be willing to come back in Monday as long as we have your commitment to start negotiating a contract. We'll get back to you this afternoon, later."

Jesse escorted them to the parking lot, gesturing like an orchestra conductor for them to keep their responses low. "They'll be watching you out the window," he said, closing them in the car to take them to the firehouse. But Folly couldn't keep the grin off her face. It had taken over and was making up for the grim hours of pacing up and down that road in front of the parking lot, worrying each time a car approached that it might turn and aim for her.

As soon as they entered the firehouse the women knew on account of the looks on their faces. The noise of them all talking excitedly rose, then fell in a hush when Martha put up her hands for attention.

"Go ahead," Folly said to Mabel.

"No, you."

"No, you."

"What?" Gilda asked in the hush, one of her hands vigorously squeezing the other. "Tell us."

"We won," Mabel called.

Folly took Mabel's hand and raised it up in the air with her own and repeated Mr. Halibut's count. "One hundred twenty-three for, eighty-nine against."

Then the noise of applause was loud in Folly's ears, almost enough to blot out feeling. Martha was right there. She put out her arms and hugged Folly the way she had the day they'd walked out. "Hey, how about that," she said in her ear. "We did right fine, didn't we."

Folly had a pain in her throat and couldn't talk. She held onto Martha, waiting for it to pass. "Better than I thought," she finally got out.

Mabel had gone off across the room. Jesse approached Folly and Martha as they moved away from the washtub filled with ice and beer. He started out to shake hands but ended up hugging them both, his blue eyes dancing with victory. "I was afraid it would be a hell of a lot closer," he said. "You guys did an incredible job."

"Wasn't just us, it was those hundred and twenty-three girls who got up the gumption to vote yes," Martha wanted to say but didn't. She didn't like the way Jesse singled them out a lot of the time. Still, he'd been very good, very helpful to them, and she didn't want to criticize, so she stood bobbing her head up and down, affirming that everything had gone well. Martha felt for Jesse—the isolation of the outside organizer. She had come to like the shine of his bald scalp and the way he left it exposed when he might have covered it. But no matter how much a part of them he might feel at that moment, he wasn't really. He'd stay until the contract was negotiated, then move on. While they were happy

85

along with him that the union had won, they were doubly happy because they were going back to work. They'd voted this at the last meeting—to work through the negotiations—as they couldn't afford not to
unless the union could come up with money for them, which it hadn't.

Jesse stood up on a chair and announced he'd take a voice vote to
see if they still agreed to go back without a contract. "We can ask them
for a final date to look to for the contract being signed, or we can leave
it open-ended and take them on good faith." There were boos from the
back and someone hollered out that it wasn't safe to presume Big Sam
had any faith. Jesse sweet talked them into letting him leave it open-
ended anyway. He said he thought the management would be willing to
negotiate for the sake of settling things back down and making up their
losses. He didn't have a rapt audience the way he'd had when he'd
started out in this firehouse.

Folly swigged her beer and felt a far distance from this man whom
she had come to put a lot of her hope in. It wasn't that she didn't trust
him to be on their side, but she had begun to see where the separation
came between him and the women. She had realized when they'd sat
in the personnel office while the ballots were being counted, that he had
been closer to a neutral party than anyone else except the man from the
Board. He had watched Fartblossom inquisitively, without the fear that
she and Mabel had needed to hold down. He hadn't felt that he didn't
belong, as Folly had. He may have come up from being a worker in a
factory himself, but he had developed a smooth tongue and an attitude
of belonging with the sort of men you found in offices. Also, there was
something peculiar to the fact that they were all women workers and
that the union didn't have a woman organizer to send out to them. Folly remembered Daisy the first time they had thought about the union,
saying, "They won't care about Cora's baby." No matter what else,
Folly thought, she'd watch Jesse on that one. He knew his union would-
n't have gotten this far if it hadn't been for Cora's baby dying. She
looked around the room. Cora was one person missing from this victory
party.

She heard the women roar a unanimous assent to go back, then more
quietly agree to the other proposals he had made, which gave him the
freedom to go forth as their representative. Then he stepped down from
the chair and the celebration began in earnest. The rest of the afternoon
Folly did nothing but bump up against one joyous woman after another.
Even the women who had adamantly opposed the union stayed and
drank beer and laughed and talked about what a hard time it had been

but still they didn't regret that day they'd all marched out. They'd do it again tomorrow. Folly kept her grin down to a flat line most of the time, until someone would come pouncing in on her, hugging and kissing her, clapping her on the back, and it would erupt as they said remember this, remember that. They told the story over and over of the day they had walked out, told of the long picket line before the injunction had stopped it, of the day Fartblossom had joined it. They told of the men who had tried to run them down, the plans that had never materialized of how they would go in and steal all the thread out of the factory, or take the tension screws out of all the machines, or paint Fartblossom's plexiglass office black.

Someone had brought records and put them on and a few women started to dance, not in couples but in groups. "Come on, y'all, come on," they said, pulling in the people nearest them. Mabel tapped Martha on the shoulder. "I can't dance," Martha said.

"Yes you can," Mabel said. "Today is the day you can. And honey, I agree, if you can't dance today, you'll never be able to." Mabel danced around Martha with her arms held out, signaling the rhythm to her. Martha gave up resisting and started to dip up and down. Mabel tapped the next woman who wasn't dancing, "Come on, c'mon join in."

Before Folly started dancing, she had been content to be watching practically the whole room moving to the music, the Black women and the white women dancing together—Fartblossom ought to see them. At the factory they hung out in separate groups and barely knew each other's names. Since the walk-out Folly had learned that the Black women were more to be trusted than she had ever realized—how they were less afraid to go against the man than most of the white women, or if they were afraid, how they had learned to contain their fear. When she was tapped, she joined without protest, and moved readily into the dance. She couldn't remember the last time she had danced, but it was way back sometime when she had still felt young, and she let herself go to feeling light and airy, let the music buoy her body as she moved her feet with the others.

The ice in the beer tub had melted, the remaining cans sunk to the bottom. Effie, drunk, wobbled up to Folly. "Hey, this is some party, don't you think so?"

"Sure is," Folly agreed.

"I want you to know I voted for. I bet you think I'm a real chickenshit. I know I was acting like one in the beginning. But when it came right down, I voted for." She swayed as she spoke.

"I'm glad," Folly said, not sure what Effie wanted from her.

Effie turned her beer upside down over her head and soaked herself, then walked off to get another. "We got a union," she giggled, though Folly had thought she was going to start to cry. The beer was out, but it was hard to end the party, even then, when it meant back to work, back to routine, back to your own shift, pay off your debts and try to start saving up again.

When is the next time they would all dance together?

13.

Lenore hesitated at the screen door from where she could see Perry and her mother sitting at the kitchen table. It was strange to come to this place where she'd grown up and not be sure she should enter without knocking first.

"Comin' in?" her ma threw out.

"Guess so. You mind?"

"Long as you got clean feet. Washed the kitchen floor just yesterday."

Lenore shook her feet to get the sand off her sneakers and went in. Perry jumped up and tackled her, holding tight around Lenore's waist, then hanging her weight on the squeeze. She bent over and kissed the top of Perry's head, then looked back up at her ma.

Evelyn held up her glass as if to toast Lenore. "Kool-Aid. Here's to you, kid. You won. Have some Kool-Aid," she slurred, imitating herself drunk.

"Won what?"

"The fight."

"What fight?"

"Come on. You know well as I. You came here to tell me you told me so. Now ain't that right. You did tell me so. And you ain't been back since."

"I don't know what you're talking about," Lenore said. It was true and at the same time, not true. She hadn't set out to go see her mother with any conscious intent of chafing wounds, but now that her mother pointed it out, she realized the reason she'd come out to see them this day rather than some other was because she knew the women were going back in to the mill Monday, and therefore, she knew her ma had been laid off, and she needed to see how she was doing.

She took a tall, skinny, plastic glass from the cupboard, filled it with Kool-Aid and sat down. "I came here to see how you were . . . and to see Perry." She put her hand on top of Perry's on the table. Perry covered it with her other hand and waited for Lenore to add another to the mound before she pulled out her bottom hand and stacked it on top of the pile. Lenore let Perry set up the rhythm of the game. Then she escalated it until they were a mass of flying hands. Perry giggled, then squealed with pleasure.

Evelyn ignored them and chewed at the nubbins of her fingernails. "Here I am . . . early retirement. I reckon that's cause for getting drunk."

Perry pulled back and turned to her mother, her face suddenly solemn. "No, Ma. We been having such a good time, you and me."

"Speak for yourself, kid."

Perry looked hurt. Lenore knew the hurt came first inside her mother. Though she didn't understand why it was there, she felt that Evelyn should keep it to herself, and it burned Lenore to see her taking it out on Perry.

"You been stayin' sober?" Lenore asked.

"That's right. You wouldn't know, would you? You ain't been around."

"I know."

"Two whole weeks," Evelyn sighed with a sound of hopelessness. "Let me tell you girls something," she said, for a moment dropping her anger. "Don't ever let the booze get you. I been shaking for two whole weeks. My body feels like I need a can of oil dripped in here and there. I ache, head to toe, for the fuel. You know how it is when you go over one of those washerboard dirt roads that jounces your insides all around? That's how I feel all the time. And it ain't worth living this way."

"Stay off longer, Ma. It'll go away," Lenore implored.

"How would you know?"

"I went to AA."

"Bullshit." Evelyn's voice was resentful. "You can't go there unless you're an alcoholic."

"You can, too. You can go when they have open meetings. I went to one."

"Rooty-toot-toot. I went to one, too . . . when I was in the hospital with my liver that time."

"I wish you'd go now, instead of going out and gettin' drunk." Lenore said this as gently as she could.

"Who needs it." Evelyn paused to light a cigarette. She tilted her head back and blew the smoke up at the ceiling. "I got enough troubles of my own without going down there and listening to a whole bunch of sob stories. And boy, let me tell you, some of them have got stories to curl your hair."

Lenore nodded. "I still wish you'd go." She remembered the stories she'd heard that night she'd gone with Gerry, one of the cashiers down at the store. She'd expected to end up in some secret room, though she couldn't have guessed where in Victory there could be one, had found herself sitting instead, her limbs pulled in close, on the couch in the waiting room of the county health clinic which was in the next town south of Victory. Gerry had introduced her, carefully specifying she was a guest, not an alcoholic. Lenore was grateful for the distinction, at the same time felt remote because of it. She felt remote from her mother now, even though they were so close, so hot together, hot enough to burn out the ability to feel. Had her mother heard the same kind of stories she'd heard? Stories with a turnaround? She remembered the people whose stories she had heard, "I'm Wanda and I'm an alcoholic . . . ." "I'm Bert and I'm an alcoholic . . . ." They had described going down a long decline, seeming to be at the bottom, then finding still more to lose, going lower. She had gone with them in their stories. Finally, washed almost totally out of sight of themselves, making the turnabout. Going sober. Lenore had gotten chills in her back, hearing, then warmth had spread through her.

The declaration, "I am an alcoholic," had rung in her ever since that meeting, so much more a definition than "I am a drunk." She had expected them to swallow the word, but they had left silence behind it, left it ringing in her head. Left her wanting it for her mother. The confusion she'd felt about looking directly at the people after the meeting, she felt with her mother now. She'd been afraid she'd recognize them and that would make them feel exposed, but then she wasn't sure if it was actually her who'd feel exposed. There had been an eye chart at the end of the hall and her eyes had kept landing on the big E of the chart, then studying the four E's beneath it situated with their legs pointing out in all directions.

Now she looked at Evelyn, felt exposed by the idea that this was her mother, looked away.

"Maybe I will go," Evelyn said. "So far I done right good on my own. Me and Perry. Perry rubs my back a little when I get home from the mill."

Lenore didn't dare say a thing. She knew her mother must be realizing again that the job was over. Evelyn refilled her Kool-Aid glass. "Don't know why I'd listen to you, anyway. I know where your loyalty lies. Drivin' them women up to vote . . . I saw you."

"I wasn't trying to hide."

"You might of stayed away . . . out of respect for your ma."

"Ma, you knew just how I felt about the strike. I told you when you went to be a scab."

"Don't use that word, child. I went to work. I sewed. I got paid. I earned every penny."

"I didn't say you didn't earn your pay."

The two of them were squared off now, their defenses rising. Beads of sweat came out on Lenore's forehead, and she wished there was a breeze, but she was sitting back to the door. This was the moment when she always wished later she could have gotten up and left, but when it was there, she never could.

She stared at the red, plastic napkin holder in the middle of the table. Why did she and her mother always provoke each other in this way? She wanted them to get along. She reached for the salt shaker and began turning it methodically with both hands. She had, at this moment, new respect for her mother for going the two weeks sober (she had come to think of her as too weak for that accomplishment) but she didn't know how to tell her.

Evelyn was so angry she couldn't keep two thoughts in her head at the same time. She'd suffered these two whole weeks without drinking. Why? She'd thought she'd known why. Now she didn't. She only knew she felt like a royal piece of shit. It was all she could do to rise in the morning, pretend she was alive, and it was getting worse with time, not better. Here she was, back on her ass without a job. She had to believe her life was worth living. Had she? She struggled to remember that she had, but the memory was vague, not something that could hold her together. The factory had lied to her and here sat her daughter who had predicted it. Here sat her other daughter begging with the big look of worry in her eyes.

Lenore thought the moment had passed with the both of them keeping their thoughts to themselves. Evelyn rose and started taking some food out of the refrigerator. Suddenly she whirled around and opened up on Lenore, her face red, her hands on her hips. "You snot. You're always going against me."

"That's not right, Ma. What I was doing to help them women didn't have a thing to do with you. I was doing it for what I believe in myself."

"Well, how do you think it made me feel?"

Lenore was silent.

"What do you think those women think of me when they see I can't even control my own daughter?"

"What women?"

"Them you was drivin'."

"If they knew you were working inside, not a one ever said a word to me about it."

"Course they didn't, they got tight mouths."

"They weren't thinking anything, either."

"How would you know. You got some kind of special radar?"

"I'm guessing, same as you." Lenore continued turning the salt shaker to keep herself calm.

"Hey, look here. Look at me when you talk to me."

She met Evelyn's stare but didn't say anything more. She felt confused about who she was looking at. Her ma. She could remember her ma back when she was growing up, letting she and Angie get in her bed on a Sunday morning and stroking their heads. She remembered Evelyn being funny and the kitchen filled with their laughter. The woman at whom she stared had a long nose; her cheeks were hollows and her eyes were pouches. And the fury that was set in her jaw froze Lenore so that she couldn't feel anything but the rage that was in both of them.

Evelyn wanted to grab hold of Lenore. She wanted to shake her silly or slap her face, snarl at her, something, but she didn't have the strength to move. She hated the way the girl had her stubbornness and couldn't ever back down. She felt as if Lenore was waiting for something from her. She couldn't tell what but she was pretty sure she didn't have it to give. She wanted her out of her sight. At the same time, she missed her all the time since she'd moved out. That contradiction fit right in with how her feelings were constantly going up and down, around and around, swinging widely. Numbness was at one end of the swing, being overwhelmed at the other. She tried to stay tuned out most of the time.

Lenore detached her eyes from Evelyn's and looked away. There was an impulse in her to reform, to find the way to be a loyal daughter, to crawl back in that bed and feel the caring hand on her head, but she dismissed it. She had to keep her own strength to herself, to be able to counteract her love for her mother, which forgave everything, even abuse that had been leveled at her or at Perry.

Perry ventured bravely into the silence between them. "What's for dinner, Ma?"

"Leftovers . . . and hotdogs."

"Can Lenore stay?"

"You asked her yet?" Evelyn responded as if she weren't sitting right there.

"Nope."

"Well, you might as well ask her first. She's very particular about the company she keeps."

"Can you?" Perry asked Lenore.

"I better not," Lenore said. "I got some things to do. Next time." She stood up and took Perry's hands and swung them with her own. "You still working on that puzzle you started?"

"It's almost all done."

She backed toward the door with Perry's hands in hers. She was stalling to try to think of a way to tell her mother she was proud of her for staying sober. Evelyn faced the stove, watching for the water to boil. There was no reason she couldn't turn around and acknowledge that Lenore was leaving, but she wouldn't. Her back was up like a cat's, and Lenore knew it wasn't going to go back down until she was out the door.

"See y'all next week," she said. "You be good, Perry." All the way home she regretted not saying more, not saying, "I'd do anything in the world to see you back to your old self, Ma." She tried to picture those words coming out of her mouth as she tried to imagine her mother allowing herself to be embraced, but she couldn't see it. She had a cat's back in her, too, which was forever up in Evelyn's presence. Besides, she was no longer sure who the old self was. Her mother's old self went with her old self, which had a child's view.

Lenore felt the heat of the late afternoon along with her confusion. She thought of going to her room and taking a cold shower, lowering the venetian blinds all the way round and lying back on her bed, no clothes, waiting for the cool of evening to fix some supper for herself. She felt remote as she drove along, remote and lonely. She should write to Betsy. She should let herself remember more the times they had enjoyed together. She realized that she hardly thought of herself as a person with a body a lot of the time, except when her mother flashed that fury, her own body winced.

She found herself pulling into the parking lot of the diner despite the fact that it wasn't a good time of day to find Sabrina idle. As long as her stool was empty it was still second home. The counter was busy but not full and no one had gone for her end. Sabrina brought her a coke. "What's up?" she asked.

"Nothing much."

Sabrina tossed the coffee grounds from the empty vat into the garbage and mechanically went about preparing for a fresh supply. She filled the pitcher with water to pour over the new grounds, while casing Lenore's face. "You look like nothing much, my foot. You look pale." She poured the water into the vat, flapped the large, aluminum lid back on as if she were clapping a cymbal and took off for the other end of the counter before Lenore gathered herself to respond. Lenore felt self-conscious, even guilty, that this woman had taken a reading of how she was from her complexion, when she had never thought of seeing Sabrina's color as one with possible variation.

Sabrina didn't have time to get back down to her end, but Lenore found herself soothed just by watching her work. She took the orders, wrote them up and shoved the tablet back in her pocket, then flowed, up and down the counter, gathering what she needed for several orders together. Her left wrist and forearm a chain of cups filled with steaming coffee, she immobilized that part of her body while flipping up the cooler cover with her right hand and dipping in for the half and half to fill the empty pitcher. Lenore had watched her mother do this work, also deftly, as if there were no effort involved. She remembered her mother coming home, setting out her ashtray and her cigarettes, her bottle and her glass, saying move over, I need the couch, my feet, my poor aching feet. That floor came right up through my feet today. In the end Evelyn had gotten dropsy. She had scalded her own arm and spilled on the customers. She had said she was sure they had put steel spurs into the concrete under the tile—spurs that had worked on her nerves.

Muriel arrived crisp and clean, her white shoes freshly polished. Sabrina came down to Lenore's end and conferred with Muriel: "Woman, am I glad to see you. Whew. They've had me running. New coffee's made. I'll finish up these few. Then I'll sit up here with Lenore 'til the tips come in." The last thing Sabrina did behind the counter was to scoop herself up a generous helping of fudge ripple ice cream, which she placed next to Lenore for herself.

"Take a load off your feet," Lenore said.

"I intend to." She brought her tip box around with her.

"Busy enough?"

"I'm not complainin'. First day in some time it might be worth counting." She unlocked the box with a key she had pinned to her pocket. When she finished counting, she stacked most of the coins in piles to be exchanged by Muriel for bills from the cash register as soon as she had the time.

"So nothing's doing, huh?" she said as she moved the piles forward.

"Nothin' except I went out to see my ma."

"Who's laid off."

"Right."

Muriel came and took the piles and gave Sabrina more change from some customers who had just left. She brought back the bills which Sabrina counted, then carefully folded and pushed to the bottom of her pocket.

"Look, I gotta get out of this joint," Sabrina said suddenly.

"Yeah, me too. I was on my way home." Lenore's need sprung the next words out of her mouth without premeditation. "Want to stop by my place?" Then she was sure Sabrina would say no, so she didn't look at her, but still she saw her in her peripheral vision, squinching up her face, making a decision.

"Okay," Sabrina said. "You're on. I'll follow. You know which is my rattletrap?"

The sun was shining in strong from the West, and Lenore closed the venetian blinds over the bed to shade the room, while saying, "Make yourself at home. Have a seat, and I'll put on water for coffee."

Sabrina perched on one of the stools that stood at the counter which divided the kitchenette from the rest of the room. She tapped her fingers on the counter. Lenore was aware that the blinds were open all across the front of the room and that Mrs. Henry could see in her kitchen window if she cared to. She tried hard to put Mrs. Henry's eyes out of her mind but didn't entirely succeed. Much as she wanted to refuse to give any credence to Mrs. Henry's views, part of her beamed from Mrs. Henry's kitchen to her own like a ray of light, landing on Sabrina. What's it to her, she thought, agitating the spirit of rebellion in herself. But still her own fears stirred in her. She had never really defined them. Mrs. Henry didn't represent the KKK to her, but those marksmen of violence and hate did stand at the far end of her fear. And she knew they still existed, knew that some of the men she worked with at the store probably belonged. Mrs. Henry, if she saw Sabrina there visiting as a friend, would not see her as Sabrina but as a large, dark woman—alien, strange. Though if she saw her working at the counter, she wouldn't think her strange—she'd think her in her place.

Lenore whistled with her nerves as she got down the mugs, placed them on the counter along with the sugar and milk. If Mrs. Henry could know Lenore's mind, she'd find her strange for being so glad Sabrina had agreed to come. She felt light, almost as if she could fly if she stepped off a high point right then, perhaps because although she still had her fears, she had left off allowing them to control her. Breaking rules that had never been spoken left her feeling the excitement of the tightrope walker. She hoped Sabrina couldn't feel all her tensions, all these eyes beaming on her. She wanted Sabrina to be comfortable here, wanted them to be friends.

"How was it, going out to your house?" Sabrina asked.

"Ma was steamin'. Pissed because I didn't come out all during the strike." Lenore poured the coffee into the mugs.

"I guess you could have predicted that."

"Woulda been smart to. Sometimes when you're too close to someone, you don't act smart, though."

Sabrina nodded agreement, but Lenore wasn't sure she really agreed since she didn't say anything more but had a questioning look on her face.

Lenore continued, "She gave up the booze two weeks ago. That's a long time for her." Sadness came into her voice. "Course now she's threatening to go back on it."

Sabrina's eyes met Lenore's then and conveyed a strong sense of understanding. "I guess if she decides to, there's not much of anything you can do."

"I know." Lenore leaned on her elbows on the counter and sipped at her coffee. Sabrina seemed to understand so much of how she suffered over her family. She realized she knew almost nothing about Sabrina's people and tried to think of a way to ask about them without seeming nosey. She looked quizzically at Sabrina. "Your ma drink?"

Play-acting, Sabrina gave a startled expression. "You kiddin'? NO WAY. My ma's the bride of Jesus, and she drinketh in the words of the Lord."

"Oh."

"My aunt, on the other hand, you look at her cross-eyed, she figures she's got cause for a binge." Sabrina laughed.

Lenore laughed along with her.

"It ain't funny, really, though she can be quite amusing at times. I do love the woman, but I fear for what'll become of her."

"She live in Victory?"

"Sure 'nough. She lives with us."

"Oh."

When the doorbell rang, the adrenalin shot Lenore's heart up like a hard ball. How Mrs. Henry or anyone could have walked right up across the yard without her noticing or hearing a thing, she couldn't believe. Her pupils were dilated so wide the paper boy looked extra small when she opened the door. "Collectin'," he said.

"Hold on," she said, going for the money and stalling for time to collect herself.

She wiped her forehead with the back of her hand. "I didn't hear him comin'," she said after he left. "Did you?"

"Nope." Sabrina moved off the stool and Lenore realized she'd been statue-still since the moment the doorbell had rung. "But I didn't jump as bad as you."

Lenore felt trapped, said nothing.

Sabrina, generously, tried to relax her. "Hey, it's okay. I been Black all my life, you know. Learned a long time ago not to get too laid back inside a white person's house."

Lenore heard what she was saying. She felt her own face still flushed with shock and embarrassment. She wanted most at that moment to be set off from white people, not connected to them, but knew that was impossible.

"I gotta get going," Sabrina said.

"I was fixin' to make myself some supper. I've got plenty if you'd like to stay."

"I'm due home, but thanks anyway. I gotta go take care of my baby."

"Sure," Lenore said. She tried to sound very casual. Why hadn't she ever realized Sabrina had a baby? This was ridiculous. She talked to her every other day. "How old's your baby?"

"He'll be two in August."

"I bet he's cute."

"He's somethin' else."

After Sabrina was gone Lenore couldn't think of anything else all evening but WOW, WOW, she's got a baby, she's had a baby ever since she's been working at the counter, must've had him right before she started, must've been pregnant when she quit school. For all she knew, maybe she had a husband, too. Now how could she get around to asking about that?

She sat down and wrote to Betsy, starting, "You wouldn't believe . . ." then telling everything including about the paper boy and Mrs. Henry's eyes. She was relieved to give over all this information to Betsy, even her own shame that she had wished the blinds had been closed before she'd brought Sabrina in. By the time she finished the letter, she was feeling her way to the realization that it wouldn't be such a shock to know Sabrina had a baby, if she weren't needing more of a mama for herself.

14.

Waking, Lenore remembered her dream of Betsy lost on some vast tundra, with only horizon in any direction she looked. There was a tunnel stretching out endlessly, which Betsy followed—tired, tense, but moving steadily. The dream was Lenore's wish to funnel Betsy back to Victory, fall asleep beside her and wake to her warmth and smell for one morning. She often felt so alone and separate from the rest of the world; that was why she didn't eat breakfast in her room. She gave herself fifteen minutes between waking and leaving her place in the morning, which left her enough time to stop at the diner for coffee and a donut before work.

"Mornin'," muttered several of the men at the counter as she entered.

"Mornin'," Sabrina said, placing a cup of coffee in front of her, then lifting the cover off the donut case and indicating the selection to Lenore.

"Sugar," Lenore said.

Sabrina brought her the sugar donut. "How's that baby?" Lenore asked.

"Just fine."

"What's his name?"

"Elijah."

With Sabrina every answer brought another question, but since she was busy at the other end, Lenore was left to ponder alone. She realized she knew most of the white people in Victory simply because they lived there and the town was small enough that word passed, within a class, at least. What she knew of the classy folks was another thing—it was speculation injected with spite. What she knew of the Blacks was next to nothing. She'd grown up side by side with them in school but been guided not to look at them as real. She was meant to have no business with them one to one, the way she was getting to know Sabrina. That message went deep, so deep she didn't know what vehicle had been used to carry it into her. She felt a huge sadness which went to the same depth and which had before only been touched by her mother. And she felt the tension she had always experienced as a child when anyone got it for being out of bounds. You're out of line, Suzy. Step back in. Look what you're doing to the line . . . . Foul ball . . . out of bounds. Even when it hadn't been her, and it usually hadn't, she'd always felt better, felt released from some unspoken confinement, when someone was breaking the rules. It wasn't that she hadn't felt fear, but with it a satisfaction, an opening out that promised fruition.

Why was she not supposed to care for Black people? What would it matter to any other white if she did? It would mess up the line. She was supposed to stay in hiding behind her own skin and fit in the place that had been made for her. In which she didn't fit, anyway. She wondered with some further trepidation if Sabrina had guessed that she was a lesbian. Not that she had ever called herself one. But since Betsy had placed the word in her head, she'd found it periodically standing up in her mind, as if it were printed on a placard. She thought of the women who had walked the picket line all those weeks out at the mill, their signs announcing what they believed in. She envied the way they had stood together.

If she were to wear a sign that said LESBIAN and parade up and down Victory with it, she would surely be parading alone.

Lenore had given *Sappho Was A Right On Woman* to Martha the day before the election and hadn't seen her since. She'd built up the nerve to do this over a couple of talks they had when Martha'd called her to do some work for the strike. She had driven several times, bringing women without transportation to the meetings, and the day before the vote, she'd babysat for one of the women who had gone out politicking. When she'd stopped by Martha's place for directions first, Martha had sat her down and offered her a cup of coffee.

"You're probably in a hurry," Lenore had said.

"Actually, I could use a chance to sit a minute."

They had sipped coffee, neither saying more for a while. Lenore had glanced back and forth from the window to the insides of Martha's trailer. It reminded her of pictures she'd seen of the insides of ships. The walls were paneled with fake wood. The couch had a yellow chenille spread neatly tucked in its crack, and the blond coffee table in front of it was cleared except for an ashtray and a paperback book. It was one of those coffee tables with a low rail around it, which would have served a purpose on a ship. The linoleum on the kitchen floor had ovals where it had worn down beneath its pattern in front of the sink and the stove. The linoleum was green but the ovals had turned to black spots. These kept catching Lenore's eye when she glanced in from the sun, these and Daisy's cane, which was propped against the wall of the hallway that must go to the bathroom and bedrooms. She didn't know whether or not to ask about Daisy. She knew from Mary Lou that she was still in bad shape in the hospital, and she worried that it would upset Martha if she asked about her.

It was Martha who broke the silence. "How you like living over there alone?"

"It's okay."

"Sometimes lonely?" she asked, her voice almost gruff and yet reassuring to Lenore.

"Sometimes."

"I know it's strange to me, here, with my mother in the hospital. I go around listenin' to my own noises."

"Yeah, sometimes you feel like the rest of the world can hear you shuffling around."

"When's Betsy coming back?" Martha asked.

She took Lenore completely off guard asking like that out of the clear blue and as if she so firmly knew that Betsy's absence was a large part of Lenore's loneliness. Lenore felt as if she were about to cry but shrugged instead and stared at the ovals on the floor. Finally, she said, "When she's ready, I reckon, or else when the job's through."

"I had a girlfriend, once, before I went down to Florida, who decided to go up North. She wanted to be an actress."

"Did she get to be one?"

"Not that I know of. She went right to New York City, though, and went around trying out for things. She ended up being a waitress at Howard Johnson's. Said that was what all the people who came to New York to be actresses did first . . . a Howard Johnson's right near the theatres. She wrote and told me about all them famous people comin' in for lunch to her tables."

Lenore had hardly been able to concentrate on anything Martha had said after the word *girlfriend.* Did that mean girlfriend the way Betsy was her girlfriend, or did that mean friend? She had to digest the idea that Martha might be telling her she was a lesbian, before she could even entertain the threat involved in the possibility that Martha's girlfriend hadn't ever come back home. She had stopped looking out the window and was keeping her eyes on Martha for any signal. "Did she ever come back home?" she finally asked outright.

Martha met her eyes. "Only once to visit, while I was still here. She wanted me to come up and see New York City, but I never did. My luck, I'd get lost in the crowd. Every once in a while I turn on T.V. and think, wouldn't it be something else if I started watching a movie and on came Lucinda—presuming I'd recognize her, of course."

Lenore was almost one hundred percent positive Martha was saying Lucinda had been her *girlfriend.* Still, she shook inside to control her cool on the outside, as she told her she had this book she'd like her to look at. "If you don't feel like reading it, that's fine with me," she said. "The only reason I have it is Betsy sent it to me and someone told her to tell each person to pass it on to someone else."

"What kind of a book?" Martha asked.

"I'll show you. I got it in the car. I better get going, too."

She got the directions for where she was supposed to babysit from Martha. She folded the paper and pushed it in the back pocket of her jeans. "I'll get the book," she said. She practically ran out to the car. How could she explain what she was doing with that book under the front seat of her car? She had taken it out of her bookcase because when folks came to her room, she felt as if they were drawn to it like a magnet. Mary Lou had seen it, she was sure, and had turned away from her somewhat after that. She fished under the driver's seat with her hand and came up with it right away, dusted it on her pants as she ran back up to Martha's door.

"Here you go," she said. "Remember, now. If it's not something you want to read, never mind. I got some good mysteries, too."

Martha was reading the title and nodding her head up and down slowly. "I hear you," she said. Lenore practically had the keys in the ignition before Martha got the words out. She felt as if she had lit a fuse and regardless of whether or not there'd be an explosion, she needed some distance.

Now plenty of time had passed; Lenore had enough distance, had fantasized every possible variation of Martha's response, didn't know why she had taken Betsy's dare anyway and let herself be taunted by it.

She followed Sabrina's graceful hands as they slipped the eggs from the grill to the plates, scraped the grease into the gutter with one wide sweep of the spatula. She liked her, and she didn't care what anyone thought. She hoped they could grow into friends. The excitement in her gut was from feeling she might be able to understand someone different from herself and that person might be able to understand her. This was true not only of Sabrina but also of Martha.

The lump in her gut which had formed around her sugar donut stayed with her most of the day while she worked. She was whistling a high note over it when Martha came by in the late afternoon and silenced everything in her but the small voice saying, "Oh, God, what if?" She did manage to smile and say Hi.

"How y'all doing?" Martha asked.

"Pretty good . . . not complaining." Lenore straightened the packages of pork chops meticulously as she stood there in order to avoid Martha's eyes. She felt as if there was only one thing Martha knew about her and that was that she was a lesbian. She felt as naked as she had been the day one of her mother's hairy boyfriends had burst through the bathroom door and caught her sitting on the toilet, pants down, red-faced with straining.

"Thanks for doing the babysitting," Martha said.

She'd practically forgotten she'd done it. "Oh, sure . . . . How is it, being back on the job?"

"Not much different, but I'm keeping my fingers crossed for when we have the contract."

"Yeah," Lenore said. Martha seemed to feel warmly toward her. Maybe it would be okay. She let herself look up.

"You got any sausage?"

"Sure. There's some out right down here."

They walked down toward one end with the meat counter between them. "If there's nothing here to suit you, let me know," Lenore said. "I can make you up what you want."

"This'll do fine," Martha said, taking a package for her basket. "Will you be around Sunday?"

"Sure, I reckon I will."

"I thought I might stop by with your book."

"Sure enough . . . okay," Lenore said, still registering Martha's words. "See you then."

As Martha moved down the dairy case with her shopping cart, Lenore saw Mary Lou go up behind her and surprise her, stamping her shoulder 59¢. Lenore kept forgetting they were neighbors. She realized she hadn't told Martha where she lived, but she must know or she would've asked. She hummed through the rest of the day, feeling inordinately happy, considering she didn't even know what Martha thought of the book. What mattered was that someone knew. She realized how little anyone else could know her if they didn't know that. And yet, it was something you couldn't just go around telling everybody.

When she got home, she closed down all the blinds. She took a shower to cool off and get the feeling of the store off her skin. She laid down before she put on clothes and let her thoughts go to Betsy. She stroked her own body the way Betsy would have, and let herself feel the way her senses wanted to come alive. She built her excitement slowly. She knew exactly where to touch, how hard, how fast. Martha *knew* about her. She felt whole and glorious. She stroked and stroked. Then the rhythm of her body took over and moved her until her insides hummed.

By the time Martha came up the walk on Sunday, Lenore had spent so much time imagining her that she felt as if she knew her real well. She had pictured her with her girlfriend, Lucinda, and she had pictured her alone, yearning for her girlfriend after she had gone off to New York. As soon as she saw the real Martha coming, she knew that back in reality they hardly knew each other at all.

Martha took the book out of her purse and placed it face up on the counter while Lenore poured the coffee.

"You read it?" Lenore asked with as casual a tone as she was capable of faking.

Martha with the gentle, gruff voice, "Yup, read it all, every last page and I thank you."

"You can keep it if you want."

"Nope. Wouldn't know where to put it around my place."

Lenore didn't tell Martha that was why she'd had it in her car to begin with.

Hesitations, long silences, and the startling interruptions of speech on tenderly self-conscious eardrums filled the next hour after Martha asked Lenore, "How did you know about yourself?"

Lenore started to say Betsy but halted. She was suddenly flooded with the many moments all across her life when she had wondered about herself—each small uprising that had erupted through and charged her with panic. With Betsy, her feelings, her desires, swollen in proportion to her fears, had muffled the panic. But she couldn't say there was any one moment when she had known unless it was now. Maybe this moment of talking to Martha, of letting those uprisings surface in her memory was the beginning of her really knowing.

"I remember when I was a kid, I wanted to be a boy. I used to sit around and pretend that I was. When kids my age started dating, I'd sit around and think about if I was a boy, which girl I'd ask out. Betsy was one and the other one was Sassy, this wild girl from out in the sticks, and I never got up the nerve to speak to her, ever."

Martha laughed warmly, quietly. Lenore wanted to ask her how she had known, but she worried she'd be asking too much. Martha was so much older than her. That was another line to cross. But Martha volunteered, "My best friend in school took me to this bar. Men and women but not together, if you know what I mean. Anyway, here I was, I knew that I was attracted to some women, but all I did in that bar was try to figure out which ones were men and which ones were women. Seemed like everybody was putting on an act. I just wanted to be plain old me. I didn't like the place, but I kept on going back, trying to fit myself in."

She told Lenore about meeting up with Lucinda there, and a couple of years later, Cookie, who was up visiting from Florida at the time. She'd moved down there with Cookie and they'd tried to live like ordinary people, no special roles. "I don't know," she added. "I guess when you think about it, that ain't right. Most ordinary people, married people, do live in roles. It's just when we do it, they think it's weird."

Lenore wanted to ask Martha if she had a girlfriend now in Victory but couldn't think of a way to phrase the question. She wanted to ask so much. Where was the bar and was it still going? Were there other women like them that Martha knew in Victory? She stared at the book cover and tried to keep her voice steady. "How was it for you . . . coming back to Victory?"

"Okay," Martha said cautiously. "I have Folly next door and I couldn't have anyone better. I don't let *that,* what we're talking about, interfere with her. And up until this last stroke, I've always had my ma at home to look after." Martha smoked a cigarette and stayed in her own thoughts. It wasn't true *that* didn't interfere anymore. It had been true for years, but now it was as if a leak had gotten started and each day more and more of her poured into those feelings. Something had come alive that she had held in dormancy after she had come home. She felt touchy, more aware of her senses. She got up and took her cup over to the sink. She noticed how neat Lenore's kitchenette was, how it smelled of cleaning smells—Ajax, a new sponge—instead of cooking odors. She wanted to tell her something that would be useful. She felt she should give something more in exchange for Lenore's courage in giving her the book, but she could neither talk about Folly nor move her mind past her. She put her cigarettes in her breast pocket, preparing to leave. "I never have regretted being the way I am," she said, "even though it's hard sometimes. You understand what I mean?"

Lenore stood up. "I reckon I do."

"We'll talk again," Martha said. "We never really talked about the book."

"I sure would like to."

Martha cupped her hands on both Lenore's shoulders and faced her squarely for a second at the door. Lenore wanted to reach back but stood with her arms inert, passively dangling at her sides. Then Martha turned and was gone. Lenore followed her in her mind's eye as she drove to the hospital to visit Daisy, as she had said she was going to do. Lenore felt the strength, the solidity of the hands that had pressed her shoulders, almost as if they were still there.

15

Folly spoke brusquely as she told the boys to mind Mary Lou. "It'll be after supper before I get home, and I don't want to find this place in no mess," she said. She felt bad about leaving them behind and regretted they'd let Jesse talk them into not bringing families to the picnic. It would defeat their purpose, he had told them. They were having the picnic to try to talk more to women who had voted against the union. If they all brought their children, Jesse reasoned, they would be too busy with them to talk—just as at the factory, they were always too busy with the work that was looking them in the face. They had decided to have the picnic in the State Park up in the mountains and, no surprise, it had turned out to be a hot, muggy day—one on which it seemed plain unfair to leave the children behind. Tiny's pout indicated his agreement. Nevertheless, Folly packed up her cooler without giving him another glance and walked off and left them. Martha was already waiting in the car. They tooted for Effie and then went around and picked up Suellen who lived on the inside loop of the trailer park.

They made the long, slow climb up the mountain with all the windows down, feeling how the air was cooling off with the increased altitude. Effie flapped her arms like wings and her laughter rippled in the back seat. Martha noticed how the temperature gauge was rising toward HOT, the red zone, and mentioned it. "Poor old car's workin' hard," Folly said, "carrying all this weight up hill."

"Good thing I'm not in the back seat, we'd be boiling," Martha said. Folly turned around and laughed with Suellen, who was nothing but bones, and Effie, who was small but plump. The road dipped down and since the temperature gauge followed it, Martha stopped worrying.

"I felt bad leaving the kids home," Folly said.

"Me too," Suellen said, "for about five minutes." They laughed. "Think of what a good time we're gonna have without them. How many Sundays have we ever gotten off both from work and from mothering—cleaning, shopping, what have you." She leaned her head back against the seat and let the wind blow part of her hair across her face. This wasn't like the quiet, reserved Suellen that Folly thought she knew.

"Whoopee," Effie hooted. "You said it, Suellen."

They all laughed more and Folly settled further into dropping her cares and joining the mood. She had resisted the idea of this picnic even though she'd been involved in the planning of it. They still didn't have a contract and as one of the union reps, she knew that was not from lack of trying on their part. It was because of the unyielding stubbornness of the management, because of the way they wanted to refuse to believe they *had* to negotiate. Jesse had confidence that they were progressing toward an agreement, if slowly, but Folly sometimes had the feeling they had no more strength than before. If this was the case, she didn't want to be wasting her time and energy trying to convince the other women they should be joining. She had argued this with Jesse. "But regardless of what has happened so far, surely you have a commitment to the ideology," he'd said, pressing the words upon her with an attitude of positive declaration of the type she sometimes used on her children. She had looked straight at him but felt as if he were somewhere distant. "If this union works, I'm for it, but if it can't work here, then I'd better be looking after my own tail," she'd said.

"We *will* get a contract," Jesse had responded, a deep, timeless patience in his voice.

She'd favored saving the picnic for after the contract, but she'd been out voted by those who had wanted it now. And as she relaxed, she began to believe they'd been right. She needed the change of scenery as much as anyone. She realized she hadn't driven up this mountain in a couple of years or more. Her ears clicked. She felt light and wondered if she felt that way because of the altitude.

Just after they entered the park, they came upon the first union sign taped to a tree trunk with a broad red arrow pointing them right at the fork. Jesse had come early to find a good spot and put up the signs. They gave a cheer. Folly felt elated about coming upon these signs, knowing they meant there was a place saved for them. They drove back through the picnic grounds on a dirt road well shaded by tall trees, following the arrows. The last sign was a placard nailed to a stake, one which Folly had carried as she walked the picket line. WOMEN OF VICTORY MILLS UNITE.

Mabel and Jesse sat side by side on top of a picnic table. The women in Martha's car unloaded and carried their gear over to put down near them. "Y'all late," Mabel announced. "I done been swimming already."

"No kidding," Martha said, not sure whether Mabel was serious. She looked hard at her magenta bathing suit to determine if it was, in fact, wet, but couldn't tell. "I better drink some of that stuff that makes you float before I go in."

"Now don't you go telling me you can't swim." Mabel shook her finger at Martha and inclined herself toward Jesse. "She already tried to tell me one other time she couldn't dance." To Folly she said, "You be my witness."

"I saw her dance," Folly said.

"You ever been baptized?" Mabel asked Martha.

"I reckon I was, but I don't remember it."

"That's right. You white folks gets dunked when y'all little bitty babies."

"Beer's there," Jesse interjected, pointing to a bench with a keg perched on it. Jesse struck Folly as more nervous than she had ever seen him, as if he thought the only thing they could talk about safely across their color lines was the union. But Mabel went on in spite of him, promising Martha she'd be ready to hit the water with her, soon as she was ready to float.

They greeted the other women already there, then more who were arriving. Soon it felt as if the area had always been theirs, the whole cluster of picnic tables scattered with the belongings of the mill women, who wandered about, talking and joking easily. Folly realized how different they all looked when you got them out of the mill. She had noticed this before, when they were out striking. Inside, each woman had a fairly set expression to her face which she held from when she arrived until she left. She geared herself to maintain a level of tension that would push against time—too little of it to get the job done, too much of it always still between the moment she had reached and the wait for the end of the shift.

Folly sat with her back pressed into the trunk of a tree and closed her eyes. She wondered if it would be possible for a mill to operate without the workers always having to be pushed the way they were. How many zippers would she sew if she were allowed to choose her own pace? She would want to keep busy, she was sure of that. She would not want to sit and dawdle with empty time. For one minute she pictured these women who moved around the picnic tables working in a factory without a boss. She could actually see them sitting at their machines, focused on their work but not tensed with concern against the clock or the man who watched them. She felt frustrated by the questions that came with the vision. What would they do with the product? Who would run things? Where would they get the machines?

Martha came with a beer for her and touching the cold cup to her leg, bounced her back to the party. They swam, Mabel seeing to Martha's promised baptism. They ate until they were stuffed. They talked union some of the time, but the fact they were all there, having a good afternoon, and that the union had put this picnic together seemed enough reason for its existence without the usual talk: power, bosses, workers, the right to have some control over their working conditions. Jesse wanted them to talk more and kept reminding them, but Martha finally told him, "C'mon, relax. We're having a good time. You're allowed to have one, too."

Late afternoon Shirley started organizing a softball game. "Who wants to be a captain?" she went around asking. She came up with Arlaine, a Black woman who was pro-union, and Nina, a white woman who was anti. Jesse muttered to Folly that he didn't want to see this union contest take place on the softball field. Folly shrugged and moved closer to the cluster of those who wanted to play. The captains chose: Arlaine chose the Black women and Nina chose the white. "No sense worrying," Folly said to Jesse as she went off to cover third base when Nina lost the toss.

Mabel had stout arms and a stance that was more remarkable for staying still than for moving, and didn't look at all like an athlete until she took up the bat, and with two women on, smacked the first home run into the picnic area beyond left field. Her teammates hooted her around the bases. This was the beginning of a trend. Two outs and the Black women hit one good grounder after another, stacking up the runs. Ten to nothing and the other side hadn't even been up yet. "This is it," Nina kept saying. "We're gonna get the next one at first."

"What you say?" Arlaine called. "We can't hear you. Ain't that right," she said to her team. "We gonna stay here, batter up, all day." Emily socked the ball straight past Gilda, the shortstop.

"Hey, come on, y'all gotta goof up sometime," Gilda hollered with frustration. "Give us a break. Where'd y'all learn to hit so good?"

Arlaine put her hands on her hips. "Right back down there at the colored school with your cracked bats, hand-me-downs from the white school. Now you see why they never let us play against y'all? They figured, turn us loose with equal stuff, no telling when we'd ever let up on you." Others on the Black team joined Arlaine in the heckling, including Freena.

Beth countered from the pitcher's mound. "Hey, just a minute, Freena. Remember me? We went to the same school together." Beth was hot and tired of pitching and sorry they didn't have an umpire to call strikes. They had asked Jesse to be one, but he had refused and now sat under a shade tree within hearing distance. She was also disappointed and embarrassed at the ineptitude of some of her teammates, the way they laughed as the ball scooted right by them.

"Wait a minute," Mabel said. "Just 'cause you used the same bats don't always put you in the same ballpark." "Yeah, okay," Beth said, feeling her face flush red and hot. "Let's play ball." She gave Freena a fast pitch and Freena hit a long drive over the heads of the fielders. Freena loped around the bases, free and proud, and lifted by the cheers of her team. Finally, the next woman hit a foul pop-up and Nina got under it. The whites were up for five minutes, then back on the field. About the fourth inning, the tension broke. The white side stopped keeping score. Mabel charged into Folly on third and they both fell down in the grass. Arlaine declared the score at the beginning of each inning, and there was no question of who was winning. Beth even started to enjoy herself though she wished she was on the other team. Folly couldn't remember a single other day in her adulthood when she'd felt so free of routine and responsibility. She got her home run in just before they quit and headed off for another swim before packing up to go home. Her eye caught Jesse giving her the victory sign as she rounded third base, and she raised her arms in return.

Folly and Martha sat in lawn chairs on the patio surrounding the kidney shaped pool of the motel. Though it was dark out, the water sparkled ocean blue because of the underground light. Folly leaned forward and hugged her own arms. "Sure is amazing how cool it gets up here at night."

"Sure is," Martha said, quietly. "I'll bring you your jacket. I was going to get mine anyway."

Folly could hear Martha whistle her way across the driveway. She leaned her head back and let out a long sigh. So this was the way people who took vacations lived. But they weren't on vacation, they were stuck. Their water pump had gone just after they'd left the park. They never would have chosen a motel with a swimming pool, but this was it, the only one near the garage where the mechanic had promised to fix their car early in the morning. Effie and Suellen had gone on with someone who'd left the picnic before them.

Folly was mesmerized by the small ripples of the blue water in the pool. Martha came behind her and slipped the jacket over her shoulders. "What a night," she said, allowing her hands to linger on Folly's shoulders. She felt the current of desire as she had so often in the recent months. Folly didn't move but tipped her head further back.

"You star gazing?" Martha said.

"Too much light in the pool," Folly said, putting both of her hands on top of Martha's and keeping them on her shoulders for a few seconds. Martha couldn't speak, she was holding her breath and feeling so full. All she could think of to say was, "I love you," and she couldn't say that outright to Folly. Her hands felt as if they had found perfect landing places and stayed in a holding pattern. How long could this go on? Would Folly be capable of breaking it?

She did. She suggested they go for a walk down the side road that started beside the motel. She let go of Martha's hands, leaving the backs of them feeling exposed to Martha, as if newly born. Folly, rising, grunted, "If I can get up. I think I ran them bases once too often."

"I hope the kids are doing okay," she said as they walked.

"I reckon Mary Lou's got the boys all settled down."

"I hope. They'll probably have themselves a wild time."

"Probably harder on you not to have them around than the other way," Martha said.

"No. I'm having a good time. I'm not even sorry we got stuck. I mean we couldn't have made it up if we'd tried, could we?"

"No," Martha said. They bumped arms with a stride and ended up with their hands clasped together. It seemed as if neither of them had initiated the move, or else they had both done so at once. They walked quietly, sneakers on blacktop, and no cars in sight.

"There's your stars," Martha said. They stopped to get their bearings in the sky, still holding hands. *I love you,* Martha silently repeated, looking at the stars, her tongue pressed firmly against the roof of her mouth. I love you, I love you, pulsed a rhythm in her body.

Folly didn't want to move. She felt infused by the warmth and energy coming from Martha's hand. She felt young and realized she had been feeling old for years. She could not remember ever feeling this young, even when Barnie had come along and ridden her on his motor scooter. She had not known what to expect, but still she had not felt innocent. She had known in some part of her that he would lead her into the woods, she had known that he was in search of a way to satisfy himself and that she would be instrumental. She would not have been able to express these things, but she had not been innocent to them. This feeling with Martha of being on this planet together, of feeling light, almost without gravity, as other planets looked on them, of not knowing of or caring for any other moment than the one that was occuring, this feeling held Folly encircled by Martha's unspoken love and seemed the closest she had ever come to a magical state. She looked at Martha in the dark and breathed deeply.

"Do you smell flowers?" she asked Martha.

"Yes." Martha sighed. Then she faced Folly squarely and enfolded her in her arms and let herself feel what came with the closeness—the flow of her desire no longer resisted, the smell of Folly's skin next to her nose, the sense of her love as being worthy of expression. Folly embraced Martha in return. She felt taken in, full with her innocence, not taken over but cared for, surrounded by Martha's large soft arms. Martha's soft, soft cheek pressed firmly against her own. She could not resist the wholeness she felt and the sense of belonging. Perhaps it had been coming all along. She didn't know. She would think later. Now it was enough to feel.

When they moved out of the embrace, she touched her own cheek with her hand. She had not realized how soft she might feel to someone else, the way her babies had felt when they were still with sleep or rocking in her lap. They started back. She walked with amazement, her other hand in Martha's. Her skin had come alive in a way she would not have believed possible. When their entwined hands touched her leg, her leg lept with an impulse that went straight to her heart, stopped her breath and made her limbs tingle.

Her sensations were so acute they were nearly painful, while exquisite, and her breath kept catching. Martha put the chain on the door. They undressed, and Martha moved all their junk onto one bed. Folly sat on the edge of the other bed, feeling dazed, wanting to help but not doing so—only watching Martha, whose body she had never seen or thought of seeing like this before. Martha went to the other side and together they folded the spread down to the foot of the bed. They did this with the ease of their habit of folding the sheets together. Then they moved into each other on top of the light, cotton blanket. Martha placed the kisses she had held in her fantasies up and down Folly's body. She stroked the length of her and felt the warmth flood to her own vulva. So long she had waited for release. She pressed against Folly and felt her own excitement travel through Folly and back inside

113

herself. She gasped at the strength of the current, licked Folly's nipples, which rose, budlike to her tongue. She wanted to move down, to part Folly's legs and taste her there, but she worried that Folly might resist. She had known women who did not like this. She put one of her legs between Folly's and it was grasped in the heat of Folly's thighs. Locked, they began to move as one in the rhythm that still pulsed in Martha's heart—I love you, I love you. Folly cried out, her head arched backwards. Martha opened her eyes and looked on her face of innocence, then melted into Folly's orgasm and joined her cry.

For a long time after, they lay perfectly still, listening to the peace inside themselves, and outside, the hoot owl somewhere off in the woods behind the motel, celebrating the silence of the night.

"Why didn't you tell me this was here," Folly asked, hours later, as they lay with the sheet draped over them, one pair of legs still entwined.

"Oh, God. Don't ask me," Martha sighed. "Why didn't I?"

Folly lit a cigarette and balanced the ashtray on the spot where her legs formed a V. She emitted smoke rings and watched them rise to the ceiling. "What does it mean? What do we do with it?"

"Take it. It means I love you." Martha had said it during the love-making, but this was her first time speaking those words outside of passion.

Folly was looking sideways at her. "Love . . . I don't have it meaning much but a word in me. I thought I should have it for Barnie, so whatever I felt, that was love. First, it was being excited that someone was riding me around on his motor scooter and feeling me up, then it was moving out of the house and in with him, then it was being fucked, cooking for him, doing his laundry and all that. Then I said, 'The hell with this, if this is what love is, I can afford to give it up.'" She turned more fully to Martha. "This is somethin' else. Whatever happened to-night, I didn't even know I was looking for it, I didn't even know it was possible."

Martha took Folly's hand, brought it to her cheek and pressed it against her face. "Are you okay with it . . . that it happened?"

"Okay? More like born. I just realize I've been dead most of my life. And there you been right next door all this time, keeping quiet about this."

"You mean to tell me you never even wondered about me?"

Folly had an impulse to deny that she had but didn't follow it. "I can't honestly say I haven't wondered about you, but it's *me* I didn't ever let myself wonder about." Maybe that wasn't actually so, but just now she couldn't really think who she had been before. She knew that her world had shifted and when things settled, she'd be standing on new ground. She looked about the room for something to hang the memory of change on, but it was your standard motel room, nothing memorable about it. The carpet had soiled spots from spilled drinks and the wallpaper was a dull green. If she needed something tangible to hold onto for the memory of this night, it would not be the walls or the floor or the ceiling but Martha's large, round breasts, the nipples darker and bigger than her own. It would be her mouth on them, the strangeness of the idea that she could do this, taste another woman's breasts, suckle them as hers had been suckled years before by her children. It would be her ear resting between the soft mounds, hearing the sounds of Martha's heart. She rolled into her again, smelling Martha's odors on her fingers.

As they walked to the garage to pick up the car the next morning, Folly said, "I guess there's times when you can live without sleep." She felt awake, light, airy, almost confused by her own lack of weight. As if she were chemically altered from her life before orgasm. She and Martha sat in a booth eating grits and eggs and smiling, grinning full face like foolish children, having to look away from each other to get themselves settled enough to swallow.

"I wish we could stay a while longer," Martha said.

"I don't know if we could stand it," Folly said, feeling so good she didn't think she could possibly have permanency.

16.

Folly had been flying since the day of the picnic. She and Martha were together all the time, and although there had only been a couple of occasions in the two weeks since when they had been able to escape to Martha's bedroom, what danced constantly in Folly's mind were the impressions and sensations of their lovemaking, and the magic of that was in their most casual touch. Frequently they snuck in these touches —at the factory, driving home, sitting at the kitchen table chopping vegetables for soup. Folly couldn't remember if they had touched before. Certainly they had cooked together often. Certainly they had bumped in the confined space of the trailer. Still, it did not seem possible that they had touched and she had not felt what she felt now. But anything was possible. She was a different person. She went about her world noticing her body. She sat at her chair in the mill and felt herself sitting squarely. She stretched her back, yawned, felt her lungs fill with air, then empty. When she chopped vegetables, she was careful, protective of her fingers.

Not until she watched Mary Lou bagging the groceries with a speed that could only mean fury did the anger of her child begin to penetrate her consciousness of bliss. Mary Lou flicked a bag open, tossed the items from her right hand to her left, then dropped them in the sack. Apple juice, rice, five pounds of flour, corned beef hash, another corned beef hash, two cans of tuna tossed and caught together, Gatorade—the bag was filling fast. Folly's eyes followed the items as they disappeared. Two dozen eggs on top. Too much, Folly was aware, wanted to say something, not the reprimand that would ride a familiar route between them, something else, but her tongue stuck against her teeth. Mary Lou grabbed the sides of the bag to heave it into the cart. Bottom brushed the lip of the counter, fell out. Apple juice poured on the bag of flour next to Mary Lou's sneaker and formed a puddle. Mary Lou grabbed another sack, flicked it open, went on packing what was left on the counter, wildly, furiously. Gerry, the cashier, stepped to the end of the counter and checked the damages. "Get yourself some replacements," she said to Folly.

"Will you go get them?" Folly asked Martha. She kept her eye on Mary Lou, who had not looked directly at her the whole time. "What's the matter?"

"Shit," Mary Lou said under her breath. "Shee-it, shit, shit." Her mouth was flat, her lips compressed tightly between her epithets. She's going to burst into tears, Folly thought, having known her all her life, but she didn't. She picked up the wet cans, the egg carton oozing yuck, put them on the counter. 'Shit," she said once more and deserted.

In the bathroom stall, Mary Lou heaved with sobs, held her hands over her face to silence herself if anyone should enter. She had never cried like this without her mother or Daisy to hold her. She tried to still her chest by breathing against her elbows. She couldn't imagine what was happening down front at the counter. Who was cleaning up her mess? Her mother? Maybe. Would she be waiting for her to come out? She couldn't leave. She was due to work the whole evening until the store closed at nine. She had to go back out there. She went to the sink and wet some paper towels with cold water. Her face was splotched red. How could she go anywhere? She set her mouth in a firm line to control her lips from quivering. Watching herself like this in the mirror, she saw her mother's face in her own. She was moved by the pride she felt in looking like her mother to the point of more tears, which she soaked up with the paper towels.

She was practicing looking normal when Lenore came in. She had squinched up her face intensely, then tried to let the cheek muscles go. She could feel a deep ache in them and a burning in her eyes. This pain seemed more tolerable to her than the hidden pain she felt about her mother, except that it showed, and she had to straighten herself out and get back to work, if she still had a job.

"You okay?" Lenore asked.

'Yeah." A tear started and she wiped it from the corner of her eye with the back of her hand in a casual gesture that she hoped Lenore wouldn't notice.

"Gerry said she thought you were upset."

Mary Lou nodded.

"What got to you?"

Mary Lou shrugged. She wasn't sure her voice was steady enough to answer. She coughed. "A little of everything." This seemed true, though it did not tell anything. She felt she owed Lenore more since she was the one who had gotten her the job. "I'm sorry. I know I shouldn't have walked off like that. Did Peters see?"

"The hell with Peters," Lenore said. "You did make one spectacular mess, according to Gerry, but she cleaned it up. She says to tell you you owe her one."

"One what?"

"One clean-up."

Mary Lou felt immensely relieved.

"Now, tell me, since I didn't see, just what did you make this spectacular mess with?"

"I was baggin' my ma's groceries . . . pissed off, tired . . . threw just about everything into one bag. Then I picked it up . . . splat . . . juice, eggs . . . ." They laughed. "Everything. I might as well have thrown it on the floor in the first place." They laughed some more. Mary Lou felt the pain in her cheeks with the laughter at the same time she felt release.

"Come over after work tomorrow and we'll cook up something."

"I'll see. If I can . . . ."

"We better get on back to work before that Peters decides to put on a dress to come in here and see what's going on. Gerry said tell you to unload the boxes of paper products, she'll handle up front."

"Okay."

Lenore grabbed Mary Lou's hand and squeezed it hard for a second. "Give yourself a break, kid. You're okay."

"Yeah," Mary Lou said, making for the door. She felt as if Lenore's squeeze of her hand was enough to start the tears running all over again, she was so full, so close to spilling.

Grateful to be doing this methodical job of opening the boxes and stacking the various brands of toilet tissue, stamping the price on each one, she felt a tenderness toward herself and toward Gerry and Lenore for understanding. She didn't let herself think directly about her mother but remembered how trapped she had felt by Skeeter calling Tiny *queer*. They'd been in the backyard playing catch and Mary Lou had been flat on her back on her bed trying to think a few things out. At first their laughter had only mildly distracted her. Then their voices had risen, Tiny's with a whine. "Too fast, Skeeter. Not so hard." Mary Lou had many times felt the sting on her own palm from Skeeter's hard ball. Tiny again, "I told you not so hard. Now look."

"Go get it," Skeeter commanded. "It was your ball." His voice was changing and went from soft to gruff each time he spoke.

Mary Lou had kneeled on her bed and looked out the window as Tiny ran over into Effie's backyard and got the ball. If it were her playing with Skeeter, she would have thrown him back a hard ball. Tiny wound up and fired, but he was too small to have any real power. Skeeter hurled another spitball and Tiny backed away. His glove tipped it, but the ball went on to the far side of Effie's yard. "I quit," he said. "You can go for that one."

"Boohoo," Skeeter said. "What's the matter? You queer? Poor little queer baby can't catch the ball."

"You leave him alone," Mary Lou had screamed. She couldn't remember getting up and running out into the backyard but she'd been there. "You don't call him names. You think you're big stuff. Sure you are, playing with someone half your size."

Skeeter had walked off to get the ball, Tiny had already gone inside, and Mary Lou felt her fury was only half dispensed. She had returned to her room and laid flat on her back again and this time the word *queer* had played like a broken record on her thoughts. A LIBERATED VIEW OF LESBIANISM—she couldn't remember the first title of the book she had seen at Lenore's. Maybe she should ask to read it because as it was, she had no view, only imaginings and suspicions. She didn't know for sure about anyone, even herself. She knew she didn't want her body blunted by some turkey like Roland. And she didn't want to go around bitter and sexless like her ma had for as long as she could remember. But something had happened to her mother recently. Her ma, who had always been pushing to get through the day, move on to the future, get the money saved, finish her shift, clean up the dishes, now all of a sudden seemed lulled by time; she was more a part of the day she was living. She shared a secret with Martha. They looked at each other all the time as if they were remembering it. At first Mary Lou had thought maybe it was about her, but by now she was sure it wasn't; it had nothing to do with her except that she was left out of it.

By the time she finished stacking all the toilet paper she felt a whole lot better, as if something had washed out of her, though she was not sure what. She went up front to thank Gerry. "I'm not usually such a clutz," she said.

"We all have our days," Gerry said, flicking her long, blonde hair over her shoulder with a jerk that excused Mary Lou.

Martha drove and Folly stayed deep in her own thoughts. She despaired of giving up any of what she was experiencing for anyone, yet she knew she had to consider what this meant to her children, at least Mary Lou, who was onto her in some way. *What* she knew was a good question. The way Folly's mind unconsciously followed the curves in the road as they moved closer to home, Martha seemed to follow her thoughts. "What're we gonna do about Mary Lou," she asked, covering Folly's hand with her own.

Folly felt the current from the touch as it made a rush direct to her heart, brain and loins simultaneously. How could she explain this to her daughter? She couldn't explain it to herself. "I've always been honest with her, except that time the counselor was worried about her hanging around with Lenore."

Martha was silent, remembering how she'd been frightened and provoked by that incident, hurt even. She wasn't ready to share this with Folly yet, not until Folly could speak more what their relationship meant to her.

"I guess I have to tell her," Folly said, her voice lacking its usual firmness.

"What will you say?"

"I don't know . . . . At least I don't know how. I'll say I found part of myself I didn't know I had. That I love you and I know that can't be bad . . . that I always did love you before, but I didn't know what it was to meet you in this other way."

Martha squeezed Folly's hand. "She's a stubborn damn kid," Folly said. "I don't know if she'll let me tell her anything."

"She will when she's ready."

If I am, Folly thought, trying to ready herself, knowing she was not. She was far from achieving a balance between fluttering and flying on her senses, a creature not of this world as she knew it, and recognizing she'd become someone supposedly despicable—perverse, peculiar, queer.

They had pulled in the driveway. Tiny came out and wanted to know if he could go down the road to play with a friend. Skeeter was doing his lawns. "Might as well come in for coffee," Martha said, steering with her head in the direction of her trailer, when they had finished unpacking Folly's groceries.

Despite the links of their talk, Folly felt the fracture that had occurred in their bond when the bottom had dropped out of the bag in the store. She felt herself moving away from Martha to make more room for telling Mary Lou. It was as if her pores had been fully opened and now she had begun to close them down, one by one. Because she felt guilty for this, she followed Martha's nod, sat at her table, drank her coffee, caught her eye from time to time, feeling hot and cold, almost sick. She was too young for menopause, but this is what she expected the change to feel like—feelings gone flip flop, moved out to the far ends of a seesaw. At the thought of losing Martha, a vast sense of isolation came on her, a view of empty terrain on which her body could not prosper.

Martha leaned over and took Folly's hand, her eyes demanding with urgency that Folly not look away. "Hey," she said, "I love you." She stood and pulled Folly in the direction of the bedroom. Folly let herself be pulled but felt her resistance come along with her. She did not feel at home in her body the way she had the other times. She wanted to, needed to. She needed to tell Mary Lou, "This is right. I know this is right because I feel I've come home to my body." The other times they'd made love in the bright light of early afternoon, her skin had felt illuminated by it. Now she went to the windows and drew the curtains tighter together, but still the room was fully light. She was not ready to tell Mary Lou or anyone. She did not know how to explain what had happened to her, even to herself, even to Martha. And she did not want to end this time of not thinking, only feeling, except already it had ended. Already the time of only feeling was a memory. Or perhaps it had never existed at all.

She fell into Martha's open arms and held her tight. She breathed her smell and let the sense of being comforted settle over her like a blanket. Martha made no moves to arouse her, only held her with her full concentration. "This is better," she said. "I felt you were moving far away."

"I was," Folly said, "only, I'm not going." She stroked Martha's back up and down. This back which had become so familiar to her by sight was now becoming familiar to the touch. The shoulder blades were blunt along their edges where Martha's large muscles attached. The bumps of her spine were more protected than Folly's, softer. The curve at the bottom of her spine was deep, and as Folly ran her hand into the hollow, she felt the light touch of Martha's belly against her own. They were much different in size, yet they fit amazingly well. Feeling the touch of their bellies together melted the last of Folly's resistance, and she found herself moving into a rhythm with Martha's body, her hand pressing the hollow.

When they lay together afterwards, still and silent, Folly felt again the sense of youth that she had not had when she was a child. She felt the strange innocence of finding love after she had long since given up belief in it. "I feel very lucky," she whispered.

"So do I."

"For the first time in my life," Folly said. "I never won nothing."

"I won Bingo once, but it wasn't anything like this," Martha said.

It was Saturday night and though Folly had the night off, Mary Lou was working till closing. Folly wrote her a note and left it on her bed when she went out to her union meeting.

Dear M.L.

If you want to talk, we can stay up late tonight. If you're too tired, never mind.

Love, Ma

When she got home all the lights were out. She looked in on Mary Lou, who was curled up facing the wall. She looked small—sweet and childlike. Not a taut wire filled with venom. Folly was relieved she did not want to talk, though perhaps it would be easier to have this discussion if Mary Lou were filled with sleep. She remembered rocking her calm after nightmares.

As soon as Folly closed the door, Mary Lou breathed deeper and started to fall asleep. It seemed as if the day had stretched out a long time, and she was glad to know that her mother was in the next room.

17.

Mary Lou turned over the note her mother had left her and wrote on the back of it in bold capital letters: GOOD MORNING MA. WORKING TIL 5, THEN GOING TO LENORE'S FOR SUPPER. PROBABLY GO BY TO SEE DAISY ON THE WAY. CALL ME AT THE STORE IF I HAVE TO COME HOME AND STAY WITH THE BOYS OR ANYTHING.

LATER, MARY LOU

She walked softly around the trailer, getting dressed and fixing herself some breakfast. She felt full of nerve, leaving this note for her mother, while she would not have told her, face to face, that she was going to Lenore's. She dared her mother to say one word about Lenore. Too old, indeed. She felt every bit as old as Lenore. She had worked full time since school let out. She went to bed tired and sometimes woke up with a yearning to stretch out and close her eyes and dream through the morning, but she hadn't missed a day of work yet. She hadn't even been late.

The enjoyable thing about being up before anyone else was the quiet. That and the coolness of the morning, the way the air seemed light though you knew it would grow heavy with the humidity by nine or ten. Mary Lou felt in charge of the sleeping household. She pictured her brothers looking innocent with sleep, her mother, too; she felt responsible for them all. This was payday. She would be getting her largest check ever for a full week plus overtime. She had tried to calculate how much the take home would be, based on the deductions that had been taken out of her previous checks, but she had little idea if her calculations were correct. She planned to cash the check at the store and give Lenore money to buy them a six-pack to take to her place. She wondered had her ma thought about the fact that Lenore was old enough to buy booze, when she'd said she was too old? She pondered again over how her ma had known to look for her at Lenore's that night Daisy had the stroke. Neither of them had brought it up afterwards. She wondered if her ma would call her at the store. She stuck the note under Folly's door, then put on her shoes and left for work.

Peters brought around the checks sealed in envelopes and stuck hers in the back pocket of her jeans while she was bagging with both hands in front of her. He reminded her of Roland butting up against her after that night she had gone to the drive-in with him. Roland had finally stopped asking her out; in fact, had even stopped speaking to her, which she didn't mind except she felt that he was often lurking somewhere, watching her, and she sensed with some fear that he might be out to get her sometime. She didn't have anything to base this on, really, just her hunch that he was a little crazy. In response to Peters she twitched her butt in irritation, a gesture which he probably took to be cute, but she didn't care—she knew what she meant by it. First chance she got she found an empty aisle and opened the envelope to check out the amount. $102.56. She had calculated $115. Everyone said she'd get the taxes back eventually, but if that was true, she didn't get the point of why they didn't just give her the money in the first place. Damn taxes. All through the rest of the day she allowed herself to day dream about where her $102.56 would go. Most of it to the grocery bill they had to pay off from the strike. She saw it next to a minus line, eating a big chunk out of the debt. Better to put it all in one place so you could see a dramatic difference like that. $313 minus $102.56 would leave . . . she tried to subtract in her head while she bagged . . . it took a long time to come up with $211. To wipe out a debt—*that* would be exciting. If you couldn't do that, maybe it would be better to spread it around more.

Just before quitting time she caught Peters in the manager's office and asked him to cash the check. "Don't spend it all in one place," he said. She refrained from telling him to mind his own business but definitely decided she would turn the whole wad over to her mother and tell her to put it against the grocery bill. She folded the bills over and pushed them deep down in her front pocket. As she walked, she was aware of the presence of the lump they made on the front of her leg, and worried about being robbed in a way she rarely had before.

When she found Lenore, she peeled a dollar off the roll and asked her to buy the beer with it. After that she felt lighter. She fantasized herself rich, pulling out rolls of bills, handing them freely, casually, without care for their dimensions, over to cashiers. Supply unlimited. No need to count the change. This fantasy turned her walk into a swagger.

Lenore drove her into the parking lot of the hospital and said, "I can go by the diner for coffee while you're visiting."

"No, that's okay. Come on in and see Daisy with me. I won't stay a minute."

The two of them stood at the side of the bed and looked down over the bed rail at Daisy. Each time Mary Lou came, she noticed how the bed looked too big for her, especially with the rails up; it looked as if she were being eaten up by the bed. Her flesh was shrinking away. Mary Lou reached over and took her hand and Daisy's eyes opened for a minute, but they were fogged over. They looked at her but didn't seem to see her. "So you're here," she said with a sigh in a far away voice.

Mary Lou felt creepy and took her hand away. Daisy must think she was someone else. She studied Daisy's face but couldn't find her, instead saw an old lady—wrinkled, wizened, dying. For a second it occurred to her she might have come into the wrong room, but Daisy's name was on the plastic bracelet on her wrist. The wrist was thin, purple spots speckling the skin. She wanted Daisy to see her with her friend and she wanted to know what Daisy would think of Lenore if she knew her. Probably she would like her . . . unless she thought she was out to put something over on Mary Lou.

Mary Lou was aware of how close she and Lenore stood to each other and of liking the feeling that came from that. She went back to concentrating on Daisy, thinking loudly to herself. *Look here, Daisy, look at me right here standing with my friend by me. I'm working all the time now. I've got a hundred and two dollars in my pocket, actually a hundred and one now. I'm turning it over to Ma later tonight. First I'm going to my friend's apartment for supper. I can think of a lot of things to buy but Ma got behind with the strike. Anyway, one more week and I get another check, same size, if I can get in some overtime. Daisy: you'd be proud of me. You look so small. I remember the year I grew to be as tall as you. Skeeter is almost as tall as me now. Tiny is still tiny. I dropped Ma's groceries all over the floor at the store yesterday. She and Martha have got a secret. Do you know it? Do you? I don't understand what's going on. They are like kids. I always thought*

125

I wanted to be the ma, but I don't. I want my ma to be the ma. She don't even tell me who not to hang out with anymore.

Daisy opened her eyes again and this time focused more clearly on Mary Lou. She worked her lips as if the words of a question were loose in her mouth. Mary Lou almost said, "Frumbled, I'm frumbled," but changed her mind. "I'm okay," she said, instead. "Are you okay?" She took Daisy's hand back in hers. The silence of Daisy's stare made it seem as if she moved from so close she could see inside Mary Lou to far, far away. Then her eyes hazed over again. What do you see behind those eyes, Mary Lou wanted to ask.

Always when she came now, she had trouble figuring out how to get away. Was Daisy finished with the visit or waiting for them to say something more? Was she tired? Was she comforted by the fact that they were standing there, or did she feel stared at and yearn for the privacy of being left alone? She wished Lenore would make a move but knew she wouldn't; she knew it was up to her.

"You ever had a bed like this, with rails?" she asked Lenore.

"Nope. My ma used to put a chair up next to mine when I was a little kid and I sleepwalked."

"Seems like to me I had a bed with a railing once, but I can't rightly remember what happened to it."

"I had my appendix out," Lenore said. "That's when I had one."

"In the hospital?"

"Yup, right here in this same hospital."

"Did it hurt?"

"After, when I laughed or coughed or something like that."

"Come on, let's go," Mary Lou said. She didn't speak to Daisy the way she usually did when they were alone. She spoke to herself again. *I'm going, Daisy. I'm going off to my friend's room. We're gonna make dinner. I think she might be a lesbian, you know, a homosexual. She sure is nice, though. I get nervous when I think about this.* She squeezed Daisy's hand. "Bye," she said out loud.

As they walked down the hall, she realized how stiff she had held her body. She let her legs stride loosely and reaching in her pocket deep, she fondled her money.

From her second beer on, Mary Lou was intent on how to let Lenore know she wanted to be seduced. She couldn't stand this low level tension, wanted to be closer to the edge, to know if it would be repugnant to her or what, if Lenore were to approach her. She had wandered around the room while Lenore was putting the supper on, checked the bookcase and found the lesbian book missing. This had seemed to fore-bode a life of frustration, given that she had finally felt she would find a way to ask to borrow it. She'd circled the room three times in her attempt to be subtle while scanning all three shelves of the bookcase and still had not found it. Finally, she'd settled into watching Lenore in the kitchen while the blank space in her mind which had counted on the book began filling in with ideas which had led to her swigging the beer faster than she should have or would have under less provoking cir-cumstances. She wanted to know—did women together start out kiss-ing like friends, then slide into something else, or what? She stopped short of letting herself feel anything sexual, but she liked watching Len-ore; she thought her body was neat. She wanted to sit up close to it, but Lenore set the places for them to eat on the counter across from each other.

After supper they sat on the floor, Lenore with her back against the bookcase, Mary Lou leaning against the chair. Lenore was telling her about how her mother was on the wagon, she hoped for good. She tried to listen closely, but her mind was too busy imagining her re-sponses to the seduction. And the consequences. Not that Lenore had made any moves. Would she be absolutely horrified if Lenore actually did? Would she walk away afterwards, changed forever? What would anybody and everybody (especially her mother) think if they knew?

She downed some more beer. Lenore was quiet now. She looked relaxed, sat with one knee pulled up to her chest, her chin resting on it. Her eyes followed Mary Lou as she stretched herself out on the floor.

"You okay?" Lenore asked.

"Yeah, just tired," Mary Lou lied. She was actually quite dizzy.

"Here we are acting like a couple of old ladies, wore out on a Friday night."

"Yup. It's a hard life." Mary Lou closed her eyes, thinking this might serve as a welcoming gesture to Lenore, but it only served to make her head spin more. She let her hand flop out to her side, close enough to Lenore that she could touch it if she wanted to. Silence. Mary Lou was tense and confused. If she let herself go loose, she feared she'd be unsure of where she was, as if she'd just done a series of under-water somersaults and lost track of her sense of horizontal and vertical.

"Daisy's sure in a bad way, isn't she?" Lenore said slowly.

"I don't want to think about it." Tears came to Mary Lou's eyes so suddenly, so out of range of her volition.

"I'm sorry," Lenore said, "but you can cry all you want here, no one will care."

About the last thing in the world Mary Lou wanted was to lay there and bawl her eyes out. She had drunk too much beer, deliberately, but not to be sad, to be brave and reckless and free. But her hotshot veneer dissolved as if it had no substance at all, and she couldn't stop herself. She remembered the hollow feeling of that moment when she suddenly hadn't recognized Daisy, had thought she was holding a stranger's hand, that she'd gone to the wrong bed, or Daisy had been switched, even died and been replaced by some other old woman. She kept her eyes closed, but the tears flowed from them anyway. As she wiped her cheeks with the backs of her hands, she bumped into Lenore who was by her side with the Kleenex box. She sat up and held a tissue to her face like a compress: Lenore put out her arms and encircled her, and held her still. She felt Lenore's strength calming her and some distant part of her was observing this was not what she had wanted, she had wanted a seduction. But another closer part said, not so, *this was* what she had wanted.

Mary Lou was back at her place against the chair, Lenore having quietly also resumed her posture in front of the bookcase. They sat without speaking and this warmed up Mary Lou's heart. She was grateful for Lenore not wanting to know everything that was going on in her. Lenore took their beer glasses and went to the kitchen.

"I don't think I better have any more," Mary Lou said.

"I know. I'm making tea. Or would you rather have coffee?"

"Tea."

"I thought so."

Mary Lou thought of her mother bringing her tea in bed once when she had been sick with a high fever and had stayed home from school. She remembered her mother's cool hand on her hot forehead. The contrast, the coolness of that hand, had made her feel exposed, as she did now. She decided she'd ask Lenore outright if she was a lesbian as soon as she brought the tea. She might as well do it while she already felt exposed.

She could tell by the smell that Lenore had made coffee for herself. She sipped at the tea and cleared her throat. "Um." She couldn't get the words to come out of her mouth. Her face ached. She blew on the hot tea and made the steam rise on her nose and cheeks. "There's something I wanted to ask you."

Lenore looked attentive, raised her eyebrows in wait. "Shoot."

"I think my mother's a lesbian."

"You do?" Lenore said with great surprise.

Mary Lou was surprised at Lenore's surprise. It had taken her a couple of weeks to put this idea into words, and it was a relief, finally, to say it, but meantime, she had gotten over her own shock. "I do," she reiterated.

Lenore was frowning. "That wasn't a question."

"I know." Mary Lou was stuck again, panic building all around her heart, but she forced the words out. "I . . . I guess I wanted to ask, are you?"

Lenore's face flushed, and Mary Lou wished she were home in bed or at least had minded the sense to keep to her own business. Lenore looked down at her feet while she spoke. "I never have called myself that, but I guess I am."

"It's okay with me. I just wanted to know."

Lenore nodded, pulled herself in tight.

"Who else do you know in Victory who's like that?"

"A few people I guess about."

"Like who?"

"Well, I wouldn't want to say names. I mean it's not something you go around telling about other people in a town like this."

"Sure," Mary Lou said, trying to sound cool. She hadn't thought this part out at all, she realized. "What I don't understand about my ma was that she was married and all. Had us three kids. Now you'd think that would prove something."

"What happened to your father?"

"He was a bastard." She said this fast, didn't want to think about her missing father, might make her cry again. "Ran off."

"Oh."

"How does a person know this about herself?"

"I don't know, she just does, or she finds out because of being close to some woman." There was still extra blood in Lenore's face which had now gone to splotches.

"My ma and Martha . . ." Mary Lou said. "They sure are close."

Lenore kept to herself. The coffee had made her cold sober and her mind raced over all the possibilities. Would Martha have told her if she were involved with Folly? Could it really be that Folly was one too? Did Mary Lou want to know about *her* because she wanted to talk about her mother or Martha or what? Would she go around telling about her? She felt worried about her knowing, lit another cigarette even though she had just put one out.

"I hope we still can be friends," Mary Lou said, "even if I'm not one."

"Of course. Of course we can."

"But I'm not sure. I might be. I sure ain't got much use for boys right now."

"You got time. Don't worry. You got plenty of time before you have to decide anything. Nobody's saying you ought to get married tomorrow."

"Me, married? You kiddin'?" The idea sobered her up totally. It was preposterous to her. When she thought of growing up, she thought of working, of having a paycheck, of learning more and being smarter, of driving a car and having her own friends. Never did she think of being married. "You are kidding, aren't you?" she said to Lenore, who laughed at her being so taken off balance. Mary Lou finally laughed, too.

"How old was your ma when she had you?"

"Jeez, you're right. She wasn't no older than I am right now. Wow. Imagine. No way," Mary Lou said, shaking her hands as if to clear herself from the possibility.

She didn't even have to ask for the book. Lenore offered it to her when she was driving her home. "Where is it? I was looking for it on your shelf."

Lenore reached down and pulled it out from under the driver's seat. "I thought that might be what you were looking for."

18.

Mabel and Folly and Jesse hunched over their table in a booth at the luncheonette out on the mill road. "I think this is going to be it," Jesse said. "It feels like the day we'll come out with a contract to me." He said it with the vigor of a person who had just had a night's sleep to the two women who had not. Mabel and Folly were both working third shift now and had just gotten off. Mabel yawned into her coffee, then leaned forward and rested her chin on her forearms, keeping her eyes trained on Jesse's face in a way she hoped would make him nervous. She could tell she wasn't succeeding, though, for a couple of reasons: one, her eyes were too droopy; and two, Jesse was too fresh and too deeply and comfortably settled in his own body—his white man's body— to look out at the world from her point of view, ever, unless he was forced to.

"I sure hope what you say is true," she said. "I'm right tired of sittin' in them sessions and listenin' to them fuss around with us. But I got a feelin' we might be doin' that a long time yet." Mabel closed her eyes as if to get some sleep in order to prepare for the tedious meeting ahead, and watching her, Folly realized what a worn down state they'd both gotten into through the course of these negotiations. They reminded each other regularly that this was the design of the management, and when they forgot, Jesse reminded them. Still, knowing this didn't keep them from feeling discouraged, and the longer the negotiations dragged on, the more they wondered if having the union really gave them any more power than they'd had before. During the organizing, they'd gone on the assumption that once they had the union they would sit down with management, hand over their demands, and no dillydallying around seven weeks later.

This crew had been functioning as a team since the election. They'd sat there in Bea Jones' beauty parlor and laid out their demands, plus extras (because Jesse said they had to have room to back down). Mabel and Folly had favored not playing games but Jesse had convinced them no one did it that way. If they wanted to negotiate for a seven percent raise they had to start by asking for ten. So they had asked for ten percent and ten days sick leave for illness of the worker or her dependent.

"Why not try for getting it all for the worker, maybe go for twelve days but keep things simple?"

"We don't want the women having to lie," Folly had said. "And furthermore, look what got us going in the first place."

"Okay. I hear you. We'll jack it up to twelve, worker or dependent."

They decided to ask for a production committee with worker representation, one woman from each shift, to establish a fair production rate."

"What else?" Jesse asked.

"Protection for us who's doing the organizing," Mabel said.

"You already have that," Jesse responded. "By law."

"You watch them wag that law at us the minute you leave town."

Having a firm sense of the way things were, Mabel called Jesse on statements like this, often. If he had more faith in what the union could do than Mabel and Folly combined, neither of them were surprised by this. After all, he got his paycheck from them. In spite of Folly's admiration for Mabel's hard and true connection with reality, when Jesse said things about the law or the union protecting them, Folly tended to believe him, out of wishful thinking maybe, out of the need to believe something that would give her the guts to be going in there negotiating.

Jesse had said they needed some throwaways, that they had to pad it and put down three extra numbers on the list. "How about better lighting? Would you be able to work better with better lighting?"

"Sure," Folly said. "And then they'd up production."

"We'll have you on the committee by then to fight that." He winked at Folly, and Mabel guffawed. "We'll also mandate your breaks so they can't be taken away arbitrarily."

"Good idea," Mabel said.

"Don't forget, these are throwaways," Jesse said.

"Well, maybe they shouldn't be. We could use a guarantee for our breaks. Maybe we should think of some others for throwaways."

Folly agreed with her. "How about increasing the meal break to forty-five minutes."

"I'm for it." Mabel sat back and rubbed her stomach. "Time for a little quiet digestion. As it is sometimes you can't hardly get through the lunchroom line 'fore it's time to go back."

Jesse put it down. "Now you're cooking." He added another number and listed job security.

"Thought you said we couldn't put that in," Mabel said.

"We weren't talking about the same thing. They can't fire you for organizing the union right now even without our contract or you'd have a good case against them. But they could make your job pretty miserable, or they could fire you for just about any other thing. We ought to try for a grievance procedure."

"As a throwaway?" Folly asked.

"No, for real. I'll work that up while you two think of more throwaways."

Mabel and Folly hadn't been any good at thinking up useless benefits. Each time one of them came up with an idea, the other rejected it as too useful. Finally, they decided to go with what they had down and try to push the whole contract through. Jesse had not been thrilled but had agreed to go along with them. "We're going to have to give a little here and there," he had said.

Before the first meeting, he'd asked them which one was going to read the demands. "You," Mabel had answered immediately, pointing at Jesse. "They won't hear them coming from us." Reluctantly, Folly had agreed. She was relieved that Jesse would be with them, directing the process, but she wished Mabel could read their demands.

She knew it would have to be practically a whole different world before Mabel could do that, but still she longed for it. She felt Mabel had the strongest presence of the three of them, but she knew this feeling was recent. It had come with Mabel saying, "Hey, listen here now, listen to the way I see it," and Folly taking some screen off of her own vision she hadn't even realized had been there, seeing with a new clarity who Mabel was, feeling also a vacancy in herself—the unreliability of her past. She had to remember that others still saw through that screen, that if she saw Mabel as beautiful—strong and furious and capable, her voice full of round tones rolling gracefully on her tongue which could compress to hisses when needed—Sam might hardly see her at all. It was not so easy to keep this understanding alive daily, since it tended to separate her from other whites. Not that she minded the separation between her and Sam or Fartblossom, which seemed like a breath of air, but there were women even among the organizers whom she didn't think really saw the Black women for who they were. Often she felt like giving up tolerance for them, grabbing them by the shoulders and shaking them, shaking them down to their roots; then other times, she knew they were her, one hair over, and knew they could learn.

What she could do now was open her eyes that had been closed and turn on the sound in her ears and not be surprised if Black folks didn't want to talk to her after all those no listening years. If things were the other way around, she doubted white folks would still be speaking.

The way the first negotiating meeting had gone was miles from the way any of them had imagined. As they entered the room, Sam had put on a great display of welcoming them, especially Jesse, whose hand he had pumped up and down. He had directed Folly and Mabel to chairs. "You all know Mr. Blossom," he said, indicating Fartblossom who was already seated. "He'll be attending these meetings as our new personnel officer."

Jesse leaned across the table and shook Fartblossom's meaty hand, then eased into a chair beside Mabel.

So that was why Fartblossom had been replaced as the night shift supervisor. Folly and Martha had been speculating all week long, had even gone to jokingly reading the obituaries. Folly had to adjust herself to the idea he would be present. There wasn't anyone anywhere she'd less like to be sitting across from, which was, of course, exactly why he was there. She squared herself in the chair and checked herself against letting Fartblossom give her the creeps. Mabel didn't really know him. She'd never worked the third shift until after the election when they'd transferred her as a form of harrassment. On Jesse's advice, Mabel had chosen not to fight this until after the contract was signed. Mabel sat, roving her hard eye from Sam to Fartblossom while Jesse read the demands. Sam closed his eyes to listen and appeared downright relaxed. Fartblossom hung his head forward and let his mouth hang open stupidly while his eyes rested on Jesse.

Jesse finished and sat back in his chair during the pause of silence. Sam rose, reached over the table and started pumping Jesse's hand again. "We'll give these some consideration before the next meeting," he said. "That'll be all for now, girls." He had turned to them without extending his hand. Mabel and Folly looked to Jesse for a signal and saw him incline his head toward the door. "We'll talk outside." He gathered them behind his arms and moved them toward the door as if they were hens who had lost their cackle. "I'll just arrange another meeting time." He stepped back into the office, leaving them at the door, slightly disoriented.

"Jesus! Wake me up to go to sleep. How'd you like that?" Mabel asked.

"I don't understand men," Folly shrugged. "Here we are ready to fight out a contract and they're shaking hands . . . smiling . . . shaking hands, sitting down, hardly getting settled . . . then they're up shaking hands again. Sneaky bastards. They got something up their sleeves, I can smell that."

Jesse came out and huddled them like the coach would his basketball team. "Come on. One last cup of coffee at the luncheonette, then you all can go home and get some sleep." Coffee nerves were something that Jesse seemed to have a natural born immunity to.

In the booth, Mabel leaned forward. "What's this—you mens lookin' so mighty friendly?"

"Oh, that's standard fare," Jesse said. "The pretext of civilization. One tries for an amicable sort of relationship in which to negotiate."

"Not this one," Folly said, anger churning her impatience. "Not with Fartblossom."

"I should have anticipated this tactic and warned you," Jesse said in a professional voice. "They want two weeks for studying the demands before they meet with us again."

Mabel moved her head in a long, slow, NO. "Two weeks for them two pages? You kiddin' me?"

"I think we have to give it to them," he answered. "It's a stalling tactic, but if we give it to them now, next time they try for one, we'll have something to squawk about. If we start squawking right away, we won't get anywhere."

They were all hurting for the settlement, hoping for the seven per-cent to go toward paying off the debts the strike had forced on them. Folly thought of Mary Lou going off and leaving her pay check, one corner of it tucked under the plate at Folly's place at the kitchen table. The week before she had left most of her earnings in crisp, new bills stuck in Folly's coffee cup. The check had sat there all day until Mary Lou came home. "You don't want this here valuable piece of paper getting dirty," Folly said. "You better put it away."

"I left it for you." Mary Lou had tried her best to sound unconnect-ed to the check. "I thought you could put it toward the grocery bill."

"Well, I could. But seems like you worked mighty hard to just be turning it over. Why don't you go down and cash it at the store and give over part of it against the charge."

"I'd rather not. I'd rather you just pay it, Ma."

"Why? What difference does it make which one of us pays it?"

"It does. It makes a difference to me. You pay it. I don't want to go in there to the same store where the money come from and say, 'Here, put this to the Burrows' account.'"

135

"Okay, okay, I'll do it," Folly had said, "but you have to endorse the check over to me."

"You mean sign it?"

"Yeah." Folly had forgotten how young Mary Lou was, she seemed so much older lately. "You have to do that if you turn a check over to someone else."

"Oh."

Folly had flipped back to hear Jesse saying, "Two weeks isn't going to make all that much difference to any of us in the long run." She decided not to comment, to just be grateful that Mary Lou had a job for the summer and didn't seem to resent giving up the money she was making.

"I suppose we ought to be used to bein' broke," Mabel said. "No, sir, won't make no difference to me. I been poor all my life." Mabel didn't conceal the sour taste this was giving her.

"I only meant it's important for us to keep in mind that we may get *more* in the long run by giving them the two weeks now," Jesse said. "I know it's been tough all the way round for you all since the strike started. I understand what you're saying."

Mabel wondered where he understood: in his head maybe, not in his belly. She and Folly exchanged looks of resolve. They were chewing on and digesting the idea of two more weeks waiting; they were also dog tired.

That was back when they'd had no idea how long this thing could be dragged out by the management, though probably someone should have predicted it. Mabel and Folly were now down to arguing for holding out longer. Jesse was saying they should make some concessions and settle, and Mabel and Folly were saying, "Hell, no. We've gone this far, now we might as well get what we came here for." After the first two week wait, they'd met once a week, every Wednesday. Folly glowered at Fartblossom throughout the meetings. After the second time, he'd appeared in her dreams to threaten her. She'd be on the picket line and suddenly look up and see the car charging her—Fartblossom popping up from the back seat just as it reached her. She'd wake up too close to the moment of being hit to know whether she had actually encountered the metal. But by the end of the third meeting, she'd gotten him down to size—big feet, big body, pea-sized brain. And meantime, since he was the personnel officer, she didn't have to put up with him on her shift. She'd be sorry when the meetings were over if that meant they'd put him back to his old job. Mabel never had been very intimidated by him and had been a considerable help to Folly in diminishing him.

Now that they were down to serious negotiating, two tables had been set up about five feet apart. Mabel and Folly and Jesse huddled around one; Sam and Fartblossom and Mr. Hart (*Sweetheart,* Mabel called him) who was the company lawyer, huddled around the other. There was no arbitrator present—though this was one of Jesse's constant threats—that if the company didn't come up with willingness to settle with them on an agreeable contract, they would move to binding arbitration. Sam and Fartblossom would confer, then the lawyer would speak for them. He came from Alabama and spoke with a sticky-sweet, melodious drawl, every word lolling on his tongue and you had to listen close to know what he was offering. He put Mabel and Folly right to sleep.

That day Jesse said it felt like the day for a contract, the lawyer had asked Folly and Mabel to leave the room. They'd really been snoozing. Sweetheart had droned out a new offer—one that included the seven per-cent raise, which was a primary point they'd been holding out for. He had run down the rest, which had sounded tediously familiar—Mabel and Folly hadn't listened that carefully as they'd been in the process of trying to disguise their glee at pulling off the seven percent. When he'd finished, Hart had made a little speech about how tired everybody was getting; how this was taking up valuable time (both ours and yours, he'd said). He'd said he had a suggestion for simplifying the negotia-tions—that if Folly and Mabel would leave the room, he'd send Sam and Fartblossom (he called them Mr. Crown and Mr. Blossom) out too. Jesse and Mabel and Folly had quickly put their heads together.

"Think we should?" Folly had asked Jesse, who had stared at her, obviously far off in his own thoughts, before answering yes, that he thought they should go along with him and see what he was up to. Fol-ly was reminded of her childhood—of playing war in the town dump and periodically conferring with the boy who assumed he was the leader to decide upon the next strategy. She turned to Mabel. "What do you think?"

"He knows what we want, well as we do," she said. "I guess if we *trust* him, we can leave him to do the job."

"We'll wait right out here," Folly suggested, "in case you want to come out and ask us about anything."

Someone started a horn beeping celebration just as Folly and Martha were pulling out of the parking lot the next morning, and most of them kept it up clear to town. It reminded Folly of being in a wedding procession, certainly not her own. She and Barney had been married in the office of the town judge—the sheriff and half a dozen hicks hanging around in the doorway, saying, "Do we get to kiss the bride now, huh?" Folly cringed, remembering.

Folly waved at women from the factory who pulled into the 7-Eleven. One woman raised her fist in the air and yelled to her: "Good work." Folly nodded. She felt outside of the mood of celebration. She had looked forward to some moment of great victory, and now, when others were acting as if they had reached it, she felt dampened with disappointment.

Jesse had burst into the hall and swooped down on Folly and Mabel, who were sick to death of waiting, success smiling all over his face. He'd put one arm around each of them, and said, "I think we've got it. I think we've got a good, solid contract we can all be proud of." They'd had one more coffee, read the copy of the contract that was all pencilled in and pencilled out. Tired. It was almost noon. They'd been up all night and all morning and had to be back in at eleven that night. They were having a victory, but Folly felt as if she'd just lost a fight. Go home, go to bed, she thought. Don't put up any more fuss now.

Her mind kept running the same track, imagining the scene after she and Mabel had left. It seemed clear now that Jesse must've known when Mr. Hart asked them to leave he was going to say they should get the business about the illness of dependents out of the way. The contract wasn't bad; in fact it was damn good. But Folly couldn't get Cora, who walked around now spindly, sad, and with a look of disconnection, out of her view. Jesse didn't have to look at her. He knew it was her baby dying that had gotten his foot in, but he was there to bring "another perspective," as he called it. "There are certain things that are traditionally negotiable," he had said. "Asking for sick time this way is highly unconventional." Remembering these statements, Folly realized Jesse had always intended to give on that part of the contract. What hurt most was her sense of personal betrayal, that he hadn't fought it out further with her and Mabel, had assured them they could trust him, even when he must have known they couldn't. Folly imagined him in there alone, acting as if he were one of the boys:

"Now, Mr. Hart, you must realize that these women were very distressed by the occurrence of the death of Mrs. Welton's baby. As a consequence, they are quite committed to this clause."

138

"Indeed, Mr. Jarvis, we are understanding of their concern. However, you and I know that this is not an appropriate clause for a contract."

"Yes, of course."

"So . . . I suggest . . . ."

She regretted they had agreed to leave the room. That was the lesson. Stay. Don't trust. The only power they had was their presence— the resistance of their bodies on the line. She wondered how Mabel felt now, having slept on it. Jesse had left them alone, said it was up to them to decide if they'd recommend ratification. They hadn't taken much time at all, couldn't afford to, too tired; they'd agreed to recommend yes while Jesse was up paying the bill at the cash register. Then Mabel had said, "Not bad, eh? What you lookin' so mad about?"

"I can't believe he didn't come out and ask us if we'd be willing to let go on the sick leave issue."

"Didn't surprise me. I always knew we was gonna lose that one. Look here—we got us six days sick leave for the first time ever in the history of this here mill or just about any other mill around."

Folly had nodded.

"You gotta learn to count your wins, woman," Mabel had said, waving the contract at her.

19.

It was Thursday evening before Folly saw Mary Lou. The day they'd
gotten the contract she'd come home, fixed some food for the kids'
supper, then slept until time to go back. This day she'd slept longer
than usual, too, but at least she'd started in the morning instead of the
afternoon. She didn't think she'd ever catch up. The place was a mess.
She couldn't remember when she'd last cleaned it.

Mary Lou was lulled by her fascination to the point of nearly forgetting where she was, when she heard Folly rattling around in the
kitchen and suddenly realized her mother was up and no telling when
she might walk through that door. Her hand moved *Sappho Was A
Right On Woman* in a reflex arc that ended under her pillow, and she
flopped over on her stomach, her belly providing the next level of insurance for covering the hot potato. She breathed rapidly, as if she'd
been caught. She *had* been caught, in a spell with this book, which she
gradually shook off.

Folly tapped softly on her door. "You awake?"

"Yeah. Comin' right out."

Although Mary Lou hadn't seen her mother since it happened, she'd
heard about the contract at the store. She'd even overheard people,
who didn't know whose daughter she was, talking about how well Folly
had done in the negotiations. "That's my ma," she'd wanted to say,
but had restrained herself, kept her smile inside and gone on bagging
the groceries. Now she went out to the kitchen and bowed to her
mother. "You're about near famous, Ma."

"Come on. What's this?"

"The honor of your presence, Madame Negotiator Mother." She
bowed again and they laughed.

Folly offered her a beer. "C'mon out back and tell me what you been hearin'?"

"Bout you getting a hotshot contract."

"Well, we got one. I hope it's worth something. Were they talking about Mabel? I hope people realize Mabel was in there with me all the way."

"Maybe. I didn't hear about anyone but you."

It robbed the possibility for joy the way people refused to recognize Mabel's contribution. Folly saw that the white man wrote up the Black man's crimes in the paper every day. You'd see his picture often enough, his hands behind his back in handcuffs, but would they see Mabel in there for the long haul, working out that contract with the others? She tried to explain this to Mary Lou. "Most of what I learned being involved in this thing is about how Black and white people have been divided, and it's surely easier to go the familiar way—the way you've been trained. A lot of life is nothing but following one habit into the next. You got to stop yourself and keep peeling your eyes open all the time if you want to see what goes on. Those people talking about me gettin' the contract, they know Mabel was there, *they know* . . . but they can't see her there. You tell them and they'll say, 'Oh, yeah, I guess she was there, but you'd a had me, that had just slipped my mind completely.' "

"I guess they gotta have a pretty lousy memory," Mary Lou said.

"That's just the point. They got a perfectly normal memory for everything else."

Martha came over and joined them, bringing with her a less pensive mood. "You figured out yet what to do with all this raise we're gonna be getting?" she asked Folly.

"Hell, it ain't gonna be much."

"What about the house?" she asked.

"Yeah, I guess I'll go back to tryin' to put something away. Don't seem so crowded around here lately, since I hardly ever see this hard workin' daughter of mine."

They all sat listening to the birds' evening song for a moment. Mary Lou tried to picture them moving off and leaving Martha but couldn't. She felt the warmth of Martha's feeling for her mother, saw them look at each other, and for a second could almost picture them touching each other the way they described in the book. But no, not her mother. Her mother might jostle with Martha but nothing else. No hugging or kissing or whatever else lesbians did. Her mother was a union representative, a mill worker, a mother, a joke teller, a mystery reader. She didn't fall into anyone's arms. She thought she had settled it for herself. It was later, after supper, when she'd gone to her room to read some more, that she'd tripped over the idea maybe she was doing to her mother what her mother said they were doing to Mabel, blanking out on her. She took the book out from where she'd hidden it under a whole mess of stuff in her bottom drawer, set her ears for the sound of someone's approach to her room, set her reflexes for a quick route to under her pillow, and resumed her reading.

Aware that Mary Lou's bedroom window was like an ear to the porch, Folly dropped her voice to a whisper. "Maybe now I can get around to talking with her, now that I don't have to be worrying about the negotiations."

Martha nodded and searched Folly's face for more understanding of what that would mean to them. She foundered in herself, knowing this was a place of rocky footing in their relationship.

"She's got her radar out all over the place," Folly said.

"I don't doubt it," Martha agreed. She went in to get them another beer, came back out and nudged Folly, "Let's move over to my place to finish these."

Folly went in and told the boys, who were watching T.V., that she'd be next door. As they crossed the back yards in the moonlight, Mary Lou could feel them moving away from her, not exactly sneaking, but pulling farther, stretching the space. Maybe Martha had something she wanted to show Folly over there, she thought. Maybe they were worried that their voices were keeping her awake. She listened for the car door or the screen door. Maybe they were going out for more beer to celebrate. But, no, they had to work that night. They had not gone inside. No doors closed. She could just barely hear their voices, talking husky-soft in the dark.

They sat on Martha's back stairs. "You know it's funny the position you get yourself in sometimes."

"What's that?" Martha asked.

"How I'm ending up defending Jesse even though I'm stitchin' mad at him. I mean these women coming up to me last night asking about what happened after we made such a fuss about how we were going to stick up for being able to stay home when our kids were sick and all. And me feeling like saying, yeah, what the fuck happened anyway, but saying, now this was the way it was, we had to take what we could get. And even the doggone words out of Jesse's mouth like, 'this is a highly unconventional demand.'"

"Well, maybe you should just say Jesse pulled out on that one."

"But the thing is, we're tryin' to build confidence in the union. What's it gonna do if we go around talking down on Jesse?"

"Yeah, I know."

"I feel like a representative . . . not myself. What bugs me is if I'd a really heard Mabel, we wouldn't of left the room. 'If we *trust* him,' she said. Not 'We trust him.' She knew. Believe me, that is one smart woman. I keep learnin' over and over again how she is keyed in, and even *knowing that,* I got to almost force myself to listen to her. Brick brain." Folly batted herself on the head with the soft side of her fist.

"Hey, go easy," Martha said, caressing the same part of Folly's head.

"Well, you know it, don't you? You know when we first went out and started organizing for the union, we didn't think much at all about the Black women. We figured, automatically, they'd fall in right behind the white women. I, for one, never had a clue how much they had their own understanding of the union thing until that day Mabel gave us the dickens and a half, hear. Remember that? Us all sittin' in our white skins havin' a gripe session over our girls that wouldn't sign."

"Yeah. I hadn't thought about it, either."

They sat, still, and the hot silence of the night mixed with Folly's melancholy mood. She broke it, saying, "You shoulda gone off to celebrate with some of the other girls. I'm a drag."

"Not to me, you're not." Martha took Folly's hand, sandwiched it between her own and rubbed it. "I'm glad to be right here with you."

Exhausted, touched by having someone to care for her, Folly let the tears rise to her eyes. It felt unfamiliar to her, this sense that she did not have to seal off her skin and toughen up more when she felt defenseless, but could let her vulnerability ride in Martha's arms. Martha held her, rocked her gently side to side on the step, saying, "It's been a long hard haul. We been pulling since June, all through the heat. Pullin' and learnin' and next time we'll know more. Now's time for rest. Now's time for takin' some rest for our tired bones." The two of them went on swaying in silence until Folly jumped.

"What's that?"

"Nothing," Folly said, looking around. "I thought I heard something." She saw it had only been Mary Lou entering her thoughts, not the back yard.

"Let's go in," Martha said, standing and lifting Folly's hand.

"I want to be home for the kids."

"I'll let you go home in a little while."

Folly followed Martha into the trailer, wondering how she had lived all the years up 'til then without anyone there for her like this. She was finally reaching the point of being ready for the celebration to start. "Count your wins," Mabel had said. This was certainly one of them, this broad, steady woman who had stormed Fartblossom's office with her the night they'd heard about Cora's baby, and had been there, engaged in this struggle ever since. How heartening it was to have such a friend, how strengthening. So much of their lives were involved in pushing against, pushing up hill. Together they could encounter a different part of themselves—they could glide, feel the summation of giving energy that would be returned. Folly experienced this energy between them as a renewable resource. What she gave to Martha she could count on having back. They sat at the table with the bowls of ice cream Martha had generously scooped up, sat close to the corner of the table, Folly with one of her legs wrapped around Martha's. This was a place they both belonged in. A place of no resistance. Trust.

Folly remembered the women in the parking lot explaining to Jesse one morning: "One thing you learn here if you're gonna stay is keep your mouth shut. Better not to say what's on your mind. The gossip is so bad here you say two words at ten o'clock, it'll be made into five clear on the other side of the room by 10:10. Sally gets a new toaster. Everybody knows it 'fore she even uses it."

"I hate it," one woman had said. "I hate the gossip. But one thing I reckon with, it's there."

"But isn't it different," Jesse had asked, "talking about the conditions of your work?"

"Different?" someone said. "More dangerous, that's all. You gonna bitch about your work, you better be damn sure who's your best friend. If you ain't damn sure, you best keep it to yourself."

"What do you think makes for all this gossip?" Jesse asked.

"Boredom. Sometimes people are just plain small, but mostly I think it's downright boredom," Freena said.

Folly realized the great ease she took from being able to trust Martha completely. She remembered that day on her porch when they'd been talking about Mary Lou hanging out with Lenore and she'd caught herself wondering about Martha. She nearly laughed, seeing who she was now. Though she hadn't spoken, Martha, following her close, felt the change in her mood and grew attentive.

"Remember when I got so upset about Mary Lou because of that guidance counselor?"

"You bet. I remember that afternoon real well. I think you stirred me up some that day."

"I didn't stick with it, but I had a flashing glimmer about you then." She reached over and stroked Martha's leg.

"Sure it wasn't a flashing glimmer about yourself?"

"Nope. I sure did cover it right up with them sheets, anyway, cause I didn't want to lose the only good friend I had. I'll put this right in with them sheets, I thought, and iron it right out straight."

They laughed. Folly went on. "I guess I was buried pretty far down myself, as far as any ideas about sex was concerned. You know, kind of like a volcano. You keep simmerin' a long time on low, when you erupt, you're gonna come forth and make up for it. When you walked me down the road that night, I tell you, I never felt such a celebration taking place inside of me. Sparklers going off every which way. Fourth of July. A little hand holding, one kiss, and hear, woman, you had my legs melting right underneath my body."

"Good thing I was there to hold you up," Martha said. She put her hand on Folly's shoulder, bent and kissed her on the lips, then sat back and smiled. "Go on . . . go on." They had taken to telling the story of that first night over and over, as a ritual.

"I thought to myself, I thought, Folly, what's happening to you? What are you fixin' to do? Is this you? Where are your legs? I said, by the light of the stars, this is you. This is you and Martha. But it ain't true. I was actually *thinkin'* all this, I was *feelin'* it. I doubt I had any circulation to the brain at all. Or to the legs."

"Where was it?"

"Come on, now. You know . . . . It was gathering force to meet you."

Martha stood and gathered Folly to her, and they moved into the bedroom. "I love the way you tell the story, it's like being there all over again."

In the moments of silence that followed their bodies moving with a swift force together, Folly reached that place in herself where there were no voices, no ideas, no limbs ready for action, no ears for the children. A quiet deep inside herself, she felt almost as if she were floating. As sleep was a requirement for resting the tissues of the body, these moments of quiet healed the wounds of daily living. She had never known she was missing this healing until she had come upon it, but now it seemed as crucial as sleep. And why should she need healing? She only spent about ninety percent of her life with her head butted up against some impenetrable wall.

She didn't stay long. She wanted to be home with the children for a while before she had to go to work. She watched T.V. with the boys. Martha's smell was still close, but her peace was gone. She felt remote from her children, though she had wanted to be with them. She was building toward doing something about the situation, which she knew could not go on. She could not balance them off with Martha like a teeter totter, herself as the fulcrum. When she was with Martha sometimes she could almost forget them and leave herself off as a mother. When she was home with them, she found herself moving off from Martha. Either way meant a pull inside her, and she did not have a joint in her middle. Somewhere there were people who managed to pull off these balancing acts, women who never told their children, Martha had told her about them, but she knew she could not be one of them. She would have to lay everything out, then see how they would deal. What would it mean to them?

Ultimately, nothing, she thought. She was the same person they'd always had for a mother, who for years now had not cared to have much truck with men. And they were the same children tomorrow or yesterday plus or minus a little growing up. They were connected to her, and yet separate. Especially Mary Lou, who was trying harder and harder to establish her separateness. Skeeter, too, held himself aloof from the family, but she didn't think he knew much of himself apart from them. Tiny had not moved off yet; he would be with her regardless of who she was.

Instinct told her Mary Lou would be the hard one to reckon with. She probably would have felt this out further if it hadn't tripped her up so with anxiety. As it was, in all her pondering about what it would be like for Mary Lou to know she had a lesbian mother, she never did cross the thought that it might be a relief to her daughter's own quandary.

20.

Lenore woke up early but lolled in bed, celebrating Sunday. She was half glad to be alone, half sorry, and wondered what Betsy was doing at that same moment. It was impossible to imagine them both in bed at the same time because the time difference was so mammoth. They had once thought they'd talk to each other on the phone but synchronizing the time was too difficult; they'd settled for letters and signals. Lenore wasn't sure how strongly she believed in ESP but concentrated hard now on Betsy, trying to hook up long distance without benefit of Carolina Telephone and Telegraph, a free wave length. She pictured Betsy relaxing with the other women, maybe playing cards. She had a momentary image of Betsy sitting down to write her a letter. That was her own intention turned around—she was planning to write, soon as she got out of bed. She laughed out loud thinking about how she was going to tell Betsy, "Wait 'til you hear all the folks I got that book passin' around to. And you thought there wasn't nobody to give it to in Victory. Whole town will have it read by the time you get back."

She was also going to ask Betsy if she ever felt touched by these ESP concentrations and if she was aware of sending them down to North Carolina, because every so often Lenore felt Betsy pop into her mind right in the middle of something else, maybe say hello, maybe hold her hand a minute, maybe touch her face. She liked the idea that she was feeling these things because Betsy was sending them. Some people would think she was going off like ripe bananas, but her reluctance in asking Betsy was not that; it was that she might say no, she wasn't sending anything, and then Lenore would have to figure she was making it all up.

The other thing she feared to ask, because she was afraid the answer wouldn't be what she wanted to hear, was when Betsy was coming home. Even if it was months away, she figured she could enjoy the countdown if Betsy's actual presence was at the end of it. Suddenly, she had more friends than she'd ever had before, and she was even able to talk about herself more deeply with them, so how could it be that she ended up feeling more lonely now than ever? Her body yearned for Betsy's return. She stretched and yawned and then curled back up, unsatisfied. She wished she had someone she could tell about her visit with Sabrina the night before.

She had gone by the diner and invited Sabrina to stop at her place again, but Sabrina had turned the invitation around, told her to come by her house after supper, and given her directions before she'd even had a chance to consider her reservations. So, she'd found herself headed in for the fifth house on the right after turning off Main. She had never in her life gone in there to visit anyone. She had been down that road a few times before, not driving herself, or suggesting it, but riding around on a Saturday night with other kids, before she had quit school, and someone had come up with the idea they should go down that road to where the church was and see if they could see some Black folks holy rolling. They had sat with the car motor off, lights off, just beyond the church, at a point where you could not exactly see because the window was up high, but you could hear, and they had listened to the singing and praising going on inside, holding their breath, slouched down low in the seats, hands over mouths against giggles. Lenore had always stared at the window even though you couldn't see anything. Finally, they would roar away, the noise of their muffler meant to disturb the people inside, and break into laughter. Lenore wished that just once, someone in the car, anyone, namely herself, would have asked what the hell they thought they were laughing at. As she turned into Sabrina's driveway, she realized she had always wanted to hear the service through.

She worried, going up to the house, that it might be the wrong one, but Sabrina was standing on the other side of the screen door. "Seen you drive up. Come on in. This here's Eli," she said of the child who held onto her leg and moved in harmony with her. "That's my father, Russell James . . . The Reverend," she threw in as an afterthought. The man sitting at the dining table, intent on a book, looked up and nodded at Lenore. "Evening," he said in a low, soft voice. Lenore stood with her hands in her pockets, nodded back and answered, "Evening, sir," barely audible. As he looked back down at his book, she realized it was a bible, one with many ribbon markers, some of which fanned out on the table. His hands, long, slender fingers, gracefully handled the markers.

"Come on in the kitchen and we'll get us some drinks to take out," Sabrina said. In the kitchen she inclined her head back toward the man. "He's getting his sermon ready. Everybody else's gone out shopping." Lenore wondered who all. Sabrina's mother and Aunt lived here and Eli and her father, obviously, but she didn't have the slightest idea who all else. The house wasn't very large, about like the house she'd grown up in, only neater. She wondered if he preached down the road at that church they had spied on. His voice was so quiet. She tried to imagine it rising, tried to imagine this tall, slender man doing antics, leading other folks in going wild with the spirits as she had figured them to do in that church, but her mind blanked. She took the glass of juice Sabrina handed her. She was so nervous about being there and trying not to show that she was nervous that she couldn't hardly follow a single thought through. She didn't know whether being in that carload of kids outside the church was something she should forgive herself for. She wished she hadn't done it. It would be nice to think she hadn't joined in the laughter, but she had.

Sabrina led her out to the front porch, Eli tagging along, still attached to her leg. "Go on, play," she told him, but he only turned his big brown eyes on her a minute, then back to Lenore.

"Hi," she said, squatting down to his level. "How ya doing?"

He broke off eye contact, then came back to staring at her. She did the same thing in return, and he smiled. He covered his eyes with his hands, then dropped them and giggled when she imitated him. His face was chubby and soft and she would have liked to pick him up and touch it to her own, but she poked his belly with her finger instead, setting off the giggle.

Neighbors out for a walk talked to Sabrina across the yard. Lenore nodded hello, then, while Sabrina conversed with them, sat, her back against the wrought iron post, feeling conspicuously white. Pale and puny and sandy, straight-haired, she didn't even have a good tan. She thought if she didn't stop feeling so conscious of her skin, she would blush, and she did. She felt the heat in her face and the sweat on her palms just as Sabrina and the neighbors were talking about how nice it had cooled off for the evening. She thought about how frequently this might happen to Sabrina, who must often find herself in a white world and feel conscious of her skin color, and for herself she had gone nineteen years without finding herself in a Black world. For that moment, at least, she thought of Blackness as a richness of color and presence, and whiteness as a blank, a quality of absence. The hum of the reverend's voice was still in her ears, and farther in the background, strong voices rising in the church, and beside that, Sabrina's directness.

The neighbors had left and Sabrina sat down opposite her. Eli moved a toy truck up and down the cement porch floor between them. "Nice kid," Lenore said.

"Yeah." Sabrina smiled. "I think I got lucky there."

They watched Eli play, Lenore still acutely aware of her color. She lost her self-consciousness only when Sabrina asked, "What's happening with your ma these days? She still sober?"

"I reckon. I hope so. I saw her about a week ago and she was, then. Bitchy, too. In a way it's easier to talk to her when she's high. Sober, she's on me all the time."

"I guess you got to expect that."

Lenore agreed, but if the truth be known she hadn't understood to expect it until the words came out of Sabrina's mouth. That was what she appreciated about her directness, it allowed her to look at things through a new view. With most kids her age you couldn't have a serious conversation without a whole lot of messing around, if then. "Someday, I sure hope she and I can hit it off better," Lenore said sadly, "since she's the only one I got."

"Yeah, it is one of them one of a kind deals."

Lenore had vowed she wouldn't go out to her mother's house that weekend. She would give them both a good long span to cool out. She silently reinforced that vow to herself, knowing there was always a temptation to break it, always a lure to the familiar, even if the familiar was only her mother's carelessly wrapped fighter's bathrobe and a fight to go with it.

"How's it for you, being a mother?"

Sabrina drew a deep breath. "Hard to say. It's a lot of different ways. Sometimes I wish I wasn't. He's getting bigger now, but in the beginning I used to hold this little thing and think about how helpless he was, except for having my protection. Now I can see that as he grows up, it turns the other way. I'm the one who's gonna need the protection from him taking over."

"That sweet little boy?" Lenore asked, looking at Eli.

"Look at what you talking about, how your ma ain't got it together."

"I guess."

Sabrina's dark eyes grew more serious. "I stepped outa messin' around in high school, scattered all over the place, didn't know what I was doing there except to try to get some education that would end me up somewhere someday, then whammy, Eli bulging up inside of me. I hadn't really given much thought to my body 'til then, and here it was producing. Kind of neat. Then here he was, produced, and that seemed real serious for a girl who didn't know much about what she was doing. Makes you grow up fast. Figure you better know what you're doing. I said, 'Shape yourself up, Sabrina, in time for this boy.' It's been real good, having him, but sometimes I think I'd like to go back to before." Sabrina looked off the end of the porch wistfully, as if she had other dreams to follow.

"Yeah, I can see that," Lenore said. "We must've dropped out of school just about the same time."

"Is that so? How come you did?"

"Oh . . . didn't seem like I was gettin' much. I thought I'd do better to work full time. My ma wasn't working . . . guess you know that since you started working her job after she left the counter. They were asking me about who I knew for the butcher's job down at the store, so I told them I'd take it myself. I guess sometimes I wish I could go back and finish school."

"I always thought it would make some big difference," Sabrina said. "Back when I was a kid, everybody said, if you just get yourself a high school diploma, you'll be somebody. Nowadays, that don't mean boo. If you're Black and you got a high school diploma these days, that means you still nobody. You got to have a trade or a college degree or something like that and a good contact won't hurt you, either. Even if you go to all that trouble to get you a college education, times like this with recession and all, you'll still get cut right back off your job. I be lucky to have what I have down at the counter."

"Yeah, me too. I reckon if I wasn't at the A & P, I'd be down at the mill."

"Least those womens got something going there now. They look pretty good to me, walking out like that, staying out like they did."

"I know, but I still think it would drive me batty to do the same thing all day long . . . or night."

"True," Sabrina said. "Least you and me, working with people, we get some variation. Not that it's always desirable."

Lenore nodded.

"Most of the people don't act like you're real anyway. Do you find that to be so?"

"What do you mean?"

"Well . . . I don't know. They'll call you down, they'll say good
morning, but that ain't really meant for you, that's just to tell them
they's awake. They puts in their order—sunnyside with grits, coffee
black. You not a person taking the order. You the hand with the pad
and the pencil, scribbling there, walking off, cracking the eggs on the
grill, fixing the plate. They not saying 'this here's Sabrina waiting on
me' or even, 'that Sabrina sure be godawful slow,' but 'where are my
eggs,' is what they be saying. Sometimes they don't even know do they
have the Black waitress or the white waitress. Now that tell you something."

Lenore laughed. "I guess I know what you mean. I had this one
lady come in last week and she said, 'Now a couple of weeks ago that
nice girl who works here fixed me up a small package of stew beef, just
right, good and lean.' I felt like saying, 'yeah, what'd she look like? I'll
see if I can find her in the back room.' "

"Least she noticed you was a girl . . . both times."

Lenore clutched more than was probably necessary, wondering if
Sabrina thought her masculine, wondering if Sabrina had ever thought
she was gay.

Shortly after that Lenore said she'd better go. Sabrina said she
ought to put Eli to bed, but she'd come out and talk some more if Lenore would wait. Another time, Lenore had said, now that she knew
where Sabrina lived, she'd come again. She was strongly aware of not
wanting to be sitting there on that porch alone, white, and maybe Sabrina's folks would be coming home.

She stretched again, closed her eyes, and tried to picture Sabrina's
face. It didn't come easy. In fact, it didn't come at all. She consciously tried to construct it. A rounded face. Eli's flashed for a moment.
Did he look like her? She hadn't noticed. She tried to get a sense of
the exact color of Sabrina's skin, how black it was? How brown? How
did black and brown merge? She could picture Betsy's cheeks, high red
after lovemaking, even when she had a tan. She could call up those colors and see them vividly in her mind, whereas, it was as if her brain cells
had never been notified of the existence of the dark tones. And now,
when she needed them, she wasn't sure how to get them. What she
could see was Sabrina's hands, long-fingered like her father's. She could
see the line where the darker backs of her hands turned to the lighter
skin of the palms. Also, she could see her eyes, the careful looking at
you that she did, and the dark brown centers. She promised herself the

next time she saw Sabrina, she'd try to get her down better in her memory. She felt ashamed for not having paid more attention to dark colors before. She wondered if others experienced this. It wasn't the type of thing she'd ever heard anyone talk about.

So many of the important things people didn't talk about, and that was one of the reasons Lenore didn't know if others had the same kind of fears. She wondered if Sabrina had been able to feel how afraid she was, to feel how she had one foot stepping in and the other foot ready to start running the other way. Even as she'd loosened up talking with her, she'd had this nervous feeling that the way she had been taught to think about Black people was cruising along just underneath the surface of her friendliness, cruising back and forth, waiting for an opening, waiting with a desire to sabotage her. She tried to get a hold of what she had learned that was cruising there, and where she had learned it, but her mind kept wanting to slip off the point. Her mother had been a Southerner through and through, but she hadn't carried any hard line on race. In fact, she'd been the first waitress to serve Blacks at the counter, after integration.

Lenore remembered her telling the story of how four Blacks had come in, two men and two women, and sat at the far end, which was Adele's section. Evelyn, down at her end, was smoking, and Adele came down and lit up, turned her large rear end toward where they were sitting, and said, "It'll be a cold day in Hell before I serve a nigger." Evelyn had sat on it a minute. The Blacks had sat, too, elbows resting on the counter. It was midafternoon and the rest of the place was empty. Finally, Evelyn moseyed on down and signaled them toward her end. "I think you'll find the service a little faster down here," she said. Later what she couldn't stop talking about was being shocked at what a good tip they'd given her. That and the fact that Adele hadn't spoken to her for a week.

Lenore wished she could have a long, slow breakfast with Betsy, who would tell her how she felt inside. Then, giving up what wasn't possible, she got up and dressed and fixed coffee for herself, and sat down to write her.

Dear Betsy,

I've gotten behind, put off writing all week because of one thing or another, and now it seems like there's too much to tell at once. Considering the usual lack of action in Victory, you must be wondering what I mean. So, I'll try to give you a summary of what's been happening here.

153

I found, not one, but two people so far to give that book to. (Ha, ha.) The first one was Martha Hurley. I don't know if you know her. She works out at the mill, lives down at the trailer park next door to Mary Lou, who's a kid (works at store) I've been hanging out with some. Her mother's name is Folly and she works out at the mill, too. In fact she's one of the ones who's worked hard on the organizing out there, both she and Martha started the walk out. Remember I told you they had a union election and last week they finally got them a con- tract settlement. I guess it's good. It's something, anyway. They never had anything like it before. I'm getting off the point but these people all count somehow, you'll see. When they were out on strike I volun- teered to do something to help, and Martha called me a couple of times to do things. Like I babysat a couple of times and I drove some wom- en to meetings and down to the mill for voting. I got wondering about Martha and one day she told me about some old girlfriend. I finally got up the nerve to give her the book. Nervous? Me? God, I was pray- ing. She's older. Not that old, but closer to my mother's age than to ours. I went around thinking–Jesus, girl, what got into you, you're crazy, passing this book around to someone your mother's age. Well, it turns out to be okay. She come to see me, and she is one. She did- n't talk a whole lot about it, but we're going to talk more. She brought the book back, and I just couldn't tell her to pass it on. So, along come Mary Lou–she's only 16–comes right out and asks me the other night if I am one. Says she might be one herself. That's enough, right. But that ain't all. The main thing she's worried about is whether her moth- er is one. Folly, that's her mother, is Martha's best friend. Now when Martha talked to me, she didn't say nothing about Folly. I don't think she would, though, even if they were together. She told me about her girlfriend who went up north to New York City and never came back. Do you ever picture yourself becoming an Alaskan? I want to know about it if you do, even though I hope it's not so.

My ma has knocked off the booze entirely. I can hardly believe it. We're still fighting, in fact more than ever. She's bitchy when she's not drinking, but then I guess she's bitchy when she's drunk, too. I hope she'll be better after a while. She goes to Alcoholics Anonymous meet- ings. I'm not supposed to tell that, but I don't get what's the big secret anyway. Everybody can see when you're drunk so what's the shame of them knowing when you're sober. Oh, well, I guess we're all hypocrites. I wouldn't want someone going around telling everyone I'm a lesbian. I tried to let Mary Lou know to keep her mouth shut without coming right out and saying it. I hope she will. She's too young to understand that we're all willing to lie sometimes to keep ourselves protected. Don't I sound like the jaded old lady?

I've been hanging out some with Sabrina. Went over to her house last night and met her father, who's a preacher. He looks real nice. Remember when we used to go back in there and try to listen in on that church? I'm not sure if that's where he preaches. Anyway, I felt so funny being there in Sabrina's house and thinking about when we did that. Like, whose idea was it anyway? This was the first time in my whole life I'd ever been inside the house of a Black person. How about you? I guess that's really not so hard to believe, considering. It's not that there was anything strange about the house. Same kind of furniture as our houses. On the wall, though, they had a picture. It was made out of something like velvet, the background was a dark maroon, like the color of drapes in a church, and then the face of a Black woman stood out on the velvet. Hard to figure out why I keep thinking of it, but if you were sleepwalking and you happened to walk into this house and open your eyes, you'd see that picture and you'd know it wasn't a white house. It's funny how I can see that picture in my mind better than I could describe what Sabrina looks like or her father, or I think I told you before, she has a two-year old son, Eli, real cute.

I've been thinking about how there's this whole bunch of people out there, the entire Black race, that I don't know hardly a dang thing about. I mean I know what we learned—a bunch of lines, but shit, sometimes I'm not even sure about that—what was in the lines and why, and who made them up? That Negroes were inferior and that's why they were poor—remember that line? So how come my mother's poor, then, and you're family ain't rich, either? Sometimes I feel real sad, thinking about how can this ever be made right. I don't know. It goes real deep. I get mad, too, at like who made up these rules. It wasn't me. I don't want to go around feeling superior. I can't stand people who act that way, but don't you think other white people assume I am 'cause I got the same skin as them? And that keeps those lines running in me, even if I don't believe in them. And it's scary to have them in me, and trying to talk to Sabrina without all this other stuff in the way. I'd like to talk to her like we were two ordinary people, alike in some ways, different in others.

Write me back about this if you can make sense of what I'm trying to say. I wish you were here so we could talk it out together. If you're thinking I might have Sabrina lined up next for "Sappho," don't worry. I don't think so, but you never know. I don't really know her that well, yet.

I miss you all the time. Oh, I almost forgot. Do you receive my ESP messages? And have you been sending some here? Describe what you send. No codes, please.

When are your bones going to be cold enough to draw you back home? I guess Victory will be ready for you. Question is, will you be ready for it?

Send me some more good books.

All my love,

Lenore

P.S. You say you're learning a lot by being so far from home, but here I am learning there are other worlds right down the street in Victory.

21.

Martha looked down over Daisy, sleeping the last of her life out in a coma. God, how you've been a fixture in my life, she thought. She skipped to a time in childhood, a spanking. She couldn't remember the lie but remembered being caught in it. Daisy had held her by the arm and spanked her rear with the thin, stringy fingers of her other hand, stinging, meaning business. She looked at the knobs Daisy's knuckles were now. Even as she watched them, she thought she saw them go a little looser, as if they were letting go. She thought she felt Daisy slip deeper in the coma. Was it Daisy letting go or was it her letting go of Daisy? Her heart swelled up as if to fill the space she forecast missing her would mean. She felt full with her memories of them together and hoped Daisy could feel that, too. Martha had, all along, been angry that her mother's old age had come too early, that she had worked too hard and worn too thin, had eaten the wrong foods for keeping her arteries clean because they were the cheapest diet. But now that Daisy seemed so close to leaving, Martha felt almost peaceful. She had the sense that death would be more of a prize than punishment.

At supper break Cora came and sat down across the table from Folly, unusual because they rarely saw each other except from a distance. She looked a little less disconnected, Folly thought. "Where's Martha tonight?" she asked.

Folly lowered her voice. "Took one of her sick days. Her mother's failing. You know she was in the hospital, anyway, not very alert, but now she's gone into a deep coma."

"Oh. I'm sorry." Cora bit at her fingernails, nervously.

"Funny you should ask about Daisy, now. She used to ask about you, right after, you know, when we had the walk out." Folly couldn't bring herself to say after your baby died. She wished she knew the name of that baby. They had always just said—Cora's baby.

"She did?" Cora's surprise sounded in her voice. She wound and unwound a strand of her hair around her finger, getting used to the idea. "That was mighty nice of her, I guess."

"She was a good woman," Folly said, vaguely realizing she was speaking of Daisy as if she'd already died. She took her sandwich out of the wax paper and started eating. Cora did, too. Folly saw how Cora's hand wasn't steady when she poured the coffee from her thermos. Neither of them said anything while they ate, though Folly was thinking that she wanted to, and as Cora closed up her thermos, she got out, "Listen, I wanted you to know, Mabel and me, we really tried to keep the clause about sick children in the contract. I never felt right that it got put out at the end. I mean, I don't know if it means anything to you or not, but I just thought I'd tell you."

Cora's eyes filled up with tears and she nodded her head up and down as she went about preparing to leave, picked up her stuff, speechless, went on nodding, then moved out for the bathroom.

When the shift was over, Folly went around to the pay phones to call home and tell Mary Lou to fix the boys some breakfast because she'd be stopping by the hospital to see how Daisy was doing. Really to see how Martha was doing because the idea that Daisy had died that night had taken strong hold in her. She wasn't going to tell that to Mary Lou, but when she told her Daisy had gone fully into a coma, Mary Lou said she had known it. "I felt it," she said. "I wouldn't be surprised if she's died already, Ma. I swear to you, I knew something was wrong. I was working away last night, stacking cans . . . a big delivery that came in late and we needed it bad. Anyway there I was, three boxes of applesauce jars to go, no reason in the world to be thinking about Daisy, and then all of a sudden she comes into my mind so clear. I could see her. You know, not the way she is now in the hospital bed, but up standing and pointing at me."

"What for?"

"Scolding me, never mind what for. Anyway, she's stayed with me ever since. For a little shriveled lady that Gramma Daisy sure can take up some space in your mind."

"I know," Folly said. "Look, I can't talk. Someone's waiting for the line. Tell the boys I'll see them later. I don't know what time I'll be home. When do you have to go in?"

"Noon. Ma, you'll call me, won't you, when you get to the hospital and find out what's going on? Maybe I can get me a ride and come over there."

"No. You stay with the boys. I'll call you, soon as I can."

Mary Lou hung up the phone and tried to convince herself what other possibilities existed besides Daisy being dead, but she kept bumping into blank spaces. She tried to talk to Daisy the way she'd taken to doing often since the last stroke, but her speaking wasn't being received. It was like trying to hit a wall through a thick, felt mat. Your punch would have neither sound nor resilience.

Martha had been right there with Daisy as she breathed a great sigh and was gone. She held both of Daisy's hands and waited for her chest to rise, knew it wouldn't but waited anyway, holding her own breath. Then leaned close up to Daisy's face, feeling for air on her cheek. Everything still but Martha's own alarm inside her about shouldn't she be doing something? She didn't want to call the nurse. She wanted to be alone with her mother. And what could possibly be done, anyway? Something to bring her back to her coma? To be done was to let go. Great, huge sobs jerked spasmodically from Martha's chest, nearly tipping her off balance and over onto Daisy. They were empty of tears. The other bed in the room was empty, a relief. Her stomach felt empty and flattened by the sobs which repeated, Mama, Mama, Mama. Martha thought of herself as always calm and steady and had not known these sobs were in her. She barely recognized herself as the woman who held on to her mother, knowing she couldn't do so much longer. She realized Daisy was turning cold. She pulled the sheet and blanket up over her hands, up to her chin. Touched Daisy's face. Skin no longer alive. If you slapped it, there would be no echo, no sting. She stepped back, swallowed the last sob, which felt hard in her throat, and became calm. She tried to think was there something she wanted to say to Daisy before she let her body be taken away? She thought of times when she wished she'd come out and told Daisy how much she was bugging her so she'd have understood why she was hiding away in her room or going over to Folly's all the time. Probably Daisy had known without the telling. The figure in the bed began to seem less and less real to her, so she went down the hall for the nurse. She was already beginning to picture her mother at different stages of her life. Daisy out of bed, on her feet, saucy and strong.

The reason Folly hadn't left work early to go to Martha was because she knew that would blow Martha's cover for her lie that she was sick.

When she got to the hospital and found the room empty, she was sorry right away. Daisy's bed was gone, even. What did they do, wash down the whole bed when someone died in it? The nurses told her the funeral parlor hadn't come for the body until six, though Daisy had died a few hours before. Folly rushed there and found Martha, collected, seated with Mr. Cowley, a pot of tea between them. Mr. Cowley had already gotten into his black suit. His crew cut stood up in front, waxed stiff. In the front of the building he sold insurance in a golf shirt. In the back, he ran the funeral parlor in a black suit. He got up and shook Folly's hand and then backed through a door that fit so inconspicuously into a wall panel, Folly hadn't even realized it was there.

"He's really the original disappearing act, ain't he?" Folly said.

Martha nodded, then stood and went into her arms. "God," Folly said into her ear, "that damn mill. I wish I'd come sooner. I'm sorry. I love you. I'm sorry."

Martha hung on to her, trying to say it was okay, but this time the tears came with the sobs, came in a flood which spilled onto Folly's neck and shoulder, and Martha's chest was held from shattering by Folly's full arms.

Later, Folly's arms went around Mary Lou and tried to comfort her but failed. Mary Lou's back was slender, lithe. She slipped away easily, and stayed inside herself. She was angry at Folly for not having called. But there had been no reason to call. Folly had simply held Martha until she had come back into control, then brought her home, left her in her trailer, and come over here. Folly sat in her rocker and rocked vigorously, looking for some comforting herself. Mary Lou sat at the table, licked her index finger, poured a little salt from the salt shaker on it, then picked it off grain by grain with her tongue. After repeating this a few times, she puckered up her lips as if her feelings were right there behind them, not to be let out. Uninvited, Folly began talking. She told everything she knew about Daisy's dying, which was whatever Martha had told her on the way home. Then she reiterated her own course of events for the day, the fact that Cora had sat across from her that night, her regrets that she hadn't followed her instincts and left work. By the end of this, Mary Lou had let the pucker out. "I sure will miss her," Folly said, finally.

Mary Lou tried to keep on looking at her mother though her vision was blurry. "Me, too." She wanted to tell her mother about the rest of what it was like for her, of how she couldn't talk to Daisy anymore, there was no receiver, like picking up the phone and getting a dead line, how lonely that was, almost like thinking it was too late to be a child. She didn't pucker, but she didn't talk, either. She sat there looking like someone surely had to be accused, and then she got up saying she had to get ready for work.

"I'm going back over to be with Martha," Folly said. "I hope you understand."

"Course."

"If you want to stop over there before you go, do."

"What for?"

"I don't know. To talk I guess. I know losing Daisy's going to be hard on us all."

"Yeah, Ma, sure," were the last words that could get around the lump in Mary Lou's throat as she walked down the hall, her back to Folly.

Mary Lou went through her closet about five times, looking for something to wear, her frustration growing to desperation as the time went on. She was supposed to be dressing for the funeral. She wanted to put on something comfortable but everything comfortable she had was dead wrong for a funeral—she knew that without ever having been to one before. She kept trying to picture what it was going to be like. Was she going to see Daisy? She was afraid to ask.

Folly called her. "Aren't you ready?"

"No, Ma, can you come here a minute?"

Her mother appeared in the door. "What?"

Mary Lou stood in her underwear, hands on her hips, pelvis tilted in a posture of insolence. She gestured to the closet. "Nothing. I ain't got nothing to wear." Maybe I'll stay home, she thought but did not say.

Folly faced the closet, pushed the hangers all back, then started flipping them forwards one by one. When she got to the end, she went back, pulled out a white blouse, a green pleated skirt, handed them to Mary Lou, who, like a robot, put out her arms to receive them. Mary Lou had a vague memory of being a child, standing between her mother's knees while she dressed her. Her mother was gone. She put on the clothes, stood in front of her bureau mirror, turned—still with the sense of a robot—a full circle, then leaned closer to the mirror. She examined herself for change. She felt the age of someone who had sustained many losses. Folly was calling them to come for scrambled eggs. She didn't understand why they were eating before the funeral. It did not seem an appropriate thing to her. Her stomach was jumping all over with her fear of the funeral, of taking her grief into public. She wished she could stay home, alone, while the rest of them went. She could cry and cry and no one would know, and then she could go say goodbye to Daisy later. But the burial was to take place right after the funeral and there was no choice but for them all to do this together.

Martha had gone early to the funeral parlor, and they were to ride over with Effie, who called while they were still in the middle of scrambled eggs and said, "Holler when y'all are ready." Mary Lou's eggs tasted chalky, and she was only able to swallow them by washing them down with orange juice. She dashed back in her room, changed to her dark blue wrap around. The waist of the green plaid had felt like a tourniquet. A relief, for at least now she could breathe.

They reached the door of the room and Folly and Effie went on in, leaving the kids standing in the hall. "What do we do?" Skeeter whispered to Mary Lou.

"We go on in and see," she whispered back, not that she really knew. Tiny had taken her hand. She could see Martha standing with people around her. The coffin was off behind her, flowers at both ends. Irises and she didn't know what. Martha looked puffy and tired but otherwise not much different. She and Skeeter and Tiny had gone through the door in their own little cluster and Mr. Cowley had spoken to them in a very low, quiet voice, so low Mary Lou hadn't caught a word he'd said. She worried that he might have made some instruction about how they should act, where they should go next.

Then Folly saved them, came and gathered them and brought them over to some of the women from the mill, and said, "These are my children—Mary Lou, Skeeter, Tiny." Everybody nodded. Were you supposed to talk? Make chit chat at these things? Mary Lou tried to hear what they were saying but her ears didn't seem to be working, her eyes kept sneaking over and lighting on the coffin. Next thing she knew she was facing Martha. Wordless, she put out her hand and tried to make a look of sympathy appear on her face for Martha, who ignored the hand and gave her a big hug. "I'm glad y'all are here," she said, as if they were cronies. Mary Lou could feel Martha's breath shudder in her chest though she remained board stiff herself. How could she possibly find comfort for somebody else even though she knew that's what she was supposed to do?

Finally Martha released her and hugged the boys, though not the same way. She asked would they like to see Daisy. "I guess," Skeeter answered, and she walked them to the coffin. Skeeter went first. He walked very slowly by it, pausing at the head for a few seconds. He had his baseball cap tucked up in his armpit. He looked as if when he got to the vase of irises, he would take off in a sprint. Mary Lou waited until he was off the platform that the coffin was on before she stepped up herself. She heard her own foot land and wondered what the step was made of. It felt like a box turned over. It seemed narrow so that she felt as if she were tightrope walking. She moved along, unaware of movement, amazed that this was actually Daisy she was seeing. This dead body. Looked like Daisy. Looked peaceful. Looked more peaceful than maybe she'd ever seen Daisy. Who are you, Daisy? Who are you now? So still. She stopped at Daisy's head. She couldn't hear anything over her own thoughts. *I'm so surprised that you almost look real, Daisy.* Like you're coming back in my memory. What you looked like before the last stroke, even before that. *I'm sorry you're not gonna get to see me grown up, Daisy; I don't know what it's gonna be like.*

She tried to memorize Daisy but her vision was blurred, and she realized again there were others in the room. She didn't know how long she had been there, so she stepped down and waited for Tiny. She held her purse in the crook of her left elbow and rocked her weight back and forth from one foot to the other. Tiny stood right up by Daisy's head, up on his tip toes, up so close his chin was sitting on the coffin. He stood and stood and stood. Mary Lou realized she hadn't touched at all, either Daisy or the coffin. She had kept a careful space between them. The longer she waited for Tiny, the heavier her purse felt, as if the strap was cutting through her arm. There wasn't much in it: her wallet, a comb, some Kleenex. It pulled on her shoulder so, she felt as if she was carrying rocks. It was embarrassing. Tiny was looking at Daisy as if she were a toy and he was home where nobody else mattered. Mary Lou tried to send him a signal that it was time to move on, but when Tiny was into his own world, that didn't work with him. There were other people lined up waiting to pay their respects, waiting for Tiny. She could just move on out herself, pretend she didn't know him. But that would be stupid. Everyone knew who they were anyway; they were the only kids at the funeral. She chewed on the inside of her lip. She wished she had stayed up there longer. Now that she was down, she thought she had probably only stayed with Daisy a few minutes, maybe it was only seconds.

She wouldn't have gone and pulled Tiny down on her own. Even though she was embarrassed to a point of wanting to disappear, she felt he was entitled, but when one of the ladies from the mill went up and joined Tiny, she did reach forward and took his hand and gently tugged him in her direction.

As she and Tiny turned away, she saw her mother and realized Folly had been there all along, watching them. She indicated another door from the one they had come in, and told them to go out in the yard until time for the service. Mary Lou was furious. Why had she worked herself up over whether Tiny would ever come down? She could have left him for her ma to attend to. Her ma could have come forward and done what she had done.

She was glad to go out in the yard. It was one of the few places in town where the grass was still green in spite of the end of summer heat. Mary Lou had always connected the green grass with dead bodies, but now she realized, of course, they weren't buried here but at the cemetery. She nearly tripped on a sprinkler that was stuck in the ground like a golf tee.

Tiny was still holding her hand, swinging it as they walked over to a tree. "That the first dead person you ever saw?" he asked.

"Yup."

"It sure did look like Daisy."

"It *was* Daisy."

"Yeah, but it looked like Daisy playing dead. I thought she was going to open her eyes to scare me."

Mary Lou laughed. She couldn't laugh very hard because she could tell the laughing would turn to crying. Tiny let go. He balled up his hand and punched Skeeter in the stomach and took off running, knowing he'd be chased and caught and punched back. Mary Lou thought about sitting under the tree, but she didn't want to mess up her skirt. She considered going back in to be with the adults, maybe taking another turn by the coffin, but the sun felt good on her back, and the idea of balancing on that box again made her feel as if her equilibrium was off. She didn't really want to see Daisy, she wanted to talk to her. And then, with a light feeling she thought she'd lost forever, she realized she had talked to Daisy, had told her about growing up, and she hadn't had the dead phone feeling at all. Her mind buzzed with all the talk she needed to have with Daisy. *This must be about the spirit, Daisy. You always said, "There's more than meets the eye, girl."* She had almost forgotten they still had to go through the service and then putting Daisy in the ground, when her mother opened the back door and signaled them to come back in.

22.

The burial was over before Mary Lou had time to digest the idea of it. The closed coffin bounced with the steps of the men who carried it. A mound of red clay beside the hole in the ground showed the stratification of the layers that had been dug. Daisy entered the earth. Too fast. The minister saying a prayer, some of them muttering Amen, the box going down. Daisy gone when they had closed the lid. Mary Lou had the feeling again of not being able to swallow her eggs. The lump grew in her throat. She fought her tears, watched the red dirt, tried not to visualize the insects, a whole culture moving underground. Folly's arm came around Mary Lou's shoulders and Mary Lou felt the sharp distinction between that arm and her own back, this back that she was trying to keep out of the ground. Why didn't they wait a minute before they threw the first spade of dirt?

Then everyone was backing away, piling into cars, holding doors, closing doors. She and Skeeter and Tiny were funnelled into the back seat of Martha's car. Home, they were going home. Martha was driving. It seemed to Mary Lou she would hear the sound of car doors closing for the rest of her life.

She went in her room and locked the door, took off her funeral clothes and put on her jeans. Sat on the bed, her back pressed against the tacky thin wall, listening to the noise in the other room. Almost like a celebration. And Daisy hadn't been buried an hour yet. She

wouldn't want them doing that if she had just died. Eating. She had
seen the women putting out food, had pictured them with covered dishes on their laps in their cars, on the way to and from the cemetery.
She'd felt like barfing when they'd removed the covers from the food.
Who could eat? Who could talk? She could hear them chattering. She
didn't want anything to do with adults. She wanted a quiet place to
think, but she had no place to go, so she stayed there, her hot head resting on the wall.

In the living room, Martha and Folly and other women who had
known Daisy well were telling stories of times with her. Skeeter and
Tiny sat on the floor, eating and listening for a while, then went outside. Folly felt Mary Lou's absence acutely. She wanted her to hear
these stories and to tell her own, but she knew not to call her out. She
could feel her disapproval coming through the wall. She thought again
of getting a house with thick walls, a place where one could wait Mary
Lou out through these moods. She thought of taking a plate of food
in to her, but decided better of it. Wait until everyone was gone.

Martha laughed, a deep belly laugh at a memory of Daisy, and Folly
followed the broad, pendulous swing of her emotion. She had never
been so close to anyone before, except perhaps her children when they
were babies. She felt as if Martha's feelings were reaching right inside
her. She didn't join the laughter but waited, as if readying to catch
Martha should she fall off at the end. She was grateful that it was Saturday and one when they had not been called to work. Otherwise they
would soon be packing up this gathering so those on second shift could
prepare to go in.

Mabel and Emily stopped by to pay their respects to Martha, and a
hush fell on the room. Folly was glad to see them. She especially
missed Mabel, who had gotten back on first shift after the contract was
signed. She missed their talk. She missed watching Mabel's sharpness
taking in all that was happening.

"Have some coffee, have some food. Let me get you a plate," Folly
said, ushering them toward the table.

"No, no," Emily said. "We had dinner. And we can't stay. We
gotta get on. We just wanted to stop in."

Mabel had gone to Martha, taken her hand, said, "I know this is a
hard one. I lost my mama a few years back and I ain't never had no
bigger loss. You take care of yourself good, hear?"

Martha nodded her head up and down, slowly released Mabel's hand,
then took Emily's.

In a few minutes they were gone, and the hum of people talking filled up the room again, but what stayed with Folly was the hush that had come with their presence—the way the white women had gone into a different gear, as if they were guarding their own mouths, and the way they so easily slipped back now into busy talk and comfort. Folly wished they'd stayed longer, but she could understand why they had not. She wanted to know them more fully. She knew Mabel had children and a husband who was gone a lot of the time, a seaman, but she didn't even know how old the children were. She wondered if Mabel had one like her own daughter, sweet and sour.

"I sure was surprised to see Cora show up," Shirley said. "I would-n't a thought she'd even know Daisy died. Must read the obituaries."

Cora's name brought Folly back. "I talked to her the other night, the night Daisy had gotten worse. So she knew."

"Oh, I see. She didn't really know my mother, so I guess she came for my sake," Martha said.

"Maybe for her own sake," Shirley said. "I reckon it might help her to grieve for someone older."

"Daisy did actually worry a lot about Cora," Folly reminded them. "That first night after the walk-out, we brought her over here for a picnic, remember Martha? We asked her what she thought about the union. She sat there and thought a minute, and then she said something like: 'Well, you can count on the fact they'll all be men, and they won't worry so much about the same things that worry the women. They won't concern themselves with Cora. But as long as you understand that, they might be worth something to you.' She was one wise woman, far as I can see."

"I'd almost forgotten about that talk," Martha said.

They were in a lull with their memories at the moment Lenore appeared. She knocked on the metal frame of the screen out of manners, though they could all see her. "Come on in," Folly said. "Hello. Won't you have something to eat with us?"

Lenore's eyes scanned the room and didn't find Mary Lou. "No, thanks," she said quickly. "I just ate." She felt conspicuous, out of place. There was no room for anyone else to sit down, except on the floor. The kitchen table had been pushed up to the wall to make room. Lenore waved and nodded at Martha. She didn't have anything she could say in front of all these women. "I thought I'd stop and see if Mary Lou was home." She wanted Martha to know she was thinking about her, too, but she couldn't think how to get that feeling to her across the room.

"She's in her room," Folly said. "Right there." She indicated the door. "Just knock."

Lenore was sorry she had come. Mary Lou kept her waiting outside the door for another awkward, long minute. She had hoped to find Mary Lou outside. Expecting all these people to have gathered at Martha's, she'd imagined she'd stop over for a second, ask to speak to Martha, say "sorry, it must be hard to lose your mother." It hadn't gone at all as planned. Did anything, ever?

When Mary Lou opened the door, she practically fell in. "Hi."
"Hi."

Mary Lou sat at one end of the bed and Lenore had no choice but to sit at the other. The room was small. The walls were covered with posters which drew Lenore's eyes. They were basically what she would consider children's posters, mostly animals. A couple were pictures of rock bands. Mary Lou followed Lenore's glance and felt foolish, looking at the room through her eyes. "Don't pay no attention to this," she said. "I'm about to take all this junk down."

"Oh," Lenore said. "I like the polar bear. Just looking at him could cool you right off on a hot day in Victory." Actually, she was thinking of Betsy, of Alaska, but at least Mary Lou grinned and the frozen rigidity of her face let go for a minute, for which Lenore was grateful.

"Summer's just about gone," Mary Lou said.

"Sure is. You gonna work right up 'til school starts or you takin' off next week?"

"Might work right on through." Mary Lou dropped her head as she said this.

"Through what?"

"Through school starting."

"Not go back?"

"That's what I'm thinking."

"Wait a minute," Lenore said. "Let me out of here."

"How come?"

"Hey, I can just hear it now. How Lenore talked you into quitting school, same as she did, just before eleventh grade. No way, kid. Listen, I'm in favor of education. I'm thinking I might go back myself and get one of those equivalencies. You got brains and you better learn to use them." Lenore recognized something close to her mother's words coming out of her mouth, so she shut it.

"I learned more working at the store this summer than all last year in school."

"I know. I know how you feel. And it's true that when you first start working, you do learn a lot. But you know the store, now. You got a job you can do blindfolded. You got nothing to look forward to but more of same. More of same, more of same, more of same." Lenore mimed the gestures of bagging groceries.

"I guess." Mary Lou looked disgruntled as she watched Lenore's act.

"I think you should be thinking about getting prepared to go on to college."

That stopped Mary Lou in her mourning. "Sure," she said, "sure. Me. Mary Lou College. I think I'd rather bag groceries."

"Well, it's *your* life," Lenore said. "I gotta be going. I really came by just to tell you I was sorry about Daisy. Stop by, when you want to talk."

"Sure, thanks."

Lenore lowered her voice. "You can come back with me now, if you want to get away from here."

"No, not now. I'm weirded out. I'm sorry. Thanks. Later."

Mary Lou was filling with tears, holding them while she locked the door again behind Lenore. She dropped on her bed, face down, and let her empty chest heave, mouth in the pillow, ears dumb with the feeling of a fist in the eustacian tubes. The women on the other side of the wall, as Lenore tried to float by, unnoticed, asked, "How's Mary Lou?"

"Okay." Lenore bobbed a hand up and down, didn't stop moving. "Bye."

Folly had that image of Lenore taking exit in her mind as she floated in her own fatigue. Everyone had left but Martha, who was napping on the couch. She wondered if Mary Lou had ever told Lenore she wasn't supposed to hang out with her. Not that she cared anymore. She was glad Mary Lou had made a friend, in spite of her. And she would like to know Lenore, once things got back to something resembling ordinary life. Right now she needed to get her feet back on her own ground. She couldn't stand so much of this everything going to fill up the losses. She thought she would miss Daisy almost as much as Martha would, but at the moment, what bothered her more was missing Mary Lou. She heard Mary Lou's door open, and held her breath, waiting for Mary Lou to come out, but she didn't. She only went to the bathroom and returned to her room. Folly felt rebuffed, fooled by her own hopefulness. She rested her head back against the chair and watched Martha sleep. Next

169

thing she knew she was fantasizing Martha on the bed, her own body pressed up warm against Martha's back, fitting her curves. A rush of feeling went through her, arousing her. It gave her a sense of being unexpectedly overtaken by joy, of dreaming a warm, sexy dream, which was something she'd never done until they had gotten together. These sensations were part of her new life, in which her sexuality was awake to whatever provoked it, and lots of times that was an inside circuit. A thought, a memory, a sense of her own vigor would bring this rush to her and through her, leaving her tingling and feeling the flutter in her heart.

She remembered Daisy looking up in one of her moments of reentry, looking at them standing together beside the bed and seeming to see the currents that traveled between them, seeming to let their sensuality evoke a smile in her. Daisy had talked after her first stroke about how she'd been able to see charges around and between people, how she'd felt like a voyeur sometimes from having this invisible information.

Folly feared she hadn't made enough room for Mary Lou to be sexual. But was her real fear that Mary Lou wouldn't be able to make enough room for her?

She fixed supper, and the boys came in. Mary Lou was called but refused. "Not eating," she said through the door. "Go ahead without me." She pictured them—cannibals chewing on drumsticks and wings. She put her radio on so she would not hear them chewing, swallowing. Folly was heartened by the sound of music coming from Mary Lou's room. She put a plate on the stove for her, covered it with a pot lid.

Martha went home, and Folly asked the boys what they thought of the funeral. 'I guess it was okay," Skeeter said. 'I guess it don't make much difference to you if you're already dead."

"I might leave our light on tonight," Tiny said. "Tell Skeeter he better let me."

"Why?" Folly asked.

"Daisy's ghost. I have a feeling Daisy's ghost might come."

"Sure, you can leave the light on, but who is this Daisy's ghost? Think she's your memory of Daisy?"

"Don't know," Tiny shrugged, "but I bet she's scary in the night." He came around and got up on Folly, hugged her, burying his face in the dark between her breasts.

"Maybe she's coming to comfort you," Folly whispered. He was comforted by the idea as well as the cocoon she made of her arms about him.

170

"What's wrong with Mary Lou?" Skeeter asked.

"Nothing that I know of," she said. "Sometimes a body just wants to be alone."

But after she put the boys to bed and Mary Lou still hadn't come out, she couldn't go on believing that. She hesitated a hundred times, then finally tapped lightly on the door.

"Who is it?"

"Your ma."

"Oh."

"You hungry?"

"Not much."

Silence. Folly hadn't tried the door, didn't know if it was locked.

"What you want?"

"Can I come in?"

"I guess so."

Folly went for the knob. It was locked, she found out as Mary Lou reached to spring it open. She closed the door behind her and went to sit at the end of the bed. She looked around at the walls, which were empty. "You getting ready to move out?"

"Nope." Mary Lou closed her mouth around the word as if she had let out too much at once.

"What happened to your room?"

"Nothing. I cleaned it up. Took the baby pictures down."

"Oh." Folly didn't want to let on how relieved she was that her first thought hadn't been right. The room looked bare, but at least it had Mary Lou in it. And for the moment it contained them both, though Folly felt the discomfort of the intruder.

"Where's Martha?"

"She went home."

"Oh."

So much for that conversation. Folly studied Mary Lou's posture which seemed to declare she was ready to live in misery for the rest of her life. Mary Lou's bones were more prominent than hers, proud of their shapes on their own, but her sad face hung over them, making policy, and Folly stopped herself short of saying anything about saving her supper.

"Is Martha okay?"

"About Daisy, you mean?"

"Yeah."

"She seems to be." Silence, then Folly continued. "How about you?"

"What about me?"

"How come you didn't come out this afternoon? All that food and we had people stopping by . . . ."

"Gross. I don't see how you can eat after a burial." She stuck her nose up in the air.

"Don't mean your body stops needing food for nurturance."

"Nurturance," Mary Lou repeated. "It's gross if you ask me."

"What's bugging you?"

Silence, again. Mary Lou worked a hand into her pants pocket, bit at her bottom lip and wouldn't look at her mother. Folly wanted to take the word *nurturance* back, away from Mary Lou, away from this room, and keep it for herself, where it was cared for, between her and Martha. She was infuriated at the hard finish on Mary Lou, shellac; she shined with a purity that Folly could not penetrate.

Finally, barely containing the spit behind her teeth, Mary Lou said, "How am I ever going to learn to drive if we don't have our own car?"

They were both fantastically relieved by the presence of this concrete problem where there had been none before and began breathing full breaths of air deep into their lungs.

"We'll have to talk to Martha about it. I don't think she'll mind."

"You don't?"

"No."

Folly saw tears flood Mary Lou's eyes. "What you crying for?"

She shrugged and tried to stop herself, grabbed a wad of tissues and held them over her eyes like sponges. She couldn't tell her ma it was because she was glad to be talking to her again. And because if she could drive she could go off and leave them when she needed to get away. She was thinking of how she would have driven off after the funeral and spent the whole day riding, watching the horizon, turning off on back roads, deciding her future. Should she go up to Alaska and make money? Quit school and keep working in the store? Go to college? She still couldn't believe Lenore had said that.

Folly realized Mary Lou was both older and younger than she had been thinking of her. She thought of her leaving the paychecks, endorsed, after that first time, week to week. Folly thought of herself, also, as being both older and younger than she had been before she and Martha had become lovers. For that moment, age seemed a lost point of reference between them.

Mary Lou sat very still, as if she knew what was coming. Folly's mouth opened and closed several times without words coming forward until she found a way to start. "I want to tell you about me and Martha. You know ever since she moved here we've been tight friends, still are. But now we're lovers, too. We love each other very much and we're havin' a time that is beautiful to us." Folly let that sit on the silence before going on. Her mouth was dry. "I hope it don't seem ugly to you. I didn't know, until now, I could love a woman like this, but I do. I haven't told Skeeter and Tiny, yet. I don't know what it will mean to you."

"I knew it." Mary Lou said. The tears squeezed out of her eyes and she blotted them again. "I knew it."

"How?"

"I could see it."

"What'd you think?"

"I thought I better grow up fast because this was coming. I thought I'd run away. I thought you'd never talk up close with me again.

"Why?"

"Cause you were all the time busy, either with the union stuff or else with hanging around with Martha, and cause I was always working at the store."

"How come you didn't run away?"

"Cause I never could get the bill paid off at the store."

Folly felt touched by this daughter, and light with the release of her secret. "Sometimes you gotta just move, regardless of the bills, but in this case, I'm mighty glad you didn't."

"So," Mary Lou said, slowly, "does this mean you and Martha are lesbians?"

"Yes." Folly was surprised at her own clarity. Until now, she had only asked this question and answered it inside herself, flinching at the naked feeling it gave her.

Mary Lou swallowed hard around the answer. She kept thinking she should say, "I'm happy for you," but that was what mothers said to daughters when they got married, not when they found out they were lesbians. Also, she was not the mother. Also, who was Martha anyway if not their friend, their next door neighbor?

"Ask anything you want," Folly offered.

Mary Lou couldn't think of a single askable question. Not that she wasn't barraged with them, but they were all too private to ask. What does this mean you do? Do you and Martha sneak off in your room and make it while I'm asleep in here? Or do you only do it in Martha's trailer? She tried to picture them sprawled out on a bed together, touching, kissing. She could see Lenore and Betsy almost clearly, (in fact it turned her on to fantasize them), one's hand stroking the other's body. Their breasts, did they touch them or avoid them, must touch them, she decided, realizing she didn't avoid her own when she masturbated. But her mother and Martha, her mind didn't stretch that far.

After a long pause, she finally came up with a question. "Does this mean you always were?"

"What?"

"A lesbian."

Folly realized it was easier for Mary Lou to say that word than for her. She felt a stranger to it and a recognition at the same time. She let the word loll around in her mind, remembering the company lawyer, the way he looked as if he kept a word in his mouth for half an hour after he pronounced it. "It's like going down a long, back road, winding round and round, getting so used to going on and on, winding along, that you don't even know you're still looking for something; then all of a sudden you're not exactly looking but you found something, you're home where you wanted to be. So I don't know if that answers you exactly. I feel like I was moving all along to this, but I sure wouldn't a known it if you'd of asked me."

"What about my father?"

"What about him? I got you and Skeeter and Tiny out of him. I ain't complainin'."

"You better tell Skeeter. He's all the time going around callin' people queer."

Folly tried to numb herself to the feeling evoked by Mary Lou using that word. It took her a second to find a voice strong enough to counteract it. "Well, I reckon this news will hush him."

"I guess," Mary Lou said.

They sat without talking for a long time. Mary Lou was tired and hungry, but she didn't want to admit that to her ma. She felt as if three days had transpired in the last few hours, breakfast (the yucky eggs) had been years ago. Her ma was her ma, but was she? She was a lesbian. She loved Martha. Lenore loved Betsy. *Daisy,* she said to herself, *who am I? What do you think of all that's going on. I don't know. I read that book and I still don't know about me. I guess my ma wouldn't mind, though, and that's kind of weird. I'm so tired and hungry. I haven't eaten since they put you down.*

174

"I saved your supper," Folly said, as if overhearing.

"You did." Mary Lou had to blot her tears of gratitude.

Folly made tea and sat at the table while Mary Lou ate rapidly, filling some of her hollows. "You know, Ma, I been thinking about some things. I wanted to ask you a question."

"What?" Folly tried to ready herself for almost anything.

"What do you think about the idea of going to college?"

"Of who going?"

"Me."

"I always sort of have it in my mind that maybe you will."

"You do?" Mary Lou was shocked. "How come you never told me, then?"

"You weren't much more than a child 'til this summer."

"Well, I was growing up . . . even when you weren't noticing."

"You watch yourself, girl. I don't miss much."

Mary Lou stopped herself from saying, "Except when you're in love with Martha." Instead, she said, "Where would I go to college?"

"I don't know. We'll have to think about it. You got two more years yet, before you have to worry."

"I know, but I'd like to have an idea where I'm going, if I'm going somewhere. I always thought I'd just end up down at the mill with everybody else."

"I wouldn't want you to. Not that I mind the work myself, but they're too hard, the way they push you now. All they care about in that place is how many stupid pairs of pants they can walk out of there."

"But how could I afford to go to college?"

"We'll get up the money somehow."

"I get my last full check at the A & P this week."

"Maybe you can get that job again next summer." Folly recalled the way Mary Lou had moped around before she'd gone to work—critical, self-centered, looking to provoke her more often than not. "I gotta say how proud I am," she said. "I guess I did miss something. I mean here you were one day, snipping around here complainin' about the length of the day, and next thing I know . . . well, I reckon you been pretty much feeding us all. And not complaining once. And I'm grateful to have you."

"Good," Mary Lou said, "cause I'm keeping this last check, the whole thing."

"What you gonna do with it?"

"Don't know yet. I'm letting my mind wander a while before I decide. Might open a savings account, start saving up for something, none of your business what." College or a car, she was thinking. "Will you take me down to the bank and show me how?" She was washing her plate in the sink.

"Sure."

Mary Lou kept her back to her mother. "Sure wish that Daisy coulda lived a while longer." She let out a long sigh and went back to her room.

23.

Folly did not go to Martha's that night. She slept alone and dreamed of herself being lifted, possibly flying. She knew there would be more to dealing with Mary Lou, but nothing as hard as the silence which had finally been shattered without fracture. She felt the coolness of the morning air, the release of another summer. That and the release of Sunday, a day of belonging to no one.

She propped herself with pillows and started on a new mystery. She was well into it when Mary Lou appeared in the doorway, her hands in her back pockets and her weight shifting back and forth from her heels to the soles of her feet. "Ain't you going over to Martha's?"

"Later, I reckon."

"See ya."

"You goin' somewhere?"

"Yeah, to town."

"Hitchin'?"

"Yup."

"Want me to drive you?"

"No thanks."

Mary Lou turned to leave. "Goin' anywhere particular?"

"Nope. Just stopping by Lenore's."

"Oh." That stopped her.

Mary Lou was already down the hall. Now what did that mean, Folly wondered as she took her book up and let herself back into the mystery.

Martha was sorting Daisy's papers. She had finished the closet already, saving little for herself. As she had taken the dresses out, one by one on their hangers, she'd been moved by how clearly she could see

Daisy in them. She'd folded each one carefully, buttoning buttons if they were open, placing them gently in the box. They were nothing but old housedresses; no one would wear them but another old lady like Daisy, but Martha would take them to the Goodwill. They were clean and well pressed. Martha remembered way back, Daisy standing stern, tapping the iron with spit on her finger, then lighting into a pile of clothes.

She remembered times when she'd thought she'd like to live with more room to expand, when her own room, her own closet had felt cramped. Now that the closet was empty, she couldn't think what use she could put it to. She kept alternating between forgetting Daisy had died, expecting her to come around the corner, saying, "What's taking you all this time, messing around in here all morning," and remembering that's why she was doing this. She'd heard people say it was hard to go through someone's possessions after they died, but it seemed to her as good a way as any to sort through your feelings. She was glad she'd been here these last few years with Daisy. Otherwise she'd have known her mainly through her childhood memories, and her childhood sat firmly in her but not forward. Also there was Folly next door. She was overwhelmed by her good fortune with Folly. She wondered if Daisy had ever felt this sense of being cared for, as she did now. Martha's father had died when she was a small child; he'd been run over by a train while working on the railroad, and Daisy'd never gone looking for another man, though she must have been young, Martha realized.

She remembered when they'd lived in Carrboro, and Daisy worked in the hosiery mill there. Martha had gone everyday after school and waited for her mother to finish work. That was the old days, before production and other ideas about efficiency had changed things. Martha captured the thought that it wasn't such a terribly long time, after all—it was Daisy's lifetime. But the changes had been extreme, and were always described in the name of progress. She remembered Daisy looping, her best friend, Hattie, sitting with her machine up next and talking the whole day, talking and laughing. What about, Martha didn't know, but she knew they'd had fun. "That Hattie could take your mind off a toothache," she remembered Daisy saying, but she'd gone and had her tooth pulled anyway. She tried to picture the hosiery mill, back then. It hadn't been very big . . . maybe twenty women looping, and the knitters upstairs, old Carl, the fixer, and Raymond, the bossman . . . . Windows up and down both sides giving plenty of light. Nowadays the windows in all the old mills had been bricked over. Martha wasn't sure why, but guessed it was to prevent the workers from looking out. But the noise must have gone out the windows at the hosiery mill then. It hadn't ever been lcud there, just a purr, enough of a purr so that she and the other kids could play after school without their mothers hearing every word they said. Seamless stockings. When was that? Seamless stockings had closed down the hosiery mill, she couldn't remember what year.

She had cleaned out the drawers and thrown out all of Daisy's old seamed stockings, wondering where the hosiery mill was that had gone on making them. In the bottom drawer she had found the shoe box of papers, taken them to the kitchen table and fortified herself with another cup of coffee. She felt more frightened of the papers than the clothes. Daisy had never done much with papers: she had not known how to read or write.

Martha unfolded the papers as carefully as she had folded the clothes, found her own birth certificate, some papers from the railroad about her father's death, and her own old report cards that she had always assumed the school kept. "Punctual and careful with her work," one said. Had she read these reports to her mother? She couldn't remember doing so, but otherwise, how would Daisy have known what they said? Behind the report cards she found a paper from the Royal Insurance Company, a life insurance policy for $3,000. She had nearly thrown it out. She had nearly thrown the whole box out without looking through it, feeling that she had no business here. Then she found another paper, which looked exactly the same but had a different date on it. It also said $3,000. Probably nothing by this time, she figured. They were old. She didn't know of Daisy ever buying anything like this since she'd lived with her. She would have to take them to someone in town. Who? Someone to tell her if they were worth anything. One thing clear was that she was the beneficiary, and Daisy had signed them; she could write that much, in fact her signature showed a good hand.

Folly came in as Martha was reading these papers for the third time, unable to convince herself that she was reading right. "Lord, woman, you came just in time. Wait'll you see what I got here."

Folly stood behind Martha and stooped down to kiss the back of her neck. "What? What y'all showing?"

"My mother's life insurance."

"I thought she didn't have none."

"So didn't I, but it's right here, sure as life."

Martha handed the two papers over to Folly who sat down to read them. "Do you think they're the same policy written out twice, or two different ones?"

"I don't know. They got two different dates."

"Yeah."

"God Bless us," Martha said, covering Folly's hand with her own. "We must of done something to deserve this."

"We better take it somewhere and find out before we get all excited about it."

"Where?"

"I guess look up this insurance company and see where they have an office."

"I doubt they have one in Victory. My luck they'll have folded ten years back," Martha said, containing herself.

"No, I don't think they can do that. I mean, someone has got to be good for the money."

That made Martha start to feel more secure about the money as reality, and her mind began wandering into the opening up of possibility that a lump of unexpected money could mean. "What do you think, Fol? What would a person like me do with that kind of money?"

"Put it aside for early retirement."

Martha was disappointed by this suggestion, which seemed dull and out of keeping with the surprise of the policy. "Me? What would I do if I was retired? Turn into an old lady?"

"Well, we both got that to look forward to some day."

"Sure, but I always thought money should lead you to feeling younger, not older."

"I suppose. Did you get some sleep last night?"

"Better than the night before," Martha said, "but I'm still tired. I went through her closet this morning and her drawers. I'm nearly done with that. This trailer'll be full of her still, even when her stuff is gone." Out of the corner of her eye she saw her mother's cane propped against the wall at the end of the hall. "I keep feeling like I'm expecting her home any minute."

"She leaves a clear memory," Folly said.

"Yeah."

An idea had begun turning in Martha's mind, and of course, it was right, it had been there all along, but she had only now reached it consciously. It was perfect. She allowed her excitement to grow while she thought of a way to broach the subject with Folly. She squeezed her hand. "Listen, I got it. If the money comes through, I mean if it's real, I want you to get the house."

"What house?"

"You know, that house you been wanting all along."

"Oh, that," Folly dismissed it, releasing Martha's hand. "Been so long since I thought about that house, I forgot all about it."

Martha felt hurt. She thought she'd known Folly better. How could she forget her dream? She crossed her arms on her chest, feeling the loss of her mother acutely. They sat this way, separate, each with her own thoughts. Folly was thinking about the house again. It wasn't true that she'd forgotten it, but she'd put it far, far back in her mind. And she wouldn't think of taking Martha's money for it. Only the day before she'd thought about putting a decent wall between her and Mary Lou. She remembered barricading herself against the threats of Fartblossom with fantasies of the house. But being in the company of Martha and Mabel and other women like them had done much more to alleviate her fears than any wall could have. She returned to feeling Martha's presence, Martha's reaction to her. She hadn't meant to push her away, but she had, she could feel her remoteness.

Martha felt she had let herself in for this hurt by crossing some unspoken boundary. She had not meant to suggest they live together, though Folly might think she had. She had gone too far, she had let her life mix up with Folly's in such a way that if she had to withdraw it, she would not know quite what to take. She remembered those weeks of the walk-out, carrying around her guard as well as her picket sign to watch over what she did, to control her reaching out for Folly, to keep the sound of her heartbeat hidden. There had been a clear line of demarcation between them then, a zone, hot with current. And she had kept moving into it and away, testing, like Daisy's spit finger sizzling on the iron.

They were both, now, painfully aware of the feeling of mental and physical separation between them. "I'm sorry," Folly said. "I guess I haven't thought much about the house because of us having such a convenient arrangement, I mean living next door, and me being able to leave the kids over there and all."

"It's true." Martha hadn't thought about where the house might be, how much traveling distance it might create between them. "I wasn't thinking of myself living in this here house we're talking about, in case that wasn't clear. Just you and the kids. Me living here in my trailer. I'd hope it wasn't too far away."

"I couldn't possibly . . . . I couldn't even think of us using your money if you weren't going in with us," Folly said.

Martha swallowed hard. "I just wanted you and the kids to have it."

Folly frowned, even though she felt moved by Martha's generosity.

"It wouldn't be any too good for your kids, living with two women loving each other. Might confuse them."

"Bullshit," Folly said. "It might be the best thing ever happened to them. Wait 'til you hear what happened with Mary Lou."

"Well, tell me. What you waiting on, woman?" Martha breathed deeply with relief. Folly got up and practically danced around the kitchen, telling about how she'd come out to Mary Lou.

"Some guts you've got, girl," Martha admired, "and so hasn't that kid. Think she's gonna be okay with it?"

"She might still brew up an explosion. That wouldn't surprise me at all. But I'm telling you where it feels real good is in me." She embraced her own belly.

"I wish I'd told Daisy, right out," Martha said. "I wanted to. I tried to, but I never just plain got it out. It's about the only thing I regret with her."

"But she knew," Folly said. "Don't you think so?"

"I believe so. I told you before about Daisy's special powers, about how she come out of that first stroke seeing lights and currents and things other people didn't see. 'Don't you ever tell that doctor,' she told me, 'less you want to have your mama put away in one of them booby traps.'"

Martha imagined her and Folly standing at her mother's bedside, the circles of light around their heads drawing them together in Daisy's eyes.

Folly was on the same memory. "I remember that day after we came back from the picnic, standing by her bed next to you. It was all we could do to keep from holding hands, anyway, and she opened her eyes and looked up at us, and clear as a bell, I thought, she knew."

24.

Lenore was in her room, jalousies open all the way round, cool breeze blowing across her, *The Heart Is A Lonely Hunter* in her lap. She felt victorious over having this book to read. Betsy had written her that one of the women in Alaska had read Carson McCullers' biography and she was a lesbian, a southern lesbian. Not that she'd disclosed this in her books, according to Betsy's report. Lenore had gone to the library just in case, and sure enough found this one, which undoubtedly meant that whoever else knew, the Victory librarian did not. She turned her chair around to face the window and propped her feet on the sill. She was deeply involved in the story when she suddenly realized someone had driven up and stopped by the curb right outside her room.

The driver got out and hesitated while the passenger came around the car; then the two women headed up Lenore's walk. The passenger was her mother; she felt dumb with taking so long to recognize that. She didn't know the other woman, but there was no question that Evelyn was Evelyn. Putting the book aside, she roused herself from the chair. She heard Sabrina's words: "Let things be a while, you'll see, pretty soon she'll come round. It's not just you needing her, it works both ways." She felt the kernel of anger which usually knotted up hard against the wall of her stomach circling around in her, like a goldfish swimming in a bowl, no place to light. It made her feel slightly off balance. Having been clued to her mother's need by Sabrina was what kept her composed enough to answer the door.

"This the right place?" Evelyn asked.

"Hi. Come on in."

"Lenore, this is Suzy Malone. She and I went to school together, back when."

"Hi."

"Way back when," she continued.

"You can say that," Suzy agreed.

Evelyn looked around at the place. Lenore went to the kitchen. "How about some coffee?"

"Sure, I'll have some."

"Me, too," Suzy added.

"Look around . . . and make yourself at home." Lenore was glad the place was picked up, but then, it always was. That was the way she had chosen to live since she'd moved away from home.

"Nice place." Suzy said.

"Where do you live?"

"Out the other side of town, near your mother."

"Oh."

"Suzy goes to meetin's with me." Lenore started to open her mouth, but before she knew what she was going to say, Evelyn added, "None of your business what meetin's." Lenore closed her mouth. "So long as we were right here in town and it was Sunday afternoon and all, I said, 'Hey, why don't we drive on by and see can we find her at home.' "

"Good. I wasn't doing much of anything, just sitting here, and I saw that car drive up and I thought, who can that be, not someone for me."

"Surprised to see your old ma, eh?"

"I'm still in shock."

"Stay that way, it makes you sweeter."

Lenore started to bristle but before she could fully react, Suzy said, "You'd better be good to this girl, Evelyn. I haven't even had my coffee yet. Besides, I think she's done right well for herself." Lenore looked at this woman, whom she had thought dull and ordinary, and began to see her whole and to feel warmly toward her. At the same time, she was embarrassed for being made fuss over. She had felt the huff go out of her back. It made her think that if there had been someone at home to take her side, maybe she would have been able to cool out, but Angie had almost always needed to side with her mother, and Perry had been too young.

Evelyn, turning away from Suzy's defense of Lenore, went to inspect the plants over by the bed. Lenore poured the coffee at the counter and put out some cookies on a plate. "I like the way you've fixed the place up," her mother said. "I reckon you've got everything you need to be comfortable here."

"I'm pretty comfortable," Lenore said, her voice calm, not betraying the excitement she felt at showing off her home, her self sufficiency. She realized she was talking to her ma in a place where she couldn't be thrown out.

Evelyn sat at the counter. "Perry's told me about your place; she's got it memorized, so I feel like I been here before."

"How is she?"

"She's fine. She's in the summer school play—one of the lead roles. She likes doing that, you know. Pretending she's someone else."

"Yeah."

"I think she's real good at it."

"Remember when we used to do that?" Lenore asked. "When you and me and Angie used to go down to the Thrift Shop and get us some stuff to dress up in, and then we used to take turns play-acting?"

Evelyn laughed. "Yeah," she said, "just barely. We used to carry on somethin' awful. You shoulda seen this one, Suzy. She used to imitate her teachers 'til I like to have died from laughing. I'd just about forgot all about that, Lenore."

Lenore smiled. "The ones I remember best was some of your customers."

"I swear," Evelyn said, "sometimes it's only making fun of people that can save you so you can go on facing another day."

"Ain't that the truth," Suzy said.

Much as it felt good to be laughing with her mother, it saddened Lenore to be reminded that this was the source of their humor.

They didn't stay much longer. They were out the door already, on the sidewalk, saying good-bye, her mother saying, "Be good"; Suzy saying, "Nice to meet you"; her mother saying, "Don't forget where we live now, come by sometime," when Mary Lou, walking with her head down, ran smack into Evelyn.

"Sorry," she said. "Excuse me. I didn't see you." Then, seeing Lenore outside, "Hi."

Mary Lou regretted not having taken a second look when she found out a few minutes later that the woman she'd run into was Lenore's mother. "I didn't recognize her because I thought she don't come here. I thought she refused."

"She did. Only I guess she's turned around and changed her mind, because she came. That was her, the only mother I got." Lenore did a series of front flips on the grass. She had a second of panic the first time over, thinking she might have forgotten how to land, but her body knew, her body did just fine on its own. She remembered the day-after-day of landing wrong learning, the noiseless thuds in her legs, the bruises, the drag of disappointment. What had made her persist had been her imagination, her idea that when she got everything down right, she would feel joy, there would be a sense of her own flexibility, and at the same time, of her control. The recoil of her landing would be the spring of her takeoff, and she would move from one flip into the next with grace rather than effort, as she did now, holding onto the exhilaration she felt that finally her mother had come.

"How'd you learn to do that?" Mary Lou asked, impressed.

"Taught myself."

"I tried in gym, but I couldn't get it."

"Takes a long time," Lenore said. "I did it and did it and did it, and one day, when I was about to give up, I got it. Same with my mother. I was just about resigned to the fact she'd never come and see me, it would mean too much giving in to her, and here I look up, and who's coming down the walk?" She did one more flip and landed on the concrete. "C'mon in."

Mary Lou apologized for the way she'd acted the day before and thanked Lenore for coming to see her.

"No matter," Lenore said. "I knew you were upset. I don't really know what it's like to go through that. I've been lucky, I guess. Never had to go to a funeral yet. Never lost anyone real close. Only my father. But he's not dead, just disappeared so he don't have to pay my ma nothing. I suppose he could be dead and we wouldn't know it."

"Mine, too," Mary Lou said. She quietly collected herself from passing the word *lost*. It still jarred her. It wasn't so much the emptiness of missing Daisy as it was the sense of who she was without her. A child who made up words with no one to hear them. She felt so tender, like a wound freshly healed that needed protection not to break open again.

Lenore tried to subdue herself to meet Mary Lou's mood, but her exuberance was hard to contain. She washed and dried the cups while Mary Lou sat on the stool and fussed with the sugar bowl. The small efficiency apartment seemed close and confined to her now, though it had seemed grand when Evelyn and Suzy had been looking around. "How about we take a ride out in the country?" she asked Mary Lou.

"Fine," Mary Lou answered. "Good idea." She pictured herself leaning back in the seat, talking with her eyes looking straight ahead or out the window, not directly on Lenore. She'd tell her about her mother and Martha, then. She'd give her the book back later, tell her she was glad she'd read it even if it hadn't answered her questions about herself.

Out past the mill, they turned up a secondary road that headed north. The countryside was hilly and the road wound in curves around the hills. Not interested in speed, but in the lushness of late summer, Lenore drove easy. She rested her eyes on the blooming flowers and the denseness of green along the tree lines bordering the pastures. The pastures were parched, burned out by the sun. They passed farms where people were harvesting vegetables from their gardens. She'd like to have a garden of her own, she thought. Maybe Mrs. Henry would let her cut up a section of lawn, a corner; she could share what she grew with her. She'd stop eating meat. She liked it less and less since she'd become a butcher. The sun was good and hot but the humidity was gone. It was a fine day, the kind that exuberance waits for, one that made Lenore feel she could do anything she wanted. Her left arm rested on the window and the air blew up her sleeve and onto her back, cool enough to feel like a friend. She glanced over at Mary Lou and saw that she was far away in her own thoughts.

Driving through a small town, Lenore waved, first at a couple of teenage girls, Black, then at an old white man. The man waved back; the girls didn't. This started her thinking how it would be if Sabrina and Eli were riding with her, and she wondered if it was something they'd like to do sometime. The Black girls probably would have waved, the white man not. But she would be the same person. Or would she? What if some redneck boys passed them and decided they didn't like what they saw and came after them? Only a few weeks before, she'd read in the paper about a white guy who'd been shot for nothing more or less than walking down the street with a Black guy, by some other white guys who'd decided to show him his place. She realized this fear was always with her, occupying territory close to her heart, something to be reckoned with first in the imagination. She rarely admitted fear, didn't want any part of her life controlled by it. But she had to know this fear, to know it had long lain dormant in her, disguised as part of her armor, if she wanted to know Sabrina better. She would *not* be the same person if she were riding with Sabrina and Eli right now.

Mary Lou broke into her thoughts. "Hey, it's real nice out here. Thanks for havin' such a good idea."

"Yeah, no problem."

"Remember what I told you about my mother?"

Lenore nodded. Mary Lou realized this was a stupid way to intro-
duce it, but she half expected Lenore to pretend the conversation had
never occurred. "Well, she told me about them last night, her and Martha, just like I thought." Once Mary Lou got started, she could hardly
stop talking. She went on and on, while Lenore listened and drove.
She liked Mary Lou, so young but so deeply exploring. She'd never
thought things through about her own lesbianism the way Mary Lou
was trying to do now. Betsy had just been there, a friend, everything
to her, and then, a lover, too. Well, maybe that wasn't so, maybe she
was skipping something. She could vaguely recall going through the
imaginings of being with Betsy before the experience of the real thing.
A step, like realizing she feared the boys riding out after her, trapping
her somewhere and punishing her for being friends with Sabrina. It was
a step she was glad she had taken.

Mary Lou's voice broke another spell of quiet with excitement.
"Guess what. I'm probably going to be learning to drive soon."

"Why probably?"

"My ma has to see if Martha will let me learn on her car."

"Teach you on mine if she won't teach you on hers," Lenore said.

"No kidding." Mary Lou was smiling. It seemed like nothing but
options opening up in front of her.

25.

Folly and Martha ended up huddled in the bathroom, smoking and fuming the way they had the night they'd led the walkout. The sun was coming up outside. Fartblossom had called Martha in, into the room where he officially performed his duties as personnel officer, even though he'd returned to being night floor supervisor.

"He's had it out for us, we knew that," Martha said.

"You can say that again."

"I shouldn't a given him the chance, though. I shoulda just taken those two nights."

Fartblossom had told Martha to sit down but had gone on standing himself, pussyfooting around his office, his belly out in front, bobbing with pleasure at his telling her he knew her mother had died. "I'm sorry to hear it," he'd said with a smirk. "Abuse of the new sick leave policy . . . strictly meant for illness of the worker . . . not for death in the family . . . not for illness of a close relative . . . sure you can see why this must be enforced, someone would consider their second-cousin-once-removed a close relative . . . no choice, I have no choice . . . I did not set the policy . . . it was set by the union contract . . . *your* union contract." Smear your nose in that union contract, he must have been saying to himself. "Contract negotiated by your friends . . . endorsed by your co-workers. I'm docking you two days . . . giving official warning . . . course we don't let no one go unless they've had three warnings . . . you're a good worker, Martha, I'm sure you'll behave."

189

"Come off it, sir," Martha had said, still in some shock. "You know I been here for years, same as you, and I bet I haven't taken five days in the last five years, and I ain't got no second cousins for y'all to be worrying about."

Fartblossom had stopped still, heavy in his shoes, and stared at her, communicating the message—you shouldn't be talking back. But she had gone on anyway, "And I don't know nothin' about these here warnings. I never had one in my life."

"Well, now we got the union, we got to keep track of things, you see. We ain't no down home mill no more."

She had relayed this all to Folly, who had looked as if she were holding her breath, then gone into a tirade. "They were laying in wait for us, any of us, but especially you and me and Mabel and anyone else they knew was working on the organizing. That Fartblossom must have had himself some time this weekend waiting to bust the news open to you, he musta been shittin' in his britches, his goddamned poly pants. You're right. We shouldn't of given him a chance. We weren't thinking. I guess we don't get no rest. I thought after all them weeks of walking, then going back in after the election, all them weeks of talking, sitting and staring at them in their meetings, Mabel and me nodding, having worked all night, saying 'pinch us, Jesse, if you see us go to sleep,' but always right there when those boys tried to pull something off. Right there until the end when Jesse said, 'Let's see what I can get for you. Let's cooperate with them. It's gone on too long, I don't think they've got anything up their sleeve.'" This part still bugged Folly, drowned out her confidence in the victory. She doused her cigarette under the faucet, threw it in the trash can, went on pacing the tiles of the restroom. "Mabel knew if you really want to be sure of something, the best thing to do is stay around and watch it. Where do you suppose that Jesse is now?"

"Sitting in some office somewhere."

"You betcha."

"Nothing to be done," Martha said, despair and grief on her face. "I wonder what good that grievance will ever be?"

"Won't do me no good if I get three warnings in one day. We better get on out there, Folly. I wouldn't want to have to lose my job to test it."

Martha felt closed in by her anger. Folly was the opposite, she practically gave off steam. Hers worked in her like an engine, pushing her toward action. "You're right. We gotta get on back. I got a few extra tickets I saved last week we can turn in if we ain't meeting production."

Martha was just about to swing open the bathroom door when Folly grabbed her hand, swung her around and hugged her tight. "I love you," she whispered in her ear.

"How many warnings you think this'd be worth?" Martha asked, her voice husky and pained.

"Enough to set us thinking."

Folly spent the whole night thinking. Thinking up one zipper and down the next, thinking just because she was mad she'd better not lean too much over the machine, she'd get a backache, better let her muscles go, think with her brains and not her muscles. Sit broad in the chair, not bony, keep her body out of this, keep it loose for lying out flat in the bed beside Martha. She thought of Daisy lying in the grave, peaceful, nothing more to put up with. But she wanted to live and not the way Fartblossom thought she should—never with any security. The liver lily. Hitting Martha with that right on top of her loss of her mother. Somebody put out all these rules—she wasn't sure who the hell it was, where the hell they started—but she'd learned them way back. A decent way to fight: don't hit below the belt; pick someone with the same weapons; keep within bounds; don't attack from behind. These cheats. They put out these rules, sure, but look what they followed themselves: attack a walker with a car; jail a woman because her baby died and you didn't let her off work; dock a woman for losing her mother.

Were they any better off than before they'd walked out? She tried to run through the whole thing from beginning to end, to answer that question for herself. "Count your wins," she kept hearing Mabel say, and it was true they'd gotten the seven percent, the sick days if anyone dared to take them now, the grievance procedure which might not be worth the piece of paper it was written on. Personally, she was better off because of the way it had brought her closer to the other women. And she had experienced a couple of weeks of feeling secure, as if the contract gave them form to feel their power as workers. But her defenses had gotten soft in this short time of false security. This power was exactly the thing Fartblossom was going after by docking Martha, and the loss of it was what left Folly feeling depleted. They were going to have to go after it again. Get smart; be alert, guarded, dogged about their next move. Pull all their energy in for the fight. And where would they come out?

She called for the fixer. Her machine was jammed. Martha looked over; her steady eyes met Folly's for a moment. Job would be fine without the management, Folly thought. She smiled at Wilbur, who put his itty bitty screw driver in his breast pocket and said, "Try it now. Should be fine."

This idea had come into her mind before, but where? She couldn't remember. Yes, at the picnic. The women sewing in their own factory. What would it take? How did someone start a mill? Even if she didn't know barely the first thing about creating things, she could at least try to think it through. What she did know to start from was that they were the basic units, the women on the line. The women and the machines for them to work on, a fixer—no bossman, no production. You'd need a seller to go out and get contracts for the things you were making. You'd need a place, you'd need to take an old building, an old mill or something and fix it into what you wanted, you'd need a maintenance man or woman.

How would a woman get paid? Each could work at her own speed. If a woman was slow and needed more, she could work more hours, as long as they had the pieces sold. When something happened like Martha's mother dying, they would have a fund for paying the person who had to take off. What if people took advantage? So what, Folly thought. Wouldn't happen very often, and she'd rather risk that chance than go around believing people didn't know how to share responsibility when to do so would work to their advantage. What if they were all owners? Nobody would be goofing off then. As soon as she hit on that idea, it seemed right, but she felt lost, too, wondering how it could be done, how could it be the answer and no examples of it anywhere to see? Co-op, co-op, it seemed as if her machine was speaking the word each time she pressed the pedal. She sewed up a storm, trying to think further. Remembered as a child, going with her mother down to the feedstore to fetch a bag of feed for the chickens. The co-op feedstore. No sign on the building, you had to know it was there. Had her ma been part owner just for that piddling little bit of feed? She hadn't been back in years, wondered if old Mrs. Butler was still waddling her enormous weight up and down behind the counter and writing up the receipts. She wondered who paid Mrs. Butler?

Wondered if Jesse could help her think past this, could he see what a place would be like without bosses. When he'd left, he'd given her a warm handshake, looked her in the eye and failed to see his betrayal reflected there. Or had she dropped it before he looked? She didn't like to think of herself as someone who held a grudge. "Call me if you need me," he'd said. "Just any question, give a call." He had not worried, as had she, of what the toll call might come to and of where in her budget there was surplus that she could cut into when the bill came. She would not call. Besides, she realized the union was dependent on having the management to fight. If they were going to have a co-op, they'd have to be on their own.

She tried to let go of the idea. Foolishness, Folly, she told herself. What you trying to do—prove your name? No sense dreaming. Here we are right here with this Fartblossom lording around us in his personnel office and trying to find a way to bust our tail. First order of business is to warn Mabel. Warn all these women the fight's not over, not at all. Here we're supposed to be convincing those who didn't vote favorably that this damn union is doing us some good, Folly thought, and now we gotta put the word out that a warning system has been started to intimidate us. And watch your moves because we don't want to have to test that goddamned grievance procedure.

She felt the arteries pulse in her temples. Mabel probably knew already, probably never did let down her guard. Just like she knew when Jesse was going to sell out. Must've learned that lesson early as a Black child in a white man's world. She remembered that first meeting. Jesse shaking hands all the way round, pumping the white flesh of their opponents. Her sitting down next to Mabel, raising her eyebrows, looking about and feeling the circle close around the two of them—aliens. Realizing now why it had been so surprising to her then. Part of her had still thought herself more one of them than being in union with Mabel. No more. She was clear on that. She wondered what Mabel would think about the idea of a co-op and set up an imaginary conversation with her.

"Here we are, Mabel. We have us a place all fixed up and we have someone to sell our stuff. We have all our workers—us, experienced seamstresses—and we're the owners, too, and ready to go to town. No bossman anywhere in sight . . . ."

"Hold on, Folly. Hold up, you movin' on woman. You all the way down to steps six, seven, eight; left out one, two, three. How you gonna buy without the dough?"

She couldn't answer. How you gonna buy without the dough? Her sewing machine had picked up the question, was asking it over and over—how-you-gon-na-buy-with-out-the-dough—everytime she hit it. Almost like a song but it wasn't a song, it was the problem. Still singing in her zipper foot when the shift bell rang, caught her unprepared so she and Martha were nearly the last ones out. First ones out were those

193

who had made an art of it. You could see how they had their pocket-books lined up by their heels, chairs turned out just so, perched but try-ing not to look it. They had their muscles set every bit as finely as the olympic runner whose toes played for advantage at the starting line.

She checked with Martha but neither of them needed the extra tick-ets to meet production; they were both over. Take it easy tomorrow night, she thought. She told Martha she'd meet her in the car, went to find Mabel in the line coming in and walked along with her a minute. She told her about Fartblossom setting up Martha. "Y'all watch your-selves. They're out for us."

"Hey," Mabel said, "we knew that would be the next move, didn't we? We watchin'." Folly felt calmed by being in reach of Mabel, grabbed her hand and squeezed it as they got to the sewing room door. She wouldn't tell Mabel her idea until she got the one, two, three.

Driving home, Folly and Martha were careful with their gestures. There was always someone from the mill in the car ahead who might be looking in the rear view mirror, someone else in the car behind. But Martha took Folly's hand on the seat between them. Folly hadn't spok-en a word. "Where are you?" she asked. "Off dreaming?"

"Some pretty furious dream," Folly said. "I'm still thinking about what a rotten bunch we work for, and how can we ever get away from that Fartblossom."

"Would it help if we could get the house?"

"I don't know."

"I'm serious," Martha said. "I'm going down later and see about that policy. I been thinking about what all we got. I mean if I was fixin' to move in the house with y'all, I could sell the trailer, and y'all could sell your trailer, too."

"How much you think they're worth?"

"I don't know, they're both old, but they're not ready for the junk heap."

"Mine's just about ready," Folly said. "It's a wonder that one wall in the boys' room hasn't fallen through."

Folly leaned back, closed her eyes, and tried to see the house she'd so often visualized. She took deep breaths of the cool, morning air into her lungs, her purifying ritual, and tried to place herself far from sewing machines, from the hum, the song, how-you-gon-na-buy-with-out-the-dough? Martha's hand was the same size as hers and strong. They could live in a house together with the children, take care of each other, curl

194

up curve to curve in the night and be restored. She was tired. She could use that kind of care. What kind of a house would it be? She tried hard to see it. But what she saw was an old factory, a line of women sewing, a sign out front: WOMEN OF VICTORY CO-OP MILL.

She sat up straight, wide awake as ever she had been. "Martha, listen, we gotta talk. I got an idea." She held Martha's hand tighter, passing her some of her adrenalin. They were pulling up between the trailers.

"Wait," Martha said. "Let's go in my place. You want to check the kids first?"

"No, I don't want to, but I better."

"You go on in. I'll do it and be right over."

Martha, I been waiting for a woman like you all my life, Folly said to herself as she went in, and I never did expect I'd be findin' you, much less right next door.

"All's quiet," Martha said, entering a few minutes later and kicking off her shoes. "Now, what's this idea that's got you all worked up?"

"A co-op mill," Folly said, simply, trying to hold down her excitement. "Owned by us, the workers."

"Us? You mean that for real?"

"Yeah, I mean you and me and the women who work on the line with us."

"But we'd have to have money to start anything like that. Who's got any money?"

"The insurance."

"But Fol . . . it ain't gonna be all that much." Martha felt confused. She sensed her own blood beginning to race to meet Folly's fervor, at the same time she held onto the vision of the house, a place for them to rest and be further from the mill.

"Hey, look here," Folly said. "Imagine working this way—no boss, no Fartblossom officiating hisself away. Goin' in and doin' your work at the pace that goes right for you and havin' time to stop and say hello to someone when you want to. Somebody dies, people offer to help you out, none of this shit we're gettin'. It would be like a dream."

The problem was seeming more and more like a song in Folly. She was up and practically dancing around Martha. She was not the same woman she used to think of herself as being, the plodding one who didn't want to be bothered with more than one day at a time.

"I guess it could be," Martha said, clasping both of Folly's hands, breaking from her own losses. She pulled her around and they sat facing each other, intent on pulling that dream down to the table in front of them, working right along with the song.

195

Martha remembered the night of the walk-out, how afraid she'd been of the feelings that had generated between them when they'd clasped each other's hands. By comparison, she felt as if she'd lost all sense of caution now, though she said, "But you know we'd have to find other ways to get money, too. Daisy's policy wouldn't really take us far."

"I know," Folly said, "we'd have to borrow. Everybody would. We wouldn't want people excluded because they couldn't put up money. Let's just figure if it *was* possible to get up the money, what then? What all could we do?"

Afterword

One of the valuable insights of the women's liberation movement is contained in its rhetorical slogan "the personal is political." Feminist scholars have continued to explore the contrasts and connections between the categories of private (the personal) and public (the political). The public sphere has always been conceptualized as male territory: work, politics, war—in short, the large and expansive world outside the self. The private world of domesticity, feelings, the family, and home, in contrast, belongs to women. Feminism, in its theories and practices, explodes this opposition, not only by claiming for women the public world and requiring from men attention to the private sphere, but also by demonstrating the ways in which similar structures and forces operate in both public and private arenas.

Folly, by Maureen Brady, is an excellent example of a novel written within the context of this feminist deconstruction of the opposition between public and private. Its plot revolves around the very public structures of factory and union local and the private territories of home and family. It requires that the reader acknowledge the similar processes at work in all locations. It refuses the split between woman as worker and woman as mother/lover. It pays close attention to issues of class and of sexuality. It locates politics in the external struggle of labor against management and in the internal struggle of white women against racist attitudes. It recognizes the way in which capitalism impacts on the home and the way the home extends into the workplace. In short, *Folly* claims that the personal is political, and the political, personal, in every social institution.

I

Maureen Brady was born June 7, 1943 in Mt. Vernon, New York.[1] Her father, she writes, identified firmly with his working-class origins, while

197

her mother held to the American myth of upward mobility—a conflict that provided Brady with the impetus for exploration of her own class identity. Her adolescence and college years were spent in Florida, giving her a knowledge of and a sensitivity to southern attitudes and values that often appear in her fiction. Since the late 1960s, Brady has made her home in New York State, where she earned a master's degree from New York University in 1977. Although she always knew she wanted to write, Brady, like the protagonist of her first novel, *Give Me Your Good Ear* (1979), also has worked as a physical therapist while devoting herself full-time to a career of writing, teaching, and conducting writing workshops.

Success was not easy at first, however. Like most novice writers, Brady collected her share of rejection slips until she began sending stories to newly established feminist and lesbian feminist literary journals. In fact, chapter one of *Folly,* then titled "Grinning Underneath," appeared in the very first issue of *Conditions* in 1977. Subsequent chapters would appear in *Sinister Wisdom* and *Southern Exposure.* Brady's career as a writer has moved in tandem with the women's liberation and lesbian feminist movements. Not only do feminist themes and issues predominate in her work, but she has also found in the feminist presses a sympathetic home for her novels, stories, and plays. Moreover, Brady, with Judith McDaniel, founded a feminist press, Spinsters, Ink, in order to publish her first novel, *Give Me Your Good Ear.* During Brady's tenure (1978-1982), Spinsters published such landmark works as *The Cancer Journals* by Audre Lorde, *Ambitious Women* by Barbara Wilson, and *The Words of a Woman Who Breathes Fire* by Kitty Tsui.

Between 1977 and 1982, the year in which *Folly* first appeared, Brady wrote and published prolificly. In addition to writing fiction, she had two plays produced (one of which, *I Know a Hundred Ways to Die,* was published in *Sinister Wisdom* 12); reviewed for feminist journals; conducted creative writing workshops throughout New York State and elsewhere; and received a number of grants, awards, and residencies, activities that she continues to pursue. She enjoyed particular success in and appreciation from lesbian and feminist readers, her chosen community or "home." But, after the publication of *Folly,* she began to find this community too restrictive. She desired wider recognition and a more diverse range of topics; she wished to stop participating in the idealization of lesbian characters, to break the rules and cross the boundaries that are inevitably established by any close-knit literary community. Of particular importance, Brady began to explore her own history as a survivor of incest. Given these new conditions and constraints, her work after 1982 has been less prolific and less visible. She began to experience the same repeated rejections from lesbian and feminist journals that she had endured from mainstream journals in the early 1970s. Since the publication of *Folly,* Maureen Brady has published only one volume of collected short stories, *The Question She Put to Herself* (1987), and two meditation books dealing with recovery from incest, *Daybreak* (1991) and *Beyond Survival: A Writing Journey for Healing Childhood Sexual Abuse* (1992). She has completed a new novel, *Rocking Bone Hollow,* and is currently at work on another.

For Maureen Brady, like many feminist and lesbian authors, writing has been a way of working through issues of personal and political importance. *Give Me Your Good Ear,* a finely etched story of one woman's coming to terms with her family history of violence and abuse and her present sexual and emotional choices, was Brady's "coming out" as a lesbian. *Folly,* in which coming out functions as an important theme and plot device, was for her most significantly a coming to terms with her internal class conflict and the movement's lack of attention to working-class women and history. When she began writing the first chapter in 1976, she thought she was writing about women who were strangers to her. In order to assuage doubts and fears that she would be accused of appropriating other women's experiences, she "would lie down, go half to sleep, then listen very hard for voices that were speaking far away."[2] These voices reminded Brady of her own working-class heritage, which had been pushed into the background by her mother's upward mobility, her own college education, and the movement's inattention to working-class women. She writes of her ambivalence about making the journey necessary to reach these voices: "Because surely we are not meant to make literature that takes its strength from the steely knowledge of our oppression. We are meant to identify with whatever access, gains, privileges we have been born into or acquired and put these to work for the further exaltation of homogenized middle-class America."[3] Fortunately, Brady made that journey, and Folly, Martha, Mabel, and Lenore were born.

Although *Folly* is not strictly autobiographical, it makes abundant use of material from Brady's past. As a hospital worker, she had been involved in labor organizing, and she also drew on stories told her by her factory-working spinster aunt. The character of Lenore, she writes, was based on the butcher at the A&P on whom she had a childhood crush. She chose to set the novel in the South because of her own adolescent experience of southern racism and because of the importance of North Carolina in the history of labor struggles. At one point she tried to relocate the labor struggle in a northern hospital, but the characters insisted on staying in Victory. These specific details are not as important, however, as her overall project, "a process of remembering for me, of finding and attaching my parts."[4] The following discussion will investigate how the novel puts those parts together into one creative whole.

II

Although Maureen Brady attempted to shift the location of the events represented in *Folly*, her original instincts were absolutely correct. Few other locales carry the same resonance in the history of twentieth-century women's labor struggles as the textile mills of the South.[5] In the 1880s, the textile industry began to shift from the mill towns of New England to new ones in the Piedmont region of southern Virginia and the Carolinas, as well as northern Georgia and Alabama. The agricultural self-sufficiency of the Piedmont, a land of small yeoman farmers rather than large slaveholding plantations, was severely disrupted by the Civil War and its aftermath. The cheap labor force produced by this disruption combined with a growing rail infrastructure and existing close-knit communities made this region perfect for the development of a new economic order based in the mill town. By 1900, almost 200 mills had been constructed, 90 percent of them in the Piedmont.

Textile mills employed "a system of job assignments based on hierarchies of sex and age" as well as race.[6] From the beginning, white women were welcomed eagerly into the new mills as spinners and seamstresses, while African-American men were restricted to the hard, dirty, non-production jobs. African-American women were kept out of the factories altogether. Not only did these hierarchies maintain social customs rooted in racism and the patriarchal family, but they maximized profits. Adult women's wages were 60 percent of those of men; wages of children and African-American men were even lower.

As southern textile mills quickly became the only real employment alternative to farming, workers poured in from around the Piedmont and the wider Appalachian region. New towns grew up around the mills, totally dependent upon them for their economic and social existence. We see in *Folly*, for example, the trailer courts built next to the mill, a contemporary version of the factory housing typical of these towns. Sabrina mentions how bad business is while the women are on strike, and how it picks up again as soon as they go back to work. Generation followed generation into the mills, much as Mary Lou expects to join her mother after high school graduation. In these one-industry towns, workers yielded little power to affect conditions on or off the job. Nevertheless, the textile mills of the Piedmont became the center of a labor movement that has taken an almost mythic place in the history of working-class struggles.

Labor organizing in the South began in the 1880s with African-American female domestic workers who were first to form associations and call strikes. In the same decade the Knights of Labor organized locals, often across race and gender lines, and even led a three-month strike in a Georgia mill town. Later, the far more racist and sexist National Union of Textile Workers led a brief insurgency that ended by 1902. Many factors militated against labor: the paternalistic control of mill towns by mill owners, the isolation of workers from the larger population, competition from a large potential work force, and government support of anti-union activities and attitudes. Faced with these conditions, workers were more likely to express their discontent by moving than by organizing unions.

World War I marked a turning point in the history of the southern textile industry. Labor shortages led to rising wages and rising expectations. After the war, however, technological changes and the loss of wartime wage gains led to a serious deterioration in working conditions, so that the 1920s was a decade of suffering and dissatisfaction in the southern mill towns. In 1929 workers responded with a spontaneous wave of strikes, the most famous of which was against the Loray Mill in Gastonia, North Carolina. Although not the largest, longest, nor bloodiest, the Gastonia strike achieved particular notoriety because of the shooting deaths of the local police chief and of Ella May Wiggins, a celebrated union organizer and balladeer who took a prominent place in the pantheon of martyrs to the cause of labor.

The strikes of 1929 did not lead to ongoing unionization nor improvement in working conditions, although union activities continued throughout the turbulent years of the 1930s and 1940s. But strike defeats, declining membership, and anti-labor legislation (the so-called right-to-work laws) made organizing increasingly difficult throughout the 1950s and 1960s. Southern women workers in particular have had a low level of sustained union participation. In part this is due to labor surplus (as we see in *Folly* where the mill owner has no trouble hiring scabs such as Lenore's mother). But the most serious obstacle to unionization in the South has always been racism: "Unity among southern workers could never be achieved as long as black and white women remained segregated both on the job and in the labor movement."[7] In fact, instead of unifying as labor against management, white workers sometimes went on strike over the hiring of African-American workers. Union locals remained segregated until 1965. Despite these problems, white women workers did conduct a famous strike against J.P. Stevens in 1958. But more recently, leadership has most often come from African-American women trained in the civil rights movement and in their churches. Since 1965, as Mary Frederickson points out, "In garment factories across the South the relationship between black and white women workers has become a critical factor in whether union elections are won or lost."[8] In this respect, as in so many others, Maureen Brady has produced a remarkably accurate picture of the southern textile mill environment.

III

Folly is a complex novel that can be read fruitfully within a number of literary traditions. To begin, it owes much to the history of the labor novel and leftist progressive fiction in general. Although that history is a proud one, it has not been sustained in American culture, not even in the contemporary feminist movement. Women writers have been central to that history even though their achievements were often denigrated by their male colleagues and overlooked by contemporary readers and critics. Deborah Rosenfelt defines this tradition as "a line of women writers, associated with the American left, who unite a class consciousness and a feminist consciousness in their lives and creative work, who are concerned with the material circumstances of people's lives, who articulate the experiences and grievances of women and of other oppressed groups—workers, national minorities, the colonized and the exploited—and who speak out of a defining commitment to social change."[9] Within this line of politically inspired women writers--among them Charlotte Perkins Gilman, Susan Glaspell, Anzia Yezierska, Meridel Le Sueur, Tess Slesinger, Josephine Herbst, Agnes Smedley, Ann Petry, and Tillie Olsen earlier in the century, and later Marge Piercy, Grace Paley, and Alice Walker—Maureen Brady takes her place.

Although progressive writers like Gilman and Glaspell date back to the turn of the century, when utopian socialist ideals were particularly strong, the most prolific period for leftist fiction was the Marxist-influenced 1930s. Novels written by women during that period conformed in some ways to male-authored proletariat literature: they tended to present noble working-class characters and clichéd villainous owners in a simple story line marked by extreme realism and verisimilitude. The protagonist journeys from political unawareness to social consciousness; in other words, the self is conceived in collective, not individualistic terms. Oftentimes, a plot structured around multiple stories and a collective protagonist undermined the bourgeois emphasis on the individual self. One entire subgenre of this leftist fiction was the strike novel, in which the industrial action functions as a symbol of social transformation, the subjugation of the individual to the masses, and the vision of ongoing work for a better society. The 1929 Gastonia strike, which produced the powerful and romantic figure of Ella May Wiggins, had a strong impact on novelists. Significantly, women wrote four of the six novels inspired by Gastonia, including *Gathering Storm* by Dorothy Myra Page (1932), which was unique in having central African-American characters and celebrating a multiracial work force—in this way anticipating the conceptualization of *Folly* fifty years later.[10]

Particularly characteristic of and unique to leftist feminist novels of the 1930s was their equal emphasis on class and gender, their intermingling of public and private. In general, proletarian realism written and theorized by men made no place for the working-class woman as subject, although she might function as adjunct or symbol. The great accomplishment of leftist feminist writers was, as Paula Rabinowitz puts it, to give equal expression to love and hunger, in other words, to represent forces of oppression and resistance that affect women as workers and as mothers and lovers.[11] Their novels were structured around a set of tensions between public and private realms: "between the longing for love and emotional fulfillment and the will to give oneself to one's work. . . . [or] between the ideal of community and the needs of the individual."[12] When Folly abandons her dream of owning a home for that of creating a cooperative mill, she is struggling with the same conflicts that have marked progressive feminist fiction for over half a century.

Proletarian fiction, including the strike novel, flourished through the mid-1940s and then, under pressure from the growing conservatism and anti-communism of the post-war era, fell into disfavor. As literary criticism emphasized aesthetic over political concerns and as McCarthyism purged radicals from academic and literary institutions, the idea of working-class literature came to be seen as either dangerous or naive. The progressive social movements of the 1960s and 1970s did for a time restore interest in leftist fiction, inspiring novelists like Marge Piercy and Alice Walker and reviving interest in earlier writers like Tillie Olsen and Agnes Smedley. But as Brady herself has pointed out, the feminist movement failed to develop a sustained commitment to the lives of working-class women. This failure is reflected in the relative paucity of fiction about their lives. And the dominance of postmodern theory in the past decade has also brought into question the value of literary realism and verisimilitude, arguably the most appropriate style for progressive fiction. In 1982, *Folly* stood as a fascinating anomaly: a political, working-class, lesbian realist novel.

IV

In addition to belonging to the tradition of leftist feminist fiction, *Folly* is firmly a part of the genre of lesbian feminist literature that began to appear concurrently with the growth of a new lesbian political movement in the late 1960s. Isolated examples of explicitly lesbian novels had appeared prior to that era, such as Radclyffe Hall's notorious *The Well of Loneliness* (1928) and Gale Wilhelm's overlooked *We Too Are Drifting* (1935). The 1950s and early 1960s saw the curious publishing phenomenon of the lesbian pulp genre: trashy soft-porn novels often written by and for men, but also including competent, lesbian (or lesbian-friendly) authors such as Ann Bannon and Valerie Taylor. In many ways these two authors paved the way for the first examples of a lesbian literary culture developed in the context of the women's liberation and gay liberation movements. Such works as Isabel Miller's *Patience and Sarah* (1969), Rita Mae Brown's *Rubyfruit Jungle* (1973), and Monique Wittig's *Les Guérillères* (1969) quickly became lesbian classics, inspiring the publication of at first dozens and then hundreds of additional novels and short stories. In addition, lesbian feminist poetry, theater, and songwriting flourished during the decades of the 1970s and 1980s. In the 1990s, as I write this afterword, lesbian and gay presses and journals continue to provide the infrastructure for a burgeoning lesbian publishing industry.

As we have seen, Maureen Brady was a part of this phenomenon as early as 1977, publishing stories and plays in literary journals and her novels with alternative presses, establishing a feminist press herself, reviewing in feminist newspapers, and even writing about mainstream novels from a lesbian feminist perspective. As a member of this lesbian feminist community, she saw herself as part of the process of bringing lesbian voices and lesbian experience out of the closet of silence and ignorance. Francie, the presumably autobiographical protagonist of *Give Me Your Good Ear,* is left pondering her first attractions to women and is at the brink of coming out when the novel closes; in *Folly,* the author takes her characters a good deal further.

In my own study of the lesbian feminist novel, I suggest that three major themes predominate in the genre: creating a lesbian identity (coming out), establishing a relationship, and forming a community.[13] *Folly* explores each of these themes, as well as the countertheme that undercuts the idealistic tendency inherent in each of these, that of the differences that separate women. Brady is particularly astute in her representation of the complexities of that simple lesbian and gay catch phrase, "coming out." It may seem to some readers that everyone in *Folly* comes out (or comes close): Folly falls in love with Martha, Lenore names herself "lesbian" and seems to be on the verge of forming a relationship with Sabrina, Mary Lou agonizes over her own sexual identity, and Martha is able to reveal her secret to at least Folly and Lenore. We see that the coming out theme in the novel is carried through on both the personal and political levels. A woman may come out when she has her first lesbian sexual or romantic experience, as Folly does, or she may be said to be in the process of coming out when she investigates her feelings for women in contrast to men, as Mary Lou does. In a political or social context, however, a woman who knows already that she desires women must come out to herself or to others. When we first see Martha, for example, she is at ease with her lesbian identity, but no one knows except herself. Her coming out process includes identifying herself as a comrade (or "family") to Lenore and as a lover to Folly. Lenore, in her turn, has been in a relationship with Betsy for years without naming herself lesbian: "She didn't like the idea of Betsy calling herself names, but in spite of not liking the idea, she was drawn to the word: *lesbian*" (23). As Lenore becomes comfortable "calling herself names," she also develops a personal pride and visibility reflected in her circulation of the book *Sappho Was a Right-On Woman* to any woman in Victory who will take it.

For each woman, coming out, whether privately or publicly, is a way of coming home. The metaphor of home is, perhaps, the single most pervasive trope in lesbian literature. In an eloquent passage, Folly explains to Mary Lou that, to her, coming out is like a long, winding journey "home where you wanted to be" (174). *Home where you wanted to be:* this is what Folly experiences with Martha, what Mary Lou reaffirms with her mother. A literal home with Folly and her children is what Martha longs for after Daisy's death. Home in Victory is also what Lenore discovers by the close of the novel; as she writes to Betsy, "You say you're learning a lot by being so far from home, but here I am learning there are other worlds right down the street in Victory" (156). And a home for the workers is precisely what Folly envisions in the collective factory: an environment that eliminates the separation between public and private spaces, that brings the warmth and human values of home into the sterile and dehumanizing factory. What may be envisioned in other lesbian novels as a bar or utopian community takes shape here as the Women of Victory Co-op Mill.

This urge toward community, whether based on gender, sexual preference, or class, is powerful for characters and author alike. But for the author, the urge has had both positive and negative consequences.

Brady writes of her tension "between the desire to write what must be written because it is true to my experience, and the desire to be part of a group, whether that group is the lesbian community, the lesbian literary subculture, or mainstream society. . . . By around 1982 [the publication date of *Folly*] I began to experience being an insider in this community as restrictive; while it was buoying me in some aspects, it seemed to suffocate me in others."[14] The consequence for Brady, as we have seen, was to slow her career as a writer. Does this conflict reflect itself in the novel? The lesbian "community" pictured there is simply too new and undeveloped to manifest as yet the tensions and conflicts that must inevitably occur. But I believe we can see Brady's awareness that "home" can exclude the outsider as readily as it includes the insider. The theme that carries the weight of difference is racism. No matter how suggestive the relationship between Lenore and Sabrina, in fact the community of known lesbians in Victory is an entirely white one. This is but one manifestation of Brady's exploration of racism as I will discuss below.

As a lesbian novel, then, *Folly* shares a number of qualities with the rest of the genre, but it is unique in a number of others. On the one hand, certainly, it is a lesbian coming out novel, it incorporates a romantic sub-plot, and it hints at the idealism and utopianism that marks the entire genre. But most lesbian novels, including those published up until now, tend to avoid such traditional political subjects as union organizing and strikes and ignore or minimize the class (and race) issues that are central to *Folly*. In a sense, lesbian feminist novels—overwhelmingly romances—have been little more successful in expressing the mutual demands of love and hunger—the personal and the political—than were the leftist novels of the 1930s, although they err on the opposite side. A very few novels, such as Valerie Miner's *Blood Sisters* (1981) and Barbara Wilson's *Ambitious Women* (1982), do defy this norm. And certainly, race and racism have been central to the texts published by women of color since 1980, including, for example, Paula Gunn Allen's *The Woman Who Owned the Shadows* (1983) and Gloria Anzaldúa's *Borderlands/La Frontera* (1987). Overall, however, in its blending of lesbian and leftist themes, its attention to the lives of working-class women, and its concern with racism and divisiveness, *Folly* stands with a small but select group of politically progressive lesbian novels.

V

I suggested above that realism is the literary form most likely to be employed by politically progressive writers. It is also the case that the large majority of lesbian novels are written in an intentionally realistic mode, although theirs is likely to be a romantic realism in which verisimilitude masks wish fulfillment. But certainly, neither the politically progressive nor the lesbian feminist novel has made a striking use of experimental, non-representational, postmodern literary techniques. The aim of each genre is to represent reality, to tell the truth, to capture experience, to stress content over aesthetic form, and to teach lessons of empathy and understanding. Hence, it is valuable to look at the place of *Folly* within the realist tradition.

Realism, a literary method associated most closely with the great English and European novels of the nineteenth century, has been defined by George Levine as "a self-conscious effort, usually in the name of some moral enterprise of truth telling and extending the limits of human sympathy, to make literature appear to be describing directly not some other language but reality itself." It is "a mode that depends heavily on our commonsense expectation that there are direct connections between word and thing."[15] In other words, realist writers contend that there is a reality outside language, that language is about that reality, and that the writer can use language to describe events and experiences as accurately as her or his skill allows. As a literary style, realism is opposed both to romance (in which language is used in a realist manner to express fantasies and desires) and to postmodernism (which denies all three of the above premises).

Maureen Brady is primarily a realist writer. Although an often elegant and imagistic writer, she uses language not for its own sake but to represent as faithfully as she can the thoughts and behaviors of women the reader may feel she knows or believes herself to be. For Brady, Folly, Lenore, and the other characters have the weight of real people who come into focus, live their lives, and then move on. In *Folly,* Brady does not experiment with plot, narration, character, or style. Most importantly, Brady's intention as a writer seems always to be to tell the truth as she understands it. None of this is to say that Brady (or any realist) is simply writing lightly fictionalized journalism. For Brady, what matters is the truth and reality of her imagination, as well as the representation of the external world.

Another way of thinking about realism is that it is "the representation of experience in a manner which approximates closely to description of similar experience in non-literary texts of the same culture."[16] This is particularly relevant to *Folly,* which begins with a quotation from Kathy Kahn's collection of oral histories, *Hillbilly Women* (1973). In researching this afterword, I have noted with interest that many books about southern mill workers are collections of or based upon oral histories.

Consider also that midway through the writing of *Folly*, Brady went to North Carolina to conduct and tape interviews with mill workers. In transcribing these tapes, Brady listened to and attempted to capture the rhythms and particularities of their speech. In a sense, then, the novel is an attempt to contextualize actual women's stories, previously presented in historical texts, within a constructed plot consistent with the leftist feminist and lesbian literary traditions. The effect is that of literary realism: a description of lived experience in language closely modeled on narratives by the women themselves.

The kind of realism that Brady uses in *Folly* may, to some extent, have contributed to the isolation she has expressed feeling as a lesbian writer and her failure to break through as a mainstream writer. On the one hand, lesbian fiction has become increasingly conventional, requiring heroic protagonists, romantic plots, abundant sex scenes, and idealized settings. As in the mainstream, formulaic fictions—mysteries, romances, adventures—are most popular with lesbian readers and thus most appealing to lesbian publishers. Although *Folly* has a lesbian hero, some sex, and an upbeat ending, its attention to issues of class and race mark it apart from the escapist fiction so beloved by lesbian readers. On the other hand, Brady's style of didactic realism does not quite fit into the stream of "serious" postmodern fiction most highly praised by the academic and critical establishments. But for those readers who value conscientious, responsible, and sensitive attempts to imaginatively represent ordinary women's lives, Maureen Brady's *Folly* is a work to be treasured.

VI

Folly (and Maureen Brady as a writer) belongs to a realist tradition not only in its formal achievements, but also in one very important thematic intention. In her informative essay on the writing of the novel, Brady explains that her motivation for writing was "the longing for wholeness and connection."[17] It is clear in her essays, interviews, and fiction that Brady—like most feminist and lesbian feminist writers—is engaged in a quest to restore or create connections that have been fragmented by the alienating conditions of modern life including patriarchy, racism, homophobia, and capitalism. The ultimate lesbian and feminist goal is a whole, healthy, and strong female self. Postmodern theorists hold a very different set of values and assumptions. Wholeness, connection, unity, self: all are perceived as illusory effects of a language structured around the words I, me, self, ego, identity. The postmodern "self" is more properly understood as a fluid, fragmented, multiple set of subject positions.

Many feminists have argued that this notion of subjectivity is produced by privilege, that women and other disenfranchised groups need to emphasize selfhood, wholeness, and integration of previously fragmented parts. Brady certainly would argue this position. Indeed, her motivation for writing *Folly* was to "re-member" herself by reclaiming her working-class heritage. On the other hand, she is not totally dissimilar to postmodernists. To her thinking, subjectivity cannot be reduced to simple categories of identity: woman, lesbian, worker, mother, white, African-American, and so on. Her characters are complex subjects, and their multiple selves do not necessarily blend in seamless harmony. Their goal may be wholeness, but the process of negotiating wholeness is difficult, contentious, and incomplete.

The number of subject positions, themes, and issues that Brady introduces—mostly successfully to my reading—is remarkable. We see Folly as mother, worker, political activist, white woman, and lesbian; Lenore as daughter, worker, lesbian, and friend. The African-American women in the novel are more thinly drawn—a problem that I will discuss below—but even Mabel and Sabrina are presented in more than one dimension. The novel interrogates issues of class consciousness, sexuality, mother–daughter relationships, community, racism, age, pregnancy, and education. Despite this topical fecundity, the novel does not feel hurried or scattered, in part because it is unified by a few specific themes: the realization of various forms of power, the creation of new ways of being, the recognition of difference and resolution of opposition, and the understanding and appreciation of alternate points of view.

The plot of *Folly* revolves around a labor strike and the acceptance of lesbian identity. Although these may seem to be very different stories, Brady connects them not only through plot devices (Folly and Martha first make love after the picnic celebrating the successful union drive, for example) but also through the theme of power. The novel contrasts abusive power with the enabling power of women uniting to change the conditions of their lives. Abusive power may take the form of bosses controlling workers, many instances of which we see in the main Fartblossom plot, but also in scenes set in the A&P; of men over women as Mary Lou discovers in her struggles with Roland; or of whites over African-Americans, the realization of which is expressed in the interior speech of Folly and Lenore, from white women's perspective, and of Mabel, from that of African-American women. In contrast, when the women walk out of the mill to protest the treatment of Cora (merging class and gender interests), when they vote in the union and negotiate better working conditions, when Folly and Martha fall in love and act upon their feelings, when Mary Lou realizes she can go to college and choose a life other than the mill, when Lenore names herself lesbian and circulates her copy of *Sappho Was a Right-On Woman,* when Evelyn stops drinking and mends fences with her daughter, when Folly and Lenore each separately reach out to understand the world from an African-American woman's point of view—when these things happen women empower themselves to create new worlds and new ways of being. Whether or not Folly, Martha, Mabel, and the others start their cooperative mill, whether or not Lenore is able to realize her fantasy of a local gay pride parade, Victory will never be the same.

Brady's characters achieve their goals by recognizing the differences that exist between them and by working to resolve their oppositions. The most important example of this is the struggle to overcome racism among the striking women, but I will first point out a smaller and more discrete example of this method. In the first chapter of the novel, Folly explains to Martha that she doesn't want Mary Lou to see Lenore because Lenore is, by reputation, "queer." There is an awkward silence, and Folly realizes that Martha is a lot like Lenore. The woman who had seemed familiarly like herself, now seemed different, alien, "other." But Folly takes one step further: Martha "was husky. She flicked her cigarette ashes with a manly gesture. 'For Christ's sake,' Folly said to herself, 'so do I'" (6). This shift in position dissolves the opposition between queer and not-queer, between friend and alien, between self and other. As a result, Folly is both open to becoming a lesbian herself and also to accepting Lenore as her daughter's friend. Characters in the novel constantly shift their position in order to understand another point of view, changing their behavior and beliefs as they change the angle from which they view the real world. In doing so, they call into question the differences and oppositions set up by various hierarchies of power and at least lay the groundwork for communities based upon equality and mutual respect. Boundaries—between lesbian and heterosexual or African-American and white—exist to separate, but they can become "borderlands" (as Gloria Anzaldúa writes) in which to transcend the separation.

The questions of perspective, separation, and borders are pursued most significantly in this novel around the racism of white women. In her essay on the writing of *Folly,* Brady discusses the firm boundaries—quoting Minnie Bruce Pratt, she calls them as charged as an electric fence—that have been drawn between the races. This novel is as much her attempt to cross these boundaries as it is to reclaim her white working-class self. But, she says, "In writing about racism in *Folly,* I found myself coming up to the fence, stopping, encountering a vast blank span in my imagination as

I considered my Black characters."[18] Her first reaction to this vast blank span was to restrict herself to writing her African-American characters from the outside, because of her fear of being presumptuous. In a novel containing so much interior monologue, however, this solution was itself racist by denying subjectivity to African-American characters. She expressed her dilemma to Audre Lorde who responded, "You cannot be presumptuous, you can only be wrong."[19] Brady tried again, writing chapter eleven from Mabel's point of view. Although this is the only place in the novel that an African-American woman is presented from the inside, Brady said in an interview that, had she written two more drafts of the novel, Mabel would have become as central a character as Folly and Lenore.

What Maureen Brady discovered in herself—an initial inability to imagine the world from the point of view of African-American women—becomes a prominent theme in the novel. Both Folly and Lenore come to understand that racism functions not only in its grossest aspects—segregation, discrimination, violence—but also in the subtle daily ways in which whites discount the equal value of being African-American. Both women come to realize that they have never really seen African-American women before, or considered them truly human, or wondered about the reality of their lives. By the end of the novel, each has made substantial steps toward doing so.

In keeping with the way the novel pursues issues on both personal and political levels, each woman comes to her epiphany from a different vantage point. Folly's transformation is initially motivated by her concern that the strike and union drive succeed. She is first shocked by her own racism in the powerful beauty shop scene in chapter eleven, when Mabel challenges the narrow view of reality held by the white women. Folly feels immediately guilty and regretful, but also immediately understands the form their racism takes: erasing the subjectivity of African-American women. Folly resolves to remedy this deficiency within herself by learning as much as she can about the experiences and perspectives of African-American women and about herself as a white woman, as marked by her color as Mabel is by hers. Although the immediate goal is a successful union drive (an accurate reflection of the history of organizing in the South), Folly comes to understand that the most insidious consequence of racism for white women is a failure in knowledge and empathy. For the rest of the novel, she attempts to remedy this epistemological deficiency.

Lenore undergoes a very similar kind of growth, motivated by personal friendship rather than political struggle. As she comes to know Sabrina, she realizes the unwritten rules that establish the boundaries between African-Americans and whites in Victory. There are the physical boundaries of neighborhood and church, but of equal importance are the psychological boundaries that prevent whites from talking to African-Americans or thinking about how they live their lives. Through Sabrina, Lenore begins to step over those boundaries and to look at life from the other woman's side of the fence.

Folly is remarkably successful in its portrayal of white women recognizing the phenomenology and consequences of racism and undergoing a transformation in consciousness and behavior. But, as Maureen Brady would no doubt agree, it is far less successful as a whole in itself transgressing the borders of the imagination. And it is worth pondering why Brady—like most white writers—was so timid in her portrayal of African-American characters. She is no doubt correct in identifying the imaginative blankness that most white people have about the lives of people of color. But the task of the writer is always to leap over barriers to the imagination. I find it interesting that Brady is very successful in creating older characters like Daisy in *Folly,* or Min in the play, *I Know a Hundred Ways to Die,* even though she herself has not experienced old age. Even though she may have known women like Folly, Lenore, and Mary Lou, it requires an extension of the imagination to bring them to life as literary characters. Why then, do many white women come up against the electric fence when they try to imagine the external and internal reality of African-American women?

This question elicits considerable debate, of course, and will not receive a final answer here. Many white women probably would agree with Cindy Patton, for example, that feminist fiction needs more honest portrayals of racism from the perspective of African-American women, but that the appropriate format might be "an autobiographical work best co-authored by a black and a white novelist."[20] She reflects the strong taboos against a member of a privileged group speaking from the perspective of the oppressed. Anna Livia, on the other hand, challenges this assumption, asking, "In whose interest is it that white women should feel Black experience is so different from ours as to be unimaginable?"[21] The answer to her rhetorical question is obvious: the racist power structure. Although she confesses to having been little more successful than Brady in overcoming the taboos, she calls upon both writers and readers to use literature to live outside the self.

Anna Livia makes a very important point. Literature is the product of imagination, as Maureen Brady contends, and the imagination is not bound by personal experience. If it were, no author could write anything but autobiography and I do not believe that to be the case. For that reason I disagree with Patton's suggestion, or the commonplace assumption that only African-American writers can create African-American characters, or that lesbians can only write about lesbians, and so on. But I also think that Brady's hesitancy—and the hesitancy of most white writers—to create an African-American character from the inside does reflect the uniquely divisive character of racism in twentieth-century America. Social divisions, although similar in many ways, are not all the same. The evidence of contemporary literature suggests that it is easier to make imaginative leaps across gender, age, social status, religion, even sexual preference, than it is across race. Racism, especially against African-Americans, is the great shame and tragedy of our nation. It is hardly surprising that its legacy should include failures in literary imagination. Although not completely successful, to Maureen Brady's credit, she struggles mightily with this legacy in *Folly*.

These discussions of lesbianism and racism return me to my initial argument that *Folly* deconstructs the opposition between personal and political or private and public in a particularly striking and effective manner. Racism is not only economic and political discrimination, it is also a legacy of not-seeing carried within every white woman. Lesbianism is not just the personal choice of sexual partner, it is a way of connecting with women that leads to political empowerment. *Folly* replaces the arguably patriarchal notion of "either/or" with the more feminist one of "both/and." Folly herself is both worker and mother, both mother and lover. Folly and Lenore are both personally racist and politically anti-racist. The women of Victory are both oppressed laborers and powerful fighters. It may be true, as some critics have argued, that the novel occasionally displays a tendency toward didacticism. But the issues raised in *Folly*—the erasure of African-American and working-class women's subjectivity, lesbians coming out and coming together, women struggling collectively to change the conditions of their lives—are of such importance and so imperfectly learned even by political activists, that we can readily forgive Maureen Brady for this touch of the pedagogue. Reading *Folly* is an educational experience in the best tradition of socially committed fiction: the novel expands our consciousness, increases our empathy, and touches our hearts.

Bonnie Zimmerman

213

Notes

1. I am indebted to Glynis Carr's biographical entry on Maureen Brady in *Contemporary Lesbian Writers of the U. S.: A Bio-Bibliographical Critical Sourcebook*, eds. Denise D. Knight and Sandra Pollack (Westport, CT: Greenwood Press, 1993), 80–84.

2. Maureen Brady, "An Exploration of Class and Race Dynamics in the Writing of *Folly,*" *13th Moon*, VII, 1 & 2 (1983): 145.

3. Ibid., 145–46.

4. Ibid., 146.

5. Historical background is taken from *Like a Family: The Making of a Southern Cotton Mill World*, ed. Jacquelyn Dowd Hall (Chapel Hill and London: University of North Carolina Press, 1987); and Mary Frederickson, "'I Know Which Side I'm On': Southern Women in the Labor Movement in the Twentieth Century," in *Women, Work and Protest: A Century of U.S. Women's Labor History*, ed. Ruth Milkman (Boston: Routledge & Kegan Paul, 1985), 156–80.

6. Hall, 67.

7. Frederickson, 160.

8. Ibid., 174.

9. Deborah Silverton Rosenfelt, "From the Thirties: Tillie Olsen and the Radical Tradition," in *Feminist Criticism and Social Change: Sex, Class and Race in Literature and Culture*, eds. Judith Newton and Deborah Silverton Rosenfelt (New York and London: Methuen, 1985), 218.

10. Candida Ann Lacey, "Striking Fictions: Women Writers and the Making of a Proletarian Realism," *Women's Studies International Forum* 9, 4 (1986): 373–84. See also Fay M. Blake, *The Strike in the American Novel* (Metuchen, N.J.: Scarecrow Press, 1972).

11. Paula Rabinowitz, *Labor and Desire: Women's Revolutionary Fiction in Depression America* (Chapel Hill and London: University of North Carolina Press, 1991), 36.

12. Deborah Silverton Rosenfelt, "Getting Into the Game: American Women Writers and the Radical Tradition," *Women's Studies International Forum* 9, 4 (1986): 364.

13. Bonnie Zimmerman, *The Safe Sea of Women: Lesbian Fiction 1969–1989* (Boston: Beacon Press, 1990).

14. Maureen Brady, "Insider Outsider Coming of Age," *Lesbian Texts and Contexts: Radical Revisions*, eds. Karla Jay and Joanne Glasgow (New York and London: New York University Press, 1990), 55.

15. George Levine, *The Realistic Imagination* (Chicago and London: University of Chicago Press, 1981), 8–9.

16. David Lodge, *The Modes of Modern Writing* (Ithaca: Cornell University Press, 1977).

17. Brady, "An Exploration," 148.

18. Ibid., 149.

19. Ibid., 150.

20. Cindy Patton, "Crackers and Queers," *Gay Community News* (June 1983): 1.

21. Anna Livia, "You Can Only Be Wrong...," *The Women's Review of Books* VI, 10–11 (July 1989): 33.

The Feminist Press at The City University of New York offers alternatives in education and in literature. Founded in 1970, this nonprofit, tax-exempt educational and publishing organization works to eliminate stereotypes in books and schools and to provide literature with a broad vision of human potential. The publishing program includes reprints of important works by women, feminist biographies of women, multicultural anthologies, a cross-cultural memoir series, and nonsexist children's books. Curricular materials, bibliographies, directories, and a quarterly journal provide information and support for students and teachers of women's studies. Through publication and projects, The Feminist Press contributes to the rediscovery of the history of women and the emergence of a more humane society.

NEW AND FORTHCOMING BOOKS

The Answer/La Respuesta: The Restored Text and Selected Poems, by Sor Juana Inés de la Cruz. Commentary and Translation by Electa Arenal and Amanda Powell. $12.95 paper, $35.00 cloth.

Australia for Women, edited by Susan Hawthorne and Renate Klein. $17.95 paper.

The Castle of Pictures: A Grandmother's Tales, by George Sand. Translated by Holly Erskine Hirko. $9.95 paper, $23.95 cloth.

Songs My Mother Taught Me: Stories, Plays, and Memoir, by Wakako Yamauchi. Edited and with an Introduction by Garrett Hongo. Afterword by Valerie Miner. $14.95 paper, $35.00 cloth.

Women Composers: The Lost Tradition Found, second edition. By Diane Peacock Jezic. Second Edition Prepared by Elizabeth Wood. $14.95 paper, $35.00 cloth.

Women of Color and the Multicultural Curriculum: Transforming the College Classroom, edited by Liza Fiol-Matta and Mariam Chamberlain. $18.95 paper, $35.00 cloth.

Prices subject to change. *Individuals:* Send check or money order (in U.S. dollars drawn on a U.S. bank) to The Feminist Press at The City University of New York, 311 East 94th Street, New York, NY 10128. Please include $3.00 postage and handling for the first book, $.75 for each additional. For VISA/MasterCard orders call (212) 360-5790. *Bookstores, libraries, wholesalers:* Feminist Press titles are distributed to the trade by Consortium Book Sales and Distribution, (800) 283-3572.